WILLIAM COLES

D0620315

MR
TWO
BOMB

Legend Press Ltd, 51 Gower Street, London, WC1E 6HJ
info@legend-paperbooks.co.uk I www.legendpress.co.uk

Contents © William Coles 2019
The right of the above author to be identified as the author of this work has
been asserted in accordance with the Copyright, Designs and Patents Act
1988. British Library Cataloguing in Publication Data available.

Print ISBN 978-1-7895508-5-6
Ebook ISBN 978-1-7895508-6-3
Set in Times. Printing managed by Jellyfish Solutions Ltd
Cover design by Rachel Lawston I www.lawstondesign.com

First published in 2010 by Legend Press

William Coles has been a journalist for 30 years and has worked for a number of papers including *The Sun, The Express, The Mail* and *The Wall Street Journal.*

Visit William at
wcoles.com

or follow him
@WilliamColes1

Other books by William Coles

The Eton Affair
Lord Lucan: My Story

Books by Bill Coles

The Spare Heir Handbook
Dave Cameron's Schooldays
Red Top: Being a Reporter
Simon Cowell: The Sex Factor

For my parents, Bob and Sarah

CHAPTER ONE

There were about twelve of us, that I know of, who survived the Atomic bombs of both Hiroshima and Nagasaki – and the question that I am asked more than any other is this: do I feel lucky? Were the Gods on my side as I lived through the nightmare of not one, but two Atomic bombs? Or were the Gods merely playing with me as I scurried from the hell of Hiroshima straight into that Seventh Circle of hell in Nagasaki?

In short, the crux of the question is: have I been blessed – or cursed?

I understand how perplexing it is for these students of wisdom as they come to me in search of knowledge. On the one hand, it might be deemed unlucky in the extreme to have been in Hiroshima on 6th August 1945. Anywhere else on earth would have been preferable to being in that city on that brilliant blue morning. But to have survived Hiroshima and then to have travelled so unerringly to Nagasaki for a second dose of atomic radiation... that, surely, must be considered 'Unlucky – to the Power of Two'. And why not add the fact that Nagasaki was never supposed to have been bombed in the first place? That second bomb was originally destined for Kokura on 9th August; at one stage, the B29 bomber was directly over Kokura and within seconds of dropping its payload. But as it was, the clouds closed in, Kokura was saved and Bock's Car turned South to drop its bomb on Nagasaki, where I had been waiting all of 90 minutes to meet my destiny.

So I appreciate that in many ways I might be considered unlucky.

I have, however, survived. I have pulled through. Not without injury, it has to be said. But I have lived to write my tale and so, in that respect, I have had the most extraordinary luck.

The bombs are how people best know me. The children on the streets would point me out and the name they gave to me was 'Two-Bomb San'. With the passing of the years, it has been shortened simply to 'Two-Bomb' – and I have come to like the name. It is not the whole of what I am, but nevertheless those two bombs are what have come to define me.

For what it is worth, this is what I believe to be true: I have been lucky. I would go further. I would say I am one of the luckiest men alive. And that is not just on account of having lived through those two bombs and come out the other side. For what I must also take into account is how those two bombs – Little Boy and Fat Man as they were called by the Yankees – have transformed my life, injuries and all.

This, by the way, is not an apology for the bombs. It is not an apology for the Americans; nor for the Japanese. It is not an analysis of the beginning of the war; nor an evaluation of whether those two bombs brought the war to a speedier end. And it is certainly not to demean, or make light of the suffering of all the hundreds of thousands of victims and their families.

Since the war, I have lived in several countries, including that of our old enemy, the Yankees. As a result, this account is not, perhaps, as solemn as many of the stories of the bombs. But then, I am not a solemn person. There has been much misery in my life, but there has been much joy with it. And although I will never forget my days in Hiroshima and Nagasaki – indeed *can* never forget my days in those ill-starred cities – I choose instead to count my blessings.

Out of the ashes of Hiroshima and Nagasaki were to spring

the most incredible shoots; not that I even remotely deserved them. Of all the Atom bomb survivors, or Hibakusha as we are known, there is not a single one who was not more deserving of happiness than myself.

So every day now I give thanks for the great good fortune that has been thrust into my lap; and when I consider also the immense grief that came from those two bombs, I can only weep at the magnitude of my own joy.

There were so many heroes at Hiroshima and Nagasaki: great men and women who rose to the occasion and gave the very best of themselves; and children too, who without complaint have struggled for decades to deal with their injuries.

But I am not like that. I was never a hero and, though I survived both bombs, have never done anything heroic. Well – possibly the once; but even that was probably more animal impulse than a conscious act of courage.

The truth was that before the bombs, I was... I was a despicable human being. How you would have despised me! And had I thought to think it, I would even have despised myself.

CHAPTER TWO

The only time I panicked was four hours after Little Boy had exploded into our lives. This was different, I understand, from the majority of Hiroshima's victims. Most tended to panic within a few minutes of the bomb being dropped, as they began to realise the size of the catastrophe engulfing them.

But during the immediate aftermath of the bomb, I was the most disciplined person in the wreckage of the building. Not even a trace of that hyper-ventilating blood-rush as panic overwhelms the head and seizes up your brain. No, my one and only moment of blind panic came as the fire-storm swept the city, razing everything in its path.

We had been trying to dig Sumie out of the ruins of her house for over an hour. I could see her, hear her, even stroke her upturned face through the wreckage. But there was too much to move, too many tiles to shift. But I was confident that, given enough time, we would be able to dig her out. I was her tenant, had been boarding with her for three months. And she was my lover.

Little by little, we had been working away at the wreckage of the house, tossing tiles and splintered beams of wood out onto the rubble of the street. After 30 minutes, I caught a glimpse of her face. She had smiled at me and, despite the grey veil of dust, was as beautiful as I had ever seen her. She was in good heart too as she patiently waited to be freed.

"Are you hurt?" she had asked me. That was the first thing

she had said. Not for a moment had she complained about her own injuries, or of being trapped in the ruins of her home.

"Don't worry about me," I said, hurling another tile over my shoulder, "Can you move?"

"My leg is trapped," she said. "Is it one of the beams?"

To the side I could see the end of a vast roof-beam poking out from the ruins. I shouted over to Shinzo, who was working on the other side of the wreckage. "Help me!" I called. "We must move it together."

We pulled and tugged, and the neighbour, that chit of a girl, added her puny weight too, but no matter how hard we hauled, nothing would shift that impossible mass of timber. The beam was square, over half-a-metre across, and perhaps 10 metres long.

"We must clear more wreckage," said Shinzo, the sweat trickling through the dust that caked his fat, jowly face.

So we continued to haul and tug at the tiles, the thousands of tiles, and all the other smashed and broken bits of wood and plaster that went to make up a standard two-storey house in Hiroshima in those days.

Every so often, I would peek through the hole that we were making towards Sumie and would give her a smile of encouragement. "You will be out in a few minutes." I tried to sound confident. I suddenly noticed a trickle of blood on her chin. She had bitten right through her lower-lip. "Are you badly hurt?"

"No," she said, though as she spoke, she winced.

"You always were a hopeless liar."

"I do not know," she said – and even then, she still smiled, beaming up at me from beneath the rubble. "I cannot feel anything below my waist."

"We will get you to the hospital."

"Do you know what it was? I saw a flash."

I continued tossing tile after tile over my shoulder. "It was a bomb like I have never seen before. Half the city is destroyed."

"A single bomb?"

"The warehouse was devastated. And we were over three kilometres away."

I picked up a piece of masonry and as I threw it onto the street, I looked about me. Carnage such as I would not have believed possible. It was as if a giant hand had smacked down from heaven and crushed everything beneath it. Save for Hiroshima's few concrete structures, there was not a building that was not either destroyed or yawing crazily to the side. Through the dust and the smoke, as far as the eye could see, Hiroshima had been turned into a wasteland of rubble.

The people, too; I haven't even begun to mention the hundreds, the thousands, of benumbed victims, so awfully burned, their clothes in shreds as they tottered aimlessly through the streets. There is so much to say about them that I hardly know where to begin; I will try to do them justice later.

But as I looked about me that I noticed the fire for the first time. Within minutes of the blast, there had been little outbreaks of fire all over Hiroshima, as power cables and kitchen stoves had set light to the tinder-dry houses. There had also been those will-o'-the-wisp flames, puffing in the air, as the radiation burnt itself out. What I saw about me, though, was much, much more than a series of individual fires across the landscape. It was a wave of fire that was sweeping north through the city, whipped up by the sea-breeze.

At first it had seemed quite far off, over a kilometre away, but as I looked, I saw the firestorm moving towards at us at the most incredible rate; galloping, devouring everything in its path.

We could already smell the sharp tang of the smoke, a harbinger of death as it flew ahead of the flames. Worse though was the noise, that crackling roar of ten thousand Hiroshima dwellings being consumed by fire.

"Quickly!" I yelled to Shinzo. The pair of us lunged again at the end of the beam. I pulled till the tears squeezed out of my eyes. Shinzo grunting, mewling, beside me as he tried to heave that massive spar of wood. The girl, even though she was only seven, straining to push beside us.

We might as well have been heaving against those once-great walls of Hiroshima castle – although even those had been destroyed by the bomb.

I scrabbled back to the hole that we had burrowed down to Sumie. Easing myself down through the masonry, I braced my feet on the rubble and grabbed her by the armpits. I pulled – how I pulled. I pulled so hard that I was on the verge of dislocating her shoulders.

All the while Sumie was staring up at me, silently willing me on. She bit savagely down on her lip, trying to stay silent through the pain. But she would not budge, the lower-half of her body trapped tight in the rubble.

"Shinzo!" I screamed. "We need rope! Get me rope!" I thought we might slip it around her chest. Together, Shinzo and I might have had a chance of pulling her out.

I bent down to caress Sumie's head. I stroked a lock of long hair out of her eyes. "It will be fine," I said, and at the time I still believed what I was saying.

She smiled up at me and stroked my leg below the knee.

"Do you still think it was a good idea to have taken me to Miyajima yesterday?" Oh, how she smiled through the pain. She must have known she was minutes from death.

"Perhaps not."

"I forgive you."

I stooped and kissed the top of Sumie's head. Over the smell of the dust and the smoke, I could even catch a trace of the oil that she used on her hair.

Sumie clasped my hands briefly. "Thank you," she said. I struggled to climb back out of the hole and gazed down at her beautiful face. It was as if she was drowning in a well of tiles and rubble.

"Will you—" she swallowed. "Will you live for me?"

"I—"

"You will live for me?"

She gazed up at me, a solitary tear rolling down her dusty cheek.

As I poked my head out of the wreckage, I caught the sound, that terrifying sound, of the firestorm. It was closer than I could have dreamed possible. In all but three minutes, it was practically upon us, tearing through the wreckage of the houses and jumping from one street to the next.

And that was when the simmering panic bubbled over and all but consumed me. I tore at the wreckage above Sumie, lunging desperately at the tiles and the snapped shards of wood. I hurled myself at the beam, screaming with rage as I tried to shift it. Trying desperately to free her; the smoke so tight in my throat I could hardly breathe; that infernal roar of the firestorm; Shinzo and the girl crying at me to save myself; and the tears of rage as I realised my utter impotence.

For a moment I stood there on the ruins of Sumie's house and howled at my own folly. She was going to die, burned alive, and there was nothing I could do to prevent it.

But the worst of it was the realisation that perhaps Sumie had been right. Perhaps it was I who had killed her. Perhaps it was I who had brought this whole disaster upon my love by taking her to the Miyajima shrine the previous day. I don't know, I don't know. But what I do know is this: that just 24 hours earlier, my dear Sumie had been cursed – and I had been the cause of it.

CHAPTER THREE

I should never have gone to Miyajima. At least, I should never have taken Sumie to Miyajima.

No-one should ever take their lover to Miyajima.

Which is a shame, because Miyajima is the perfect place for lovers. To my mind, this little island shrine is the most romantic, the most picturesque spot in the whole of Japan. In fact, I go further: I have travelled to many countries in the world, but I have yet to see a place of such outstanding beauty as Miyajima. It is a perfect synthesis of man and nature, with a cluster of shrines on stilts that nestle on the shoreline. It is most famous for its towering Torii Gate, a vast camphor wood gate that stands in the water, 100 metres out from the bay. At high tide, the lacquered orange gate and the vermilion shrine seem to be actually floating on the water. Behind the shrine are the verdant green woods that rise up 530 metres to Mount Kisen.

From the first time my father took me there, 25 years earlier, I have thought it quite magical. It is better still at night, when the visitors have departed and the candles shimmer in the shrine.

My father was a merchant seaman and an immensely practical man. He would have laughed in your face if you had accused him of being superstitious. Yet even he, that most capable and straightforward of men, would not have dreamed of taking my mother to Miyajima. There are some things you just do not do.

Only a maniac would think to take his lover to Miyajima; and only a woman who was brimful with love would accede to her man's demands and accompany him there.

Every fibre in Sumie's being told her not to join me on the ferry. But she loved me.

It was a brilliant blue Sunday and, especially in times of war, you take your chances when you can. You seize every moment of happiness exactly as it comes along, for who knows what the morrow will bring.

How ironic that phrase seems now. Although we do not know what tomorrow will bring, we usually have a good idea of what is going to occur: tomorrow, more than likely, will be just like today, and likewise the day before it. But every so often, something really different does happen. Something so extraordinary, so outside your experience, that it changes your entire world-view. And, perhaps once a century, something occurs that changes not just your world-view, but the world's view. Something so monumental that no single human being's perception of life will ever be the same again.

If there was one single benefit to our country being at war, it was that it had heightened my desire to live in the moment. This attitude, to savour every single taste of happiness that passed me by, had been forming throughout my life. But after four years of war, it had crystallised into the position where I snatched at everything that came my way, whether a kiss, a joke, a shot of Sake, or the delicious ecstasy of sex. Yes, especially that sweet delight.

I should mention, by the way, that I was very different from my fellow citizens. Perhaps they were just like beasts of burden, bowed down by the war. For we were in the middle of not just a war, but the war of wars – the biggest war the world had ever seen. There was no end in sight. There was never any end in sight.

All we had was this relentless barrage of propaganda from

the papers and the radio, which claimed that we were driving the Yankees off the face of the earth. But all we knew for certain was that food was scarce, the Nazis were finished, and that even the children had stopped going to school in order to join the war effort.

When Japan had launched her attack on Pearl Harbour in 1941, Sumie had been as much of a proud patriot as anyone else. But since we had become lovers, some of my natural cynicism had rubbed off on her. She had started to be more sceptical of what she read in the papers. She had become greedy to seize not just the day, but every minute, every second; she wanted to grab every magical moment.

Even so, even considering the fragile state of our existence during those climactic closing stages of the war... only the most foolhardy would have deliberately courted misfortune by travelling to Miyajima.

"Come on!" I said. "The ferry is leaving in five minutes!"

Sumie laughed at me. "I'm not coming!"

I had leaned out over the side of the boat and beckoned her with my little finger. "But it is beautiful!"

"I know it is beautiful!" She giggled as she stood not five metres away on the dock at the far end of the gang-plank. "I know it well."

"Come on!" I said. "You are feeble!" I was laughing, but I was still desperate for her to come. Around me were 30 daytrippers, lining the decks of that battered old ferry as they made the most of the summer sun. There were clusters of benches to the fore and aft, as well as a small functional cabin. Black wood smoke spumed out of the funnel.

"I said I would come to wave you off and that is what I am doing," she said. "You will enjoy yourself without me and I will be waiting here for you when you get back."

"I want you to come. Come! Come with me!"

She laughed at the thought of it. How fine it was to be in the middle of that most gruesome of wars and yet still to be able to laugh.

"You are incorrigible!"

"That is why you adore me!"

"I adore you despite that, not because of it!" She looked quite lovely, standing there laughing in the sunshine. Even though she was wearing just a simple patterned shirt, frayed trousers and straw-sandals, on that day, with her long, oiled hair curling back over her shoulders, she seemed more beautiful than I had ever seen her. Not a line on her face, not a bag under her eyes, an exquisite porcelain doll that I longed to cradle in my hands. And just to the side of her mouth, a beautiful black mole. To some it might have been a blemish, but I loved to kiss that little beauty spot as much as I loved to kiss her glistening lips.

"Dearest one, there is a war on," I said. "I am sure the Goddess has more important things on her mind."

"After all – why should she be jealous over you?"

"You are right," I said, "I would not be to her taste."

Sumie stepped aside to allow the last of the passengers on. A girl, barely a teenager, was readying to cast off. She was one of the tens of thousands of schoolgirls who'd been forced to join the war effort. Other children had been put to work doing hard manual labour, but this girl, with her quick easy movements and her deft fingers, was serving her time as a cabin-girl. I observed with cool professional detachment how she coiled the ropes; she had the makings of a competent sailor.

Sumie, hand still on the plank-rail, stared down as she placed her toe onto the ground, suddenly coy. Or more precisely, she was playing at being coy. "And why do you want me to come?"

"Why? Because you are beautiful; because it will be a wonderful day; and... because when we make love, I feel that I am savouring a little taste of heaven." Yes, I could be quite the charmer when I was so minded. It is a very useful tool for manipulation. And I may as well be candid: women liked me. I had a breezy patter which never dried up in the face of beauty.

Two elderly men, bent and bald, shuffled onto the boat, staring at me as they walked past. I did not care what they thought. I did not care that, in those days of thrifty hardship, it was not considered seemly for a man and woman to be in love. But then I did not care much what anyone thought.

"A taste of heaven?" Sumie asked, echoing my words. One foot strayed onto the gang-plank.

The captain, oily and belligerent, had limped out of his rathole of a cabin and was standing beside me.

"Are you coming or staying?" he yelled at Sumie, spitting over the side of his boat. "Either get off the gang-plank or get on board."

Sumie stared at the surly captain for a moment. "Yes," she said. "Yes, I think I will come."

"With your boyfriend?" The captain shook his head as he slunk back to the cabin. The ship's whistle blew, the lines were cast off, and just as the gang-plank was about to be raised, Sumie scuttled over onto the ship and took my hand. How we laughed, like a pair of truants who had skived off school to go exploring in the woods.

Few ferries were then operating out to the islands. Fuel was scarce and what little there was left was needed, as always, for the bottomless pit that was the war effort. But occasionally at the weekends, an old boat might steam out from Ujina, in a little bit of make-believe that some vestiges of our lives were still continuing as normal.

As we glided out of Hiroshima City, we could see squads of soldiers digging holes for their wretched boats. How astonishing it all now seems – that while America was on the very verge of dropping the world's biggest bomb, Japan had in her turn devised our very own top-secret weapon. Like many of our inventions, this weapon was uniquely Japanese, and spoke volumes about both our country and our ideals. No-one but a Japanese General could have dreamt up this extraordinary machine, combining as it did Japan's warped sense of patriotism with the most ludicrous impracticality. So I ask in all seriousness, was there ever such a senseless weapon as the suicide boat?

By now the Yankee invasion of Japan was an absolute certainty; even the most sanguine patriots knew it was going to occur before the end of the year. We did not have much to fight the Yankees with, apart from our bamboo spears, which even the schoolgirls were learning to master.

It was still hoped, however, that we might yet take the fight to the Yankees with our scores of suicide boats. The Special Attack Forces, who were in charge of Japan's Kamikaze pilots, had been building hundreds of the wretched things. We may not have had many conventional weapons, such as guns or warships, but we did have whole fleets of those rickety suicide boats.

Each boat was packed with 250kg of explosives. I suppose that if they had hit a US warship plumb, then a few GIs might have been killed. But, even though I was a mere merchant seaman, I had always believed there to be a fatal flaw with the very concept of a suicide boat. The Kamikaze pilots, at least, were almost unstoppable. Once they started in on their final death-dive, they arrowed in on the US ships like a guided missile.

But as for the suicide boats, with their top speed of perhaps 30 knots, they were never going to work in the first place. They would not have got within 300 metres of a US battleship before being blown out of the water.

Still, the suicide boats were the one secret weapon that Japan had left, and we certainly did not want them destroyed before the invasion had started. So the Special Attack Forces were proving their devotion to the Emperor by digging holes to hide their pitiful craft.

How pathetic it all seemed, those patriots determined to throw away their lives in the face of an unstoppable Yankee tide. Thinking back though, there was very little in Japan that was not pathetic by the end of the War. We were like a punch-drunk prize-fighter: battered, bloody and tottering blindly on our feet, yet still out of misplaced pride determined to continue the fight.

As we watched those benighted soldiers digging the holes that might as well have been their graves, I had never felt so grateful to be alive. For the first time in four months, I was back at sea again. Hiroshima City was receding into the distance and, for a short while, the World War with it. We sat on a bench by the aft passenger rail, and I offered Sumie one of the rice-balls and some of the cucumber that she had packed for me earlier. The food in those days was frugal. You thought yourself lucky if you had a piece of fish to eat. As for meat, it was so long since I had eaten it that I had almost forgotten what it tasted like. Our diets largely consisted of unpolished rice and whatever vegetables were at hand.

Sumie took a bite of the rice-ball and delicately patted a crumb off her lips. "This is very stupid," she said. "My sister would be very unhappy if she knew that I was visiting Miyajima with you."

"She would be very unhappy whatever I was doing with you."

"That is so." She swept her mane of hair off her forehead and behind her ear, where it streamed like a scarf over the passenger rail. "Will the Goddess forgive me?"

"Probably not," I replied. "I will try to make it worth your while."

The story goes that the island's shrine is inhabited by the sea goddess Ichikishima, who is fiercely jealous of any couple who comes to visit her. The shrine was built in 593 and legend has it that Ichikishima has been separating couples ever since – usually by arranging some cataclysmic event for the women. The island is so sacred that neither births nor burials are allowed there, and weddings are obviously out of the question.

"You know that this story of the jealous goddess was made up by the local sailors?" I said.

"Why would they do that?"

"It was a Red-Light district," I said. "They first built a shrine here to protect the local seamen and the prostitutes followed soon after. The sailors made up this tale of the jealous goddess because it was the only way they could stop their wives from accompanying them."

"Stop it!" she laughed and slapped me on the knee. "That is ridiculous."

"It is true," I said. "My father told me."

"As if he would know! And doubtless you were planning to visit one of these brothels when you got there."

"Well – now that you mention it ... "

My actual reason for visiting Miyajima was rather less joyous. My father had died the year before and that Sunday, that Sunday 5th August 1945, would have been his 80th birthday. I was going to this old seaman's shrine to give thanks for his life. After my mother had died when I was two, my father had brought me up almost single-handed. There was my grandmother, too, helping out during the day, but the bulk of what I have learned about life I have learned from him. He had wisdom such as I could only dream of. Long, long before Pearl Harbour, this gnarly old merchant seaman, who had seen so much of the world, was already querying the correctness, the direction, of this crazy unquestioning jingoism that had swept the nation.

I will return to my father later. But the reason why I was travelling to Miyajima on that bright blue morning was to give thanks for his life, and to honour everything that he had given to me.

At length, Miyajima's century-old Torii gate came into view, while Hiroshima was just a grey speck 15 kilometres away on the horizon. The tide was high and, with its green backdrop, the floating shrine truly looked like something from another planet; certainly a world away from the war and the grinding poverty and endless air raid sirens that had us daily scurrying for our bunkers. They said that the Miyajima's vermilion pagoda was so sacred that it could not be sited on normal soil – and for a moment, even a complete non-believer such as myself could scent a faint whiff of spirituality.

Sumie marvelled at the site of the shrine, clutching at my

hand. Since she was brazening it out and visiting this Holy of Holies with her lover, then why should she not have held my hand? How much more could it have provoked that island's jealous goddess?

"I have never seen it so beautiful," she said.

"Nor I." I wish I could have boxed up that time, as for a single moment everything about us seemed so simple and so refreshingly uncomplicated: the clear blue sky, not a cloud on the horizon; the verdant forest, as green as I had ever seen it; the almost turquoise blue of the cove; and then, in stunning contrast to all else, the red shrine, like a ruby gemstone set in the middle of the most gorgeous crown.

"Could I... would you mind if I stayed on board?" Sumie asked.

"It will be all right." We stood among the swirl of passengers that was disgorging onto the shore.

"You know how superstitious I am," she said, tugging at her baggy trousers.

"Do not worry," I said, and, like a father leading a recalcitrant child, I took Sumie firmly by the hand and led her onto the gang-plank. And she, still filled with such terrible foreboding, followed.

Even before I had set foot on the land, even as I walked down the gang-plank, the omens were disastrous. I had walked but three steps when a shriek of intense pain rent the air. We all stopped and turned, and there by the anchor chain was the young cabin-girl, her mouth a perfect 'O' of horror as she stared at her mashed and bloody arm. Her hand had somehow got caught in the winch mechanism of the anchor chain, and she had lost two, three fingers, the blood already streaming onto the deck.

All she could do was stand there, stock still, and stare at the wreckage of her arm. She was whimpering, her brain numb with shock, little severed fingers lying at her feet.

And it says so much of Japan as a nation that not one of us, not one, moved to help her. We stood and watched, bowed down by the weight of national apathy. I, like the sheep I was, did not move a muscle towards her. Was not I the perfect wretch? Now, now I would do anything at all to have helped. But then, I was still so self-centred as to think that her pain had nothing to do with me. I could watch. I could observe. But I was not a part of it and it was not for me to help her.

I shudder to think of the utter callowness of that man that was myself. I may well have been doing what all of us had been conditioned to do. We did nothing out of the ordinary unless we had received a direct order. But it is not a humane way to behave; it denies every natural impulse to help your fellow man.

One person did finally go over to the girl. It was that captain, that monstrosity of a man. Yet rather than embrace her, or tend to her injuries, he merely launched into the most terrible harangue. "You!" he shrieked. "What do you think you are doing? Why did you not take more care? Go into the cabin and bind up your hand."

The girl, still with her bleeding limb outstretched in front of her, cowered as if he was about to hit her.

"Get off my deck!" he said. "Get off my deck and get into the cabin! And stop crying! Stop crying! What are your injuries compared to those who have given their lives for their country? Stop crying, you hear me?"

But even then, even then, it was not too late. I could still have stepped in, could have comforted that shattered, bleeding girl – and, at the very least, defended her from the foul-mouthed captain.

I should have and it still makes me wince that I did not. Perhaps it was just in our nature in those days. We had about us a natural reserve which meant you did not get involved; you let people sort out their own problems.

But my cold-hearted inaction was down to much more than mere conditioning. The truth was: I did not care. It was not my problem. The girl was in pain and had been maimed for life. But what could I do? What could anyone do?

The other passengers remained glued to the spot. Sumie at least was trembling at the horror of it all. Everything inside her was telling her to get back onto the ship and to go to the girl. But even Sumie could not find it in herself to go against a lifetime of conditioning. That was how it was in Japan: you knuckled under. You obeyed orders. You did not think for yourself. And you played the part of the good citizen by stifling the slightest impulse of emotion.

We stood for a moment longer, watching as the girl tottered to the cabin, the stump of her hand in her mouth. The captain showed his disgust by spitting over the side.

"What are you all looking at? Have you not got anything better to do?" With that, he kicked at the severed fingers, those pathetic little scraps of bone and flesh, knocking them into the sea. "Be off with you!" he said, not bothering to look up. "Go say your prayers."

I have so many regrets in my life, but one of my greatest is my complete spinelessness in the face of that awful monster. What did I have to lose? I could, at the very least, have berated the man. Better yet I should have knocked him down and forced him to clean up the blood with his own tongue. But I did not and I despise myself for it. No, like all the other peasants on the ship, I registered that the show was over and I tramped onto the landing-stage. Not my problem. None of it was my problem. But how much horror does one have to witness before, eventually, it does become your problem?

Sumie was actually crying as she stepped off the gangplank, making no attempt to dry her tears. "That poor girl," she said.

"Yes." That was all I thought fit to reply.

We sat on one of the benches outside the shrine and in time Sumie's tears dried. With one last decisive sniff, she gave herself a shake and squared her shoulders. "I think I am ready," she said.

"Good."

If only I had been more attuned to portents and signs, I

would then and there have led Sumie back to the ferry. For sometimes I do believe the heavens give us due warning of what is to come. And if ever there had been a warning sign that Miyajima was not for us, that cabin-girl's accident was it.

But we stayed, digging ourselves deeper into our hole until we were drenched from top to toe in misfortune. Now that I think of it, even Miyajima's famous plum tree, planted by the great Saint Kobo Daishi, had been against us. That spring the tree had failed to produce any of its legendary double-petalled red flowers. That alone was a sign of extraordinary ill-omen.

Sumie followed me into the vermillion shrine, washing her hands and mouth before entering the portal. Although I went through the motions, I have never much been one for religious ritual myself.

Like my father before me, my heart had been turned against religion – whether it were Buddhism, Christianity, Mohammedanism, or any faith you can think of. All of them, in their own fanatical ways, are as bad as each other. Why is it that all of the greatest outrages that have been inflicted on this world have always been in the name of 'religion'? And the Buddhists, with their protestations of peace and goodwill, were no better than anyone else; who was it, after all, who launched the attack on Pearl Harbour? But I had not gone to the shrine for religious purposes. I was there purely as a mark of respect for my father.

I walked alone down colonnaded corridors that were hung with lanterns. The main shrine was gloomy after the bright sunlight, with that eternal musk of religious devotion. From below, I could hear the water slapping on the stilts, while all around were the muttered chants of the penitents next to me. I knelt and said a prayer of thanks for my father. In every way, he had been a much better man than myself.

Unlike the rest of the pilgrims, I was not going to waste my time on praying for my own good fortune; if it happened, it happened. I could not conceive how my future could be even remotely altered by a prayer on Miyajima.

I left after only a few minutes and was thankful to be back in the sunshine and away from that stifling atmosphere of religious zeal. As I had left the shrine, I had taken one of the fortune-telling paper slips, an Omikuji. I had been playing with it in my hand and had scrumpled it up into a little ball before forgetting about it.

A deer, one of Miyajima's 600-odd tame deer, came over and nuzzled my hand. Deer, along with the monkeys that infest the island, are said to be messengers of the Gods. The doe thought I had some food and as I opened my fingers I saw the fortune-slip. I flattened out the paper to find out my destiny. But it had nothing at all about my future – and everything about my way of life. 'Can you be kinder?'

I remember how aggrieved I felt. Could I be kinder? What did that mean? All of us could, perhaps, be kinder, but we have other things to do: family, lovers, work, commitments, obligations and traditions that must be kept. Did they not know there was a war on?

I fed the slip of paper to the deer, but still it rankled. Why me? Had I been especially unkind? Was I more unkind than anyone else? Not that I was superstitious, but still it vexed me and that, of course, was because it had so precisely hit the mark.

I waited for Sumie and tried to distract myself by reading the Hiroshima paper, the *Chugoku Shimbun*. You would not believe the drivel they used to serve us. We had been at war for four years, we were being beaten out of sight, and yet still the *Chugoku Shimbun* and all the other festering newspapers in Japan were claiming that ultimate victory was just around the corner. Well, perhaps it might have been – if it had been us who had spent the last five years developing the atomic bomb. But Japan's atomic weapons programme was nothing, nothing at all; just a dozen men wandering blind in the very foothills of atomic research. As it was, all we could fall back on were our bamboo spears, our suicide boats and our indomitable pluck.

But the editors of the *Chugoku Shimbun* were never in any

doubt. Every day, they ran pictures of girls eating bramble shoots, as well as delicious recipes to make the most of the grass and acorns. And always the countless stories about how we were on the very brink of winning the war. What was going on? Did they think we were imbeciles? How could anyone swallow this twaddle, this outrageous claptrap, when we were on the verge of a full-scale Yankee invasion?

Some people believed it; I suppose they must have, in much the same way that some people believed the Emperor was divine. I remember how, after it was all over, one of the army's most senior men, a Major General Masakazu Amano, had bleated: "We were absolutely sure of victory. It was the first and the only battle in which the main strength of the air, land and sea forces were to be joined. The geographical advantages of the homeland were to be utilised to the highest degree."

But I never bought it. Not for one moment.

I flicked to another page – more lies. As I simmered with resentment, I didn't notice the man at my feet. He was a war veteran and had lost both his legs. He sat on a cushioned wooden pallet and used his arms as crutches, pivoting on the knuckles of his gloved hands.

I lowered my paper and looked at the man. He was in his early-thirties, practically the same age as me. But with a face that was unlined, serene, as if he had found contentment on Miyajima.

"Yes?" I asked.

He proffered up a wooden bowl that had been tucked under his shirt. "Alms for a war veteran? Alms for a man who lost his legs fighting for the Emperor?"

"Perhaps," I folded up the paper, "If you can tell me one thing."

"Yes?" he smiled up at me, his teeth gleaming in the sunlight and his scuffed hands hanging limp by his side.

"Tell me honestly. Are we going to win the war?"

"Yes," he said. "Without question. We will win the war."

"And how are we going to do that?"

"I do not know."

I stood up. "Well I know. We are getting a beating. And if we do not surrender soon, your beloved motherland will be nothing but scorched earth—"

"How?"

"Have you not heard what happened to Tokyo five months ago? Do you know nothing? Half the capital has been burned to the ground. Every day, hundreds of bombers are pulverizing our cities."

"But Hiroshima has not been attacked. Be thankful for that."

"I will not be thankful for that! Be damned to you!"

The beggar shuffled at my feet. He was wearing the most pristine white shirt that hung loose over the stumps of his legs. "Alms for an old soldier?"

"No." I tossed that useless copy of the *Chugoku Shimbun* into his bowl. "You have lost your legs and still you have learned nothing."

He raised his hands anyway, as if in prayer, nodding towards me. "May the Goddess protect you."

"To hell with you." I stormed back to the water's edge, seething with rage at the war and at what the beggar had told me. For I knew that in one respect, at least, he was quite right. And I had long dreaded the consequences.

Just as he had said, throughout the duration of the war Hiroshima had hardly been hit by a single bomb – and meanwhile every other city in Japan was being pummelled to ruins by the Yankees' B29 bombers. Some believed that the Yankees had somehow forgotten about us; that our wonderful port city was blessed. Some idiots even thought – and I do not make this up – that President Harry Truman's mother had been captured by the Japanese and that she was being held prisoner in Hiroshima.

Truly it was as if we had built our city on the verdant South-facing slopes of a simmering Vesuvius and were revelling in our great good fortune. But just as they say in the West: beware Greeks bearing gifts.

There were a few cynics like myself, though, who believed there was only one reason why the Yankees were not bombing Hiroshima. And that had nothing to do with some slight cartographical oversight on the part of the American High Command. Rather it was because something special was being prepared just for us.

If I had had more sense, I would have followed my instincts. I would have left Hiroshima that very afternoon. But, come to think of it, I would only have been returning to my wife and son in Nagasaki, so I was going to be blown up whatever happened. Does it make any difference if you are blown up by two atomic bombs rather than one?

CHAPTER FOUR

My wife and child? Yes, among my many defects I also happened to be a faithless swine. But I can assure you that marital infidelity was the very least of my sins.

I had a wife and child waiting back home for me – in, of course, Nagasaki. The boy, Toshiaki, I loved to distraction; his mother Mako I had loved once, but my love had withered and died and was now nothing but a bare husk, like a shrivelled grape that has been left out on the autumn vine.

It was not solely because of my loveless marriage that I had taken up with Sumie after my posting to Nagasaki – but it had certainly helped. Alhough even if Mako had been the most affectionate of wives and a houri in the bedroom, I would still have more than likely taken up with all of my lovers. That is just the way of war. If you know that you might be nothing but ashes tomorrow, you are hardly going to be restrained by old-style notions of marital fidelity. So if a woman let it be known, by glance or deed, that she was interested then I saw it as a point of principle to take her up on the matter.

Since I'd married four years earlier, just a month before Pearl Harbour, I'd had seven lovers. Some were nothing more than a back alley tryst, feverishly panting out our lust against the walls before we went our separate ways, and some were full-blown affairs, with a proper beginning, middle and end.

Most of my affairs ended cordially enough and, if the opportunity arose, could be rekindled.

But of all of them, of my wife, my mistresses, and my flings-in-the-night, it was Sumie who was my favourite.

I had not noticed her as she glided up behind me at the water's edge. She had been in the shrine for nearly half-an-hour, praying for good fortune, health, wealth and happiness, and all the other little boons that we beg of our Gods – as if they cared one jot what we asked for.

In my total self-absorption, I did not recognise her agitation. She sat at the water's edge beside me, her feet a few centimetres above the water but not quite touching; just like death, now that I think of it, which also perpetually hovers over our heads.

She stared again at the fortune-slip in her hand before tucking it back into her pocket. How she twitched, first burying her hands between her entwined legs and then running her fingers through that rich, long mane.

"What does it say?" I asked.

"Everything is fine," she snapped. "Thank you for bringing me here."

She looked as if she was about to burst into tears. If there is one thing I cannot handle, it is a woman crying. It turns my heart to flint.

"Shall we go," I said, standing up, and the deer followed as we shuffled from the shrine complex and onto the island proper. Perhaps I could have been kinder, just as my own fortune-slip had suggested. But are we all supposed to turn our lives upside down just at the say-so of a scrap of paper? No, of course we do not. If we are going to change our selfish ways and shallow mindset, it is going to require something much, much more substantial than some injunction to kindliness on a random fortune-slip.

The mountain is said to have seven wonders, including a cherry tree beneath which the ground never dries, and a fire which has been burning for over 1,200 years. Not that those weren't interesting enough, along with the hollow rock that was perpetually replenished with sea-water, but for me it was pleasure enough to walk through the maples with Sumie's hand in my own.

The sweat was slick on my face, my shirt sticking to my back before we had even walked halfway up the hill. Sumie had at least stopped crying, but I left her alone with her thoughts. I did not wish to pry and I hoped that in time she would come out of it.

There was a bench by the path and wordlessly we sat on it. I offered her my water bottle.

She sipped, rolling the water round her mouth before swallowing. "I wish they would stop the war," she said.

"I wish they had never started it." Through the trees I could just catch a glimmer of the Inland Sea; how tranquil it all seemed.

"I do not understand why they go on. They talk about victory, but what are we hoping to achieve?"

"That is Ketsu-Go. We will kill so many of their soldiers that eventually they will realise we cannot be beaten. Ever! And then they will give up and go home."

"How many of us are they going to kill?"

"Does it matter? Does it matter if every man, woman and child is killed in defence of our country? It is an irrelevance. The aim of Ketsu-Go is to administer such a blood-letting as has never been witnessed before in recorded history. Ketsu-Go will give the Western Imperialists a perfect display of Oriental inscrutability."

She laughed and cuffed my leg. "Do you always have to make light of these things?"

"I would have gone mad if I didn't." I laughed and kissed her on the neck. "What else am I supposed to do? There is death all around us, hundreds of thousands of people burned alive in Tokyo. And yet still we are supposed to be cheering this blind charge over the cliff-edge? Laughter, I tell you Sumie. It is the only way."

"The only way?" She kissed me full on the lips, her hand slipping beneath my shirt to my waist.

"As always, you are right," I said, and dutifully followed her into a cluster of trees about 50 metres from the path. We took off her clothes with practised ease, tossing them onto the ground to make a bed of sorts. How easy it was making love in those days. I hardly remember a pause in the conversation as we began to make love in the matter-of-fact way of new lovers for whom sex is a daily requirement.

How she wriggled and teased beneath me, smiling up as the dappled shadows flecked across her face. "The war did bring you into my life," she mused. "Should I be grateful for that?"

"Perhaps we would have met even if there had not been a war?"

"But without the war, I probably would not have become your lover."

I paused for a moment to kiss that exquisite mole beside her mouth. I have never so loved an imperfection on a woman's body as that little mole, its vivid blackness in stunning contrast to her perfect white teeth. "How could you deny your instincts?"

She sighed with contentment, lifting her knees off the ground. "Did you ever joke around with your wife like this?"

"No. She doesn't like my jokes. She never has," I stroked some hair out of Sumie's face. "What about your husband?"

"What do you think? He was a soldier. He did what he was ordered – and he was certainly not ordered to think—"

"Stop," I whispered. We were being watched. In a bush not five metres ahead of us, I could see a pair of unblinking black eyes. For a moment I thought we were being stalked by a child.

"What is it?" Sumie said, trying to turn her head.

"One second." I rolled back onto my knees and picked up a stone, hefting it once before hurling it at the bush. There was a flat wet thud, followed by a shriek of pain. The monkey screamed as it clambered up a tree, a young buck calling out for its mother. It sat on one of the upper branches of a maple, rubbing its chest as it chattered insults down upon my head.

Sumie, so at ease with her nakedness, her hair a perfect shimmering black waterfall, rolled onto her side and stared at the enraged monkey. "Was that a good idea?"

"You wanted to put on a sex show for him?"

"He was just interested, the poor thing."

"I will throw another if he stays there."

"You will do no such thing. Come here and make love to me."

"Watched by that monkey?"

"I am sure you have done worse."

By now a second monkey, a larger one, had come swooping through the tree-tops in all its long-limbed glory. And there on the high branch the two monkeys sat, squawking to themselves like a pair of hunched crones.

Despite my lust and despite Sumie's extraordinary beauty, the moment had gone. The monkeys had killed my ardour and there was nothing that Sumie could do to recover it.

"I didn't know you were shy," she teased me.

"There is a difference between being shy and wanting to put on a floor show for a troupe of monkeys."

"And would you be able to teach them anything?" How gaily she laughed as she put her top on.

"How about this?"

I picked up a handful of stones, each about the size of a hen's egg, and then and there bombarded the monkeys. How they shrieked as the stones whistled round their ears.

"Stop that," she said. "You might hurt them."

"That's what I am trying to do." I must have been mad – standing there naked amid the trees, hurling stones at two monkeys who had unwittingly spoiled my fun.

"Please stop," she said. By now she had pulled on her trousers and was slipping on her shoes.

"And one for luck." I tossed the stone lightly in my hand, remembering how I had used to scare the crows off my father's vegetable plot. I hurled it with all my might, as heedless as a schoolboy of the consequences. The stone arcked up through the branches and clouted the smaller monkey full in the face. For a moment, the screeching stopped and then the animal slowly toppled head-first out of the tree. It caromed off two branches before thudding headfirst into the ground just a few metres from where I stood.

I stood there, naked, staring at the dead monkey. I could hardly believed I had killed it. From the top of the tree there started a great wailing.

Sumie had rushed over to the frail corpse that a moment earlier had been so full of life. The monkey was now nothing but a broken rag doll, its limbs splayed limp on the leaves.

"Oh, but that was unkind," said Sumie, tears in her eyes as she stroked the animal. "You can be so thoughtless."

I was both stunned and embarrassed by what I had done. I tried to make light of it, though, as I pulled my clothes on. "That is what happens to anything that gets in the way of our love-making."

"Please do not joke." She gazed into the monkey's pulped face, searching for any sign of life. "That was awful."

I did not know what to say, or how to handle the situation. I had just killed a dumb animal and I felt like an idiot. So, not knowing what else to do, I continued to joke. "Bush-meat," I said. "We should take it home. I've not eaten meat in months."

"I should never have come," Sumie said, walking back to the path.

I hurried after her, the screams of the other monkey following me through the trees. "I'm sorry," I said, snatching at her elbow. "Sumie, I'm sorry."

"I am cursed now. I know it," she said. "I was cursed when I set foot on the island and now I am doubly cursed."

"I'm sorry," I repeated, as I followed her down the path and back towards the shrine.

"Those monkeys are messengers!" She stopped suddenly on the path, turning to me. "Do you not understand?"

I reached out and tried to pull her close, but she slipped from my fingers and continued down the hill. How I hated her for crying like that. "What more can I say? What do you want me to say?"

"I should never have come," she said once more, though it was almost as if she were talking to herself. "Why could I not have followed my instincts? Why did I have to listen to you?"

How I squirmed, how I writhed, as I scuttled after her down the hill, only too aware of how badly I had behaved. I also knew that I had blown any chance of having sex on Miyajima. Perhaps it was that which irked me more than anything else.

Sumie strode on ahead of me, arms swinging briskly as she bounded back to the shrine.

"It is only an old wives' tale," I called out after her. "It is just a superstition!"

"So I am superstitious," she called back. "What are you going to do? Throw a stone at me?"

"Sumie – please."

"The shrine has been here for over a thousand years!" She stopped and turned again, the tears still bright on her cheeks. "And I let you bring me here. We even had sex."

"It is all right." I stretched a hand, trying to soothe her.

"I should never have come."

She was still seething as we climbed onto the ferry later that afternoon – but by then not so much cross with me as angry with herself for being cajoled into visiting Miyajima. On the way back, I made a few conversational sallies and tried to be bubbly, but it was as if she'd had a glimpse of her own death because nothing could rally her.

Back at her home, that lovely old guest-house where Shinzo and I had spent the last three months, she busied herself putting some rice onto the brazier. It was so unlike her to be like that. Normally after a disagreement, she bounced back in a matter of minutes. But this time, she was so dispirited that soon after our desultory supper she went to sleep.

I went for a walk by myself on that last evening in Hiroshima. Like everywhere else in Japan, there was a total black-out; the little light that there was came from the stars and the new moon. It was a cool, delicious evening, the mountains bathed a gorgeous vermillion red in the dusk light.

Despite the war, Hiroshima had still retained a few cinemas and a few brothels, now that I think of it. What better way for a soldier to spend his wages than to buy a few minutes of love? In those harsh days, you took what you could get.

I joined the queue at the Kotobuki theatre to watch a movie. I still remember the name: *Four Weddings* – a comedy, I think, about four sisters all desperate to marry the same eligible bachelor. I was not in the mood for humour; still annoyed, in fact angry, about the dead monkey.

I might have enjoyed walking back through Hiroshima's sedate streets with its mass of waterways if Sumie had been at my side. It was a heavenly night, the perfect night; as if the city somehow knew that she was about to take leave of her citizens. Without anyone to share it, though, and with no hand to hold, no lips to kiss, the evening left me unmoved.

Shinzo was already snoring on his futon in the room that we shared. Occasionally in his sleep he would scratch at his groin or his head. All of us were infested with lice in those days, though I think Shinzo had them worse than most. Even if you did get the lice out of your hair, your clothes would still be riddled with them, lying snug in the seams.

I undressed silently, leaving my clothes on the floor where they fell, and slipped across the landing to Sumie's bedroom. She was asleep on the futon, her back curled to the door, but a gas-lamp was burning low for me on the table. Her clothes were hung up neatly by the door. I was about to turn out the light when I paused. I wondered. Was it still there?

I padded back to the door and went through her pockets.

At first I thought she had thrown it away, but then my fingers touched it, crushed into a crisp ball at the bottom of her trouser pocket.

I took the fortune-slip over to the lamp, flattening it out between thumb and forefinger. I could not imagine what had made her so tearful.

There was no getting round it. Even I would have been unnerved. Some fortune slips are ambiguous, but this was quite unequivocal: "Very bad luck".

Though now I think of it, the fortune slip was more than just a prediction for the future. It was also a note of sympathy, or regret, as if to say how unfortunate it was that Sumie was about to be caught up in the hell that was Hiroshima.

CHAPTER FIVE

I wrote earlier that those pitiful suicide boats were Japan's most useless invention of the war.

I correct myself. There was, I believe, one other weapon that was even more ridiculous – and I was one of the few men who were helping to make it.

I was a kite-maker.

The irony of it all still amuses me. Sometimes I laugh so much that the tears run down my cheeks; so much that my wife will come hurrying out to the balcony as if I am in some terrible pain. But I am not in any discomfort. More often than not these days, I am deliriously, senselessly overjoyed to be alive, and to still find myself with the ability to laugh at the stupidity of it all.

I used to be told that my humour was inappropriate and out of place. But now I am an old man and am perceived to have wisdom, I can laugh at whatever I please. To my mind, one of the more hilarious facts about the end of World War II is that, while America was spending approximately $2 billion building the world's first atomic bomb, we had gone into overdrive with our production of bamboo spears. In the last few months of the war, we may not have had the steel to produce many guns or conventional ordnance, but our production of bamboo spears had sky-rocketed. Never before in recorded history had we produced so many of the things, and everyone, right down to the fresh-faced 15-year-old schoolgirls, was being trained how to use them.

And along with our millions of spears, we were also hoping to fend off the Yankee offensive with our hundreds of box kites. The kite scheme had been dreamed up by the Tiger of Malaya, General Tomoyuki Yamashita, as a means to protect our convoys from Yankee fighters. Yamashita's plan was that each ship would have up to 20 heavy-duty kites, which would be attached by strong twine and then sent spiralling 500 metres into the sky. Rather like the great barrage balloons that flew over Europe in World War I, each kite was to have a number of grenades attached to its underbelly. It was hoped that when the Yankee fighters swooped to attack, they would hit the kites and be blown out of the sky.

I do not believe that a single one of our kites was ever used in action. For a start, we did not have any ships. The few ships that were left in the Combined Fleet, including the great battleship Yamato, had been sunk off southern Kyushu four months earlier.

But aside from not having any ships, there were so many flaws to the kite bombs I would have been staggered if they had killed a single Yankee. Apart from anything else, the kites were largely made of bamboo, paper, paste and string: hopeless in the wet.

Still, we all of us had to play our part in the war effort, even the 12-year-old girls who were put to work as telephonists. And since I was not just a kite-maker but a Nagasaki kite-maker, I was deemed to have the necessary levels of expertise to be allowed to make kites for the service of the Emperor.

My love affair with kites had started when I was just six years old, ever since my father had first put a little square Hata kite into my hands. Kite-flying is a national hobby in Japan, but in Nagasaki it has risen almost to the level of a religion. We're so fanatical we even have our own kite festival every March; what a sight for my tired old eyes to see those thousands of kites, a riot of colour, bobbing in the breeze.

My kite-making had only ever been a hobby and for the previous seven years I had been a merchant seaman. But as the tide of war had turned against Japan, I was out of a job. We had no ships left, no fuel to power them – and next to nothing that was worth transporting in the first place.

That spring I had arrived back in Nagasaki after my final tour to China and, like everyone else in Japan, was immediately put to work. The whole country, young, old and infirm, was doing its bit for the war effort. For me, this meant making kites to protect our ships.

I know it sounds completely crazy; welcome to the insane world of Imperial Japan during the last few months of the war.

Three months earlier, in May, Shinzo, I and a handful of other Nagasaki kite-makers had taken the train 240 kilometres North-East to Hiroshima. We were billeted out to various boarding houses around the city and spent our days mired in bamboo, string and paste. It was strange to think that those little works of art were not going to be used for play but as weapons of war. For the first time I was an arms manufacturer and therefore a legitimate enemy target. But I was one of the few Japanese who enjoyed my war work. For me, kite-making was a joy in its own right. Once the kites were finished, the army could have used them for firewood for all I cared.

From the start, it was apparent that the whole kite scheme was ridiculous. But it would not have been politic to have mentioned my scepticism to anyone except Shinzo and a few select friends. Every town and every work place was infested with secret informers, who were just thirsting for the chance to report you to the Kempai-Tai – as if that would somehow prove their patriotism. So, although we all had our doubts about the kites, in public at least we pronounced our delight at finally being able to play our part in the great war that would bring such glory to the Emperor.

Hiroshima, with its neat streets of wooden tiled houses and its seven arterial waterways, was a gem of a city; very different from how it is today. And that bright, clear Monday morning – Monday 6th August 1945 – I had never seen it so beautiful. I was up at 6.40 and, as I threw open the first-floor shutters, the glistering city was spread all before me, like a rolling patchwork of brown and beige that slipped into the sea. Little tendrils of grey kitchen smoke were already puffing up from its hundreds of chimneys, as our daily fare of unpolished rice was boiled up on the charcoal burners. Far off, I could make out great flocks of seagulls, a flurry of white against a clear blue sky; could smell the salt tang of the Inland Sea, even though it was perhaps five kilometres away. Our waterways were tidal, so wherever you were in Hiroshima, you always had that scent of the sea.

Compared to Japan's other great cities, Hiroshima was in a fabulous state of repair – but that was solely so the full potency of Little Boy could be properly tested on virgin bombing ground. Or, as the man in charge of America's atomic bomb project, General Leslie Groves, pithily recommended to his superiors: "The targets should not have been previously damaged by air attacks, to enable us to assess accurately the effects of the bomb."

The only obvious damage to Hiroshima had been an epic piece of self-mutilation. Three enormous fire-breaks had been carved out East-West across the city, as some 70,000 houses, cafes, shops and offices had been razed to the ground. Over 7,000 school-children had been put to work, pulling down our houses with nothing more than ropes and brute force. It was hoped that the breaks might stem the firestorm when the inevitable bombing raids finally rained down on Hiroshima.

I still find it astonishing to think that not one of us had realised the true import of why we had never been bombed. There we were imagining that somehow we had been blessed; that Japan's seventh largest city, ripe with its munitions factories and army installations, had somehow just slipped beneath the Yankees' radar. We believed that if we kept quiet, kept our noses down, then we might be allowed to carry on going about our mild-mannered business. Whereas we had been the primary, or 'AA', target for the world's first atomic bomb for at least the previous three months. Oh yes, they knew all about Hiroshima. We had been hand-picked by a special 'Target Selection Committee', before being personally approved by the President; as Truman said, the buck stopped with him.

On almost every count, Hiroshima was the perfect target. We had over 43,000 troops which qualified us as an army city; we had scores of munitions and explosives factories (not forgetting, of course, our lethal kite-bomb warehouse); and, unlike the only other 'AA' target, Kyoto, we had no especial 'religious significance' to save us.

In fact, the more the Target Committee studied Hiroshima, the better she looked. The city had the perfect dimensions, roughly five kilometres by seven kilometres, to be totally annihilated by a 13.5 kiloton bomb such as Little Boy. Even our mountains, those breathtaking mountains, were against us with the Target Committee deeming them 'likely to produce a focusing effect which would considerably increase the blast damage'. And then, the icing on the cake, our distinctive pattern of waterways meant that the Yankee bombardier Tom Ferebee could have spotted us blindfold.

No, our destiny had been decided long ago in Washington, and there was only one thing that could have saved us that Monday: thick cloud cover. Tom Ferebee could only make his drop if he had visual contact with the city nine kilometres beneath him. The clouds were certainly thick enough to save Kokura three days later. But that morning, with the wind calm and temperatures already soaring into the 80s, I can hardly remember seeing the sky so blue. It was going to be another glorious summer's day.

That last image that I have of Hiroshima, the epitome of a peaceful city stretching itself awake, is freeze-framed in my mind. I remember it well because it was the last time I ever saw her. And there is always an especial poignancy to that last picture we have of an old, dear friend before they are taken away from us.

In just 96 minutes, Hiroshima would be blown off the face of the earth by that black screaming horror that was Little Boy. Shinzo was still asleep, his stubbled jowl glistening with sweat. I watched him twitch in the half-light, like an old hunting dog at the hearth, his snoring now as rhythmic as waves on the beach. A hand moved to scratch at the lice in his armpit. In a rare moment of tenderness, I let him be.

By the side of his futon, there was another painfully ridiculous invention of the war: the personal bamboo life-raft, comprising four struts of bamboo that had been lashed together into a square. Now if ever you doubted it, the construct of the bamboo life-raft truly reveals that we were being led by headless chickens.

For some reason, it had been conceived that the Yankees were going to bomb the dams about 50 kilometres inland, and that in the ensuing flood Hiroshima was to be wiped off the face of the earth. That being the case, the military had issued 200,000 'life-rafts'. When the great flood came, we were to strap the life-rafts to our backs and bob merrily into the Inland Sea until the waters had abated. You may imagine that I am exaggerating this point, but every word of it is true.

I barely know where to begin as I try to express my contempt for the woolly thinking that went into creating all those thousands of bamboo squares. It was farcical. Even if the dams were bombed – which was never going to happen – it would have taken eight hours for the floods to reach Hiroshima. And, when that occurred, were we seriously going to trust those bamboo life-rafts?

Sometimes it felt like the authorities were just trying to keep us busy, running us off our feet from one moment to the next so that we could never stand still, be calm, look at the problem rationally. If any of us had done that, we would have surrendered in the blink of an eye.

After I had washed and shaved, I put on my work-clothes;

just the usual patched shirt and trousers that were standard in Japan in those days. All clothing was rationed by then, our annual allowance buying a single shirt and pair of trousers. I will say this for the war though – it had made all of us equal. We were all wearing the same tatty clothes and all of us, even the Emperor, were eating the same miserable food.

The last thing I did before I left the room was to slip on my money-belt, which we were all encouraged to wear – just in case we lost everything we owned. It contained over 3,000 Yen, equal to about six months' pay. Half of the money was Shinzo's. We had decided to take out an insurance of sorts, by dividing up our money between us so that, even if I lost everything, I would still have half my purse lying snug round his ample belly. That is how much I trusted the man – and in that respect, at least, I showed surprisingly good judge of character.

I popped in on Sumie. She was still asleep, but smiled and cupped my cheek when I knelt and kissed her goodbye. And, like my last image of Hiroshima, I will never forget the sight of her sprawled on her front, arms and legs splayed in wanton abandon, exuding that childlike innocence that comes to all of us in sleep.

Sumie's white-tiled kitchen was spotless, but I did not linger, wolfing down some rice-balls and a piece of left over pumpkin. In the vestibule, I put on my favourite footwear, my old leather boots, weathered by many years at sea but still far more durable than the usual straw slippers we wore. I had worn them during my days as a merchant seaman, but I loved them because they had belonged to my father. Every time I put them on, I thought of him.

My bicycle was in the shed by the vegetable patch. I wheeled it out and, just as I knew she would be, the neighbour's girl was already there to wave me off.

She was only seven years old and, like many children of the war, had a precociousness and self-sufficiency that was way beyond her years. She was an orphan and was looked after by her grandmother, who worked long hours as a nurse at the Shima Hospital in the centre of Hiroshima. There were no uncles, aunts or cousins, so the girl spent her days as she pleased; like a young mongrel that scavenges constantly about her patch in search of excitement.

"Good morning," she called.

I peered about me to see where the voice was coming from, studying the shadows and the alleyways for a sight of her, but still she eluded me. "Good morning yourself, wherever you are."

"I'm up here," she laughed. She was right on the top of her home, sitting astride the very apex of the roof-tiles.

"Is that as dangerous as it looks?"

"Not for a dancer," she said, and with that she got up and starting skipping along the roof-ridge. She was over two storeys high but was parading herself as easily as if she had been on the pavement. I remember how surreal it was to see that circus act silhouetted against the sun, with the girl's pig-tails flying behind her as she danced in the sky. What a picture of carefree abandon, so unaware that she was teetering on the very edge of disaster. She danced along the roof, skipping, one step, two step, as blithe as a ballerina. With a final twirl, she landed against the chimney stack and curtseyed to me.

"Very impressive," I said, clapping lightly. "What would your grandmother say?"

"She's gone to work."

"So you'll be getting up to mischief?"

She laughed and twirled again. "I thought I would join the local schoolgirls. You have never heard a sound like it when we pull the houses down. And the dust, it gets everywhere! It gets into your mouth, your nose and your eyes. It's very exciting."

I laughed at the thought of the girl tugging away at the cables. I could almost picture the fierce frown of concentration as she joined 30 other toiling schoolgirls in this ceaseless tug-of-war. "I am sure you are very good at it."

"I am," she said, and with that she grabbed hold of a drain-pipe and shimmied down the side of the house as effortlessly as a monkey. She jumped the last metre and then skipped over to me, hands clasped behind her back, skirt billowing about her. "They say we're pulling down many more houses now that I'm with them."

"I am sure they are." I climbed onto my bicycle, kicked up the pedal.

"When are you going to make me a kite? You promised me one weeks ago."

"Every time I make a kite for you, the Navy takes it off me. They say they need them for their ships."

"To kill more Yankees?"

"That is the idea."

"That is good then. I hope we kill every one of them."

"They are not that bad. I think you would quite like them."

"Never! They killed my father!"

"I will see about that kite."

I was about to push off, when the city's siren opened up in a series of short blasts. It was more an alert signal than the full alarm. High up in the sky was a single B-29, a gleaming streak of silver set against the most brilliant blue; I am told that the sight of it moved some people to poetry. The name of that particular B-29 was 'Straight Flush', and it was in the very act of signing our death warrant – its radio operator was reporting back that the weather conditions over Hiroshima were perfect.

Over the previous weeks we had seen scores of these B-29s, and – just as Colonel Paul Tibbets had planned – were so used to them that we barely gave them a second glance. We had seen so many of these passive planes drifting high over Hiroshima that we had all but forgotten that they were the world's most advanced killing machines.

"A single Mr B," I said, using the affectionate 'B-san' name by which the children called the B29s. "Will you go to the shelter?"

The girl kicked at a stone in front of her, scuffing up the dust. "If I die, I die," she said, squinting at the innocuous single plane.

"It would be nice to think we had some control over our future," I said.

"It is fate."

I have often wondered about that since. All of us like to believe that we are masters of our own destinies. But once you have been caught up in something like Hiroshima, when small matters of happenstance mean the difference between life and death, you can start to believe that fate may have lent a hand. This is exponentially so if you have also survived Nagasaki; it is fate squared. For most of our lives, there is not much of true import. It makes no odds if we go into work early, or if we have a leisurely breakfast at home. It does not matter if we spend all day in bed, or if we diligently go about our chores. But, for one single second that day, fate ruled the world and every chance decision that we made that morning would determine whether we lived or died.

It is best not to dwell on these matters; it plays havoc with your brain. If you have survived not one but two atomic bombs, you can be constantly tormented over whether the small things do matter. Should I boil some rice, or should I go for a walk? Will it make a difference? Will my life depend on it?

With luck, though, you will eventually come to the serene conclusion that, most likely, nothing will make a blind bit of difference; and, even if it did, there is nothing you could do about it anyway.

I waved to the girl as I weaved off down the dusty lane, with not an inkling that we were but an hour from Armageddon. With the wind in my face, it felt like I was in a safe haven, a world away from the death and destruction that was daily being visited on Toyko.

Out on one of the Drill Fields, soldiers were already going about their training, thrusting with bayonets at the stuffed straw bags that were our make-believe Yankee enemy. Cherry trees, peach trees and the great willows by the rivers, all of them verdant, green, lush with life. The teeming waterways, so full of energy – destined by noon-time to be so clogged with death that you could have walked the water on a bridge of corpses.

It is difficult to think back to that 30-minute bike ride through the city without also remembering how in a single second Hiroshima was turned into a wasteland. The clusters of schoolgirls, devoted to their duty, were already hauling at their ropes to create ever bigger fire-breaks. I watched as a team of 20 of them hauled at a rope attached to a wooden pillar. At first nothing seemed to happen, and then suddenly the front of the house tumbled down in a rumble of dust, tiles and wooden planks.

The Aioi T-bridge, the biggest of our 49 bridges, so broad, so impregnable and within the hour set to become the very aiming point for Bombardier Tom Ferebee. Already the bridge was alive with cyclists, pedestrians, wooden push-carts, all of them going about their business, not knowing that the wheel of fate was on its final spin. I can especially recall the sight of a lone beggar, squatting on the stone steps of what might have been a bank. He was on a blanket, wooden stick by his side, tranquilly watching the world go by. Four hours later I walked past him again. He was still staring sightlessly out over Hiroshima, his shrunken body turned into a solid piece of black charcoal, incinerated from head to toe. His shadow was etched into the stone wall behind him, an eerie echo of his last moment on earth. I remember the shock as I recognised him. I had stooped to touch his hand; his charcoaled arm snapped in half like a dry twig.

The sedate streets, with their long lines of tinder-dry wood houses – just perfect for a city-wide fire-storm. It did not really need Little Boy to destroy us. I am sure we could have been just as effectively wiped out by the incendiary bombs that had worked so well on Tokyo. But what was the point of spending $2 billion on a new atomic toy if you were not going to use it?

And those posters; how I remember those posters. As I think back to Hiroshima before the bomb, I get these little snap-shots of memory. Plastered on every available piece of wall-space were these jingoistic posters, which constantly bleated that the end was in sight: 'Victory is definitely with us! Our sacred country will repel the hated enemy!'; 'The enemy must be defeated!'; 'We ask for nothing but to win the war!'

Yes, indeed – just give us the chance to get stuck in with our bamboo spears and we would grind the Yankees to dust. Forgive me if my words do sometimes drip with sarcasm, but if you could not laugh at the irony of it all, it would make you weep. And I have done that too; many times.

I had cycled about five or six kilometres south through the city before I came to the vast Mitsubishi Shipbuilding Company, which lies on one of the fingers of Hiroshima that stretches out into the Inland Sea. Warehouses were dotted all about the waterfront, the relics of what had once been a thriving war industry. But the place had long since turned into a ghost town.

The bomb alert ended as I pedalled up to the kite-makers' warehouse. A few cautious souls emerged from the bomb-shelters, but most had not bothered to take cover. Hiroshima had not been targeted in months, so why were the Yankees going to start now?

From one of the bunkers stepped Takuo, a woman who I had flirted with and who I would definitely have kissed if she had not been so happily married. I think she worked as a secretary for one of the senior officers, though I never talked about work with her. A lovely smile and, what I remember best, the loveliest breasts, which, though kept under wraps, seemed constantly straining to break through her patterned shirt. In those lean times, it was rare indeed to see a beautiful woman so amply endowed.

"Good morning, Takuo," I said, leaning my bike against the wall.

"Did I miss anything?"

"Only 20 minutes of sunshine." I locked my eyes on hers.

"Oh – but the bunker can be quite nice in the morning."

"With you, Takuo dearest, the bunker would be wonderful at any time of the day." It was cheesy, I know, but she giggled delightedly all the same.

"Why are you in so early? You're never in at this hour."

"All for the greater good of the Emperor and our beloved Motherland."

"How is it that when you say such things, I never believe you?"

By now I had walked to the warehouse, where I lingered by the door. "Do you believe anything I say?"

"From you?" She raised her finger coquettishly to her lips. "Probably not."

I opened the door. "One of these days I would like to go on a picnic with you. Can you believe that?"

Takuo tittered in the manner of a Geisha girl, hands in front of her mouth, almost as if she was embarrassed at this unseemly display of humour. "I am a married woman!" she said. She then ruined the effect by giving me the most brilliant smile, and I fluttered my fingers as I walked into the gloom of the warehouse.

I think our warehouse might once been used for army stores, but these had long since gone. Instead, all about the high walls and stretching the length of a tennis court were the hundreds of box kites that we had so lovingly constructed for the Japanese Imperial Fleet. I did, I suppose, feel some little pride as I walked in and inspected my handiwork of the previous three months; though, even before Little Boy, I was aware of the futility of it all.

High in the walls were a few dirty windows. The dust spangled as the weak sunlight glimmered through the murk. After the brilliant sunshine, it took a few seconds for my eyes to adjust. I was surprised to find that one of the other kite-makers, Motoji, was already hunched over his work-bench, softly sawing off lengths of bamboo.

He had the radio on and was listening to the glib patter of Masanobu Furuta, one of Hiroshima Radio Station's 'sweet-sounding voices of reason'. Furuta possessed, said the newspapers, a voice 'which calmed our anxieties'. I could not stand the man.

"Good morning," I called out to Motoji. "Enjoy yourself yesterday?"

"I came here to work," said Motoji, peering up at me over the tops of his little round glasses. His brow was drawn and furrowed, and he had an almost perpetual stoop, the mark of a man who had spent too long indoors. And what a low-slung weasel of a man he was. Motoji was one of the few kite-makers who came from Hiroshima, and I had met him three months earlier. As it was, I think I would only have needed two minutes with him to have come up with a complete character analysis.

The war seemed to have cemented all the most loathsome aspects of his personality. Under the mantle of the war effort, this stifling killjoy was able to vaunt himself as the most ardent patriot. Eating the most frugal food was proof that he was a patriot; arriving early to work and leaving late was proof that he loved his country; and working on Sundays meant he was a devout nationalist who worshipped the Emperor.

There were many like him, though thankfully I rarely came into daily contact with them. To me, Motoji was nothing more than a hamster on his wheel, blindly scurrying onward, onward, because that was his masters' bidding.

I laughed as I sauntered through the warehouse, my fingers stretching out to trace over the kite-frames. I have always loved the feel of the parchment-dry paper of a new kite.

"You know what they say – a day away from the warehouse is a day wasted."

"That is so," Motoji replied, ignoring my irony.

I stopped by the door at the far end and called out to him. "Tell me, Motoji. Do you think any of your kites will ever be used in action?"

"Without doubt. They will help us to ultimate victory." He stood up to look at me, his round shoulders continuing in a smooth curve from his neck.

"And where are the ships on which your kites are going to fly?"

"They are out fighting on the oceans. We are making more of them as we speak. Our armaments factories are working through the night."

"Strange how none of the ships ever put in to Hiroshima anymore," I goaded.

"The fighting spirit of the people lives on," he said, as if repeating some hallowed piece of wisdom.

"Is that another line you are spouting from that rag *Chugoku Shimbun*?"

"It is," he said, toying with the saw in his hands. "It is a paper that I am proud to buy. You would do well to read it."

"So that they can tell me about all the fleets of Yankee ships that we have sunk?"

"The Yankee ships have been sunk. I know it."

"So I can read more uplifting stories about the life and times of a Kamikaze hero? So I can garner more delicious recipes for grass soup?"

Motoji bristled, the saw quivering as it flexed between his fingers. "That is disgraceful," he said. "You are a disgrace. You are disloyal to your country and you are a disgrace to your Emperor."

I could have said more, but I saved my breath. I could not be bothered. It would have been easier to talk a pig into denying his constant appetite for food. Yet there were so many like Motoji, people for whom it was easier to believe the government's lies than to deny the evidence of their own eyes. How cleverly our leaders had dressed up the war effort, as if it was our patriotic duty to believe in Japan's ultimate victory, and that to doubt it for even a moment was tantamount to treason.

I clicked the metal door shut behind me and walked into the small common room that adjoined the main warehouse. Shinzo and I would occasionally have lunch there. It had a few bamboo chairs and a low table, as well as the sacred picture of our Emperor Hirohito, his chest dripping with medals, braid and bejewelled honours. How singularly out of place all that gilt and gold looked on our mild-mannered Emperor. With his wisp of a moustache and thick pebble glasses, Hirohito gave every appearance of being an earnest academic.

And indeed he was – before the war, he had been a world expert on marine microbiology.

Actually, though once I may have sneered at Hirohito and everything he stood for, I do now admire the man. From the very first, he had been against the war. Just before Pearl Harbour, Hirohito had read out a poem to that blood-thirsty band of warmongers that ruled our country:

'When I regard all the world
'As my own brothers
'Why is it that its tranquillity
'Should be so thoughtlessly disturbed?'

Wise words from the great man. Not that anyone listened to him but, in the end, Hirohito did manage to bring about a speedier close to the war – and I have always been grateful for that. If he had not, I would have been shot dead, and what a tragic end that would have been for a man who had just survived two atomic bombs.

You may wonder what I was doing at the warehouse so early on a Monday morning when I had little interest in making kites. The reason was simple enough: I was there to nose round the foreman's office. Like Motoji, our foreman was another upstanding Japanese patriot, but the difference with Major Akiba was that he had power with it. He was a short thug of a man in charge not just of our kite-making operation but the entire complex. With his smooth, waxen face and trim little moustache, he was a blistering cauldron of rage. Even for a civilian like me, he could make life very unpleasant.

Akiba is now dead and so I will strive to be fair to the man. He was a typical product of Japan's 'no surrender' school of army training. There were thousands like him and I do not doubt that I would have loathed them too. I was so sick of the daily diet of lies fed to us, and Akiba and his ilk were all part of the system which kept the entire 100 million population under heel.

I do not especially blame Akiba; he was doing just exactly what he had been trained to do. But I certainly did not have to like him either. For the past three months I had been in almost daily contact with that barking martinet, with his shrieked orders and his eye-watering petty sanctions, and I had come to loathe the man.

So that morning, while he was off for some meeting at Hiroshima's old castle, it was the perfect opportunity for me to delve and pry. I have always been a snooper; perhaps I should have become a journalist.

I walked across the common-room and lifted the Emperor's portrait off the wall. Behind it, just as I expected, was a little hole which contained the key to Akiba's room. It had never once occurred to the brute that one of his staff might venture into his office.

I took the key and carefully replaced the picture, before letting myself into Akiba's office. Should have taken the trouble to lock the door behind me. Or perhaps not, seeing as how events turned out.

Just as you would expect from a disciplinarian like Akiba, his corner-office was immaculate. The room was high and airy, with two spectacular walls of windows that stretched from waist height all the way up to the ceiling. As befitted someone of Akiba's rank, they were cleaned weekly. Behind his wooden desk was a view of the entire city of Hiroshima, and beyond it the cocooning embrace of the mountains.

For the moment, I ignored the four grey filing cabinets that were standing against the wall underneath another picture of the Emperor. If Akiba had anything of value, he would keep it in his desk. I pulled up the sturdy wooden chair and made myself at home. He didn't have the imagination to lock his desk; it was beyond his comprehension that someone might dare to rifle through his personal possessions. How little he knew me.

I hit gold with the first drawer that I opened. It was a broad drawer, a full 40 centimetres wide, and I had thought it might contain some of Akiba's more personal jottings. But as the drawer squeaked open, I realised with delight that it was his personal drinks cabinet. It contained not one but two bottles of Sake, as well as a single cut crystal glass. Why have two glasses when you had no intention of ever sharing your drink?

Sake! How I love the stuff, and, even now that I am in my nineties, I still treat myself to a daily tot. In the latter days of the war, good Sake was fantastically difficult to come by. It could not be bought for love nor money. Some friends back in Nagasaki had attempted to distil their own rice spirit, but it was so rough that the headache had kicked in long before I'd felt even remotely inebriated.

But this Sake, I could see from the label, was of the very best quality Kamoizumi. As stated earlier, it was in my nature to snatch up every gift the very moment it passed me by. Though perhaps I did have a tingle of what was about to befall us, for I was suddenly possessed by the most reckless abandon. I poured out three fingers into Akiba's cut-crystal glass and, leaning back on his chair, I kicked my big seaman's boots up onto the polished desk. I delighted at the sight of those ugly old boots on his black-lacquered desk; how that pompous piece of puffery would have exploded if he had seen me!

I had a stunning view of the Tenma River, the water so dazzling it might have been carpeted with jewels. I took a long sip of the Sake, holding it in my mouth before letting it razor down the back of my throat. It had been so long since I had tasted decent Sake that I had quite forgotten its soft kick, which seems to mainline those intoxicating earthy fumes straight to your brain.

How blissful it was to sit there with a glass of Akiba's Sake in my hand, making myself at home in his spit-polished office. Was this, I wondered, how my indignant little master liked to spend his evenings, admiring the view and quietly filling out the interminable paperwork that came with rank?

In another drawer, I found, of all things, a number of red onions. I ate one of them there and then, stuffing the wispy peelings into my pocket. And even six hours later, as I tried to dig Sumie out of the rubble, I could still smell the onion on my breath; just a tiny reminder of my life before Little Boy.

I found some personal files and was leafing through them. There was one with Motoji's dour face clipped to the cover. Along with all his service details, there was a single word summary at the top: 'Diligent'. I snorted in derision.

My own file, complete with a similarly wan photo, was a little further down the pile. Akiba had used two words, not one, to sum me up: 'Lazy. Insubordinate.' Perhaps he knew me better than I thought. I helped myself to more Sake, delighting in the rainbow hue of the cut crystal.

It was just after 8am and I was gazing out over the port waterway that once had been so brimful of activity. An old man was rowing across the river, squat arms as rhythmic as a marionette. His wife was with him at the back of the boat, trawling for their supper. Like many of the people I saw that day, I never found out if they survived the bomb. They were just another fleeting glimpse of humanity before Hiroshima's slate was wiped clean.

Akiba was into the room so fast that I did not even have time to get my boots off his desk. One moment I was staring out over the dock and the next the door had exploded open and striding into the office was Akiba in all his martial grandeur.

I was so startled that I dropped the glass of Sake. It smashed on the floor as I whipped my boots off the desk.

Akiba, small and perfectly turned out in his crisp khaki uniform, was so wild with rage that he could barely speak Behind him, cringeing in the common room like some malign toad, I could just make out the hunched figure of Motoji.

I quickly got to my feet. I still had one of the files in my hand. I returned it to the desk and then, not knowing what else to do, stood to attention.

"You!" Akiba shrieked, slowly stalking the desk towards me. "You dog! You devil!"

I continued to stand at attention, eyes lightly focused not on Akiba but on the wall ahead of me. I wondered what, if anything, to say.

Akiba cracked me across the face with the swagger stick that he carried for effect. "Get out from there! Get away from my desk! Get away! I could shoot you on the spot!"

I moved around the desk and was about to quit the room. "Close the door!" he screamed past me. Then to me: "Stand there! Stand there! Don't move!" He was pacing now, up and down by the window, backwards and forwards, slapping his swagger stick into the palm of his hand. He was so agitated that he was still wearing his army cap.

He suddenly noticed the shards of cut-crystal grinding beneath his boots and howled with rage. "My glass!" he said. "You drank my Sake! You broke my glass!"

He was more annoyed by that than anything else. He started thrashing me about the head with his stick. "You will pay for this! Dog! You piece of filth! You whoreson!" He was stamping his feet with rage as he lashed at me over and over again. "I will see you court martialled for this. I will have you shot! I will shoot you myself, you treacherous cur!"

I tried to protect myself, shielding my head with my hands. I sometimes wonder why I did not hit him. I suppose that old instincts die hard. Even in my parlous position, I could not bring myself to strike a commanding officer.

Eventually, after Akiba had beaten out his rage with his swagger stick, he had calmed enough to sit behind his desk. Very precisely he placed his stick next to the telephone. After the storm, the calm. For a full minute he stared at me, hands clasped lightly in front of him on the black-lacquered desk, his smooth face now a wax mask. The blows ached a little, but were not yet painful. I had been staring out of the window, but my eyes momentarily flickered down.

In that one minute before the bomb exploded, it is odd what still lingers. I remember gazing at that thin strip of a moustache above his top lip and wondering to myself just how much time he needed every morning to shave it quite so precisely.

At length, Akiba got to his feet and, turning his back on me, stared out of the window. His short figure, hands clasped behind his back, was almost silhouetted against the bright lines of Hiroshima city.

"I have always known you were like this," he said with icy control. "And I wish to God I had acted upon it. You will leave this room now. When the guard arrives, you will return here. You will be put under close arrest and taken to the military prison. I will see that you face every conceivable charge that can be brought against you."

I continued to stare out of the window, dully registering Akiba's words. Not that I felt anything, other than mild resignation – these threats of punishment take time to sink in.

Of all the things to look at, I was staring at the domed top of the Industry Promotion Hall, built in 1915 by the Czech architect Jan Letzel. Normally you could not see it from the warehouse, but the firebreaks had completely opened up the view. It was said to be a masterpiece of modern architecture. Perhaps so.

I wonder what that Czech architect would have thought had he known that his dome was about to be immortalised and would stand for all time as Hiroshima's sole relic of the bomb.

At that very moment, nine kilometres above Hiroshima,

Tom Ferebee was lining up the cross-hairs of his M-9B Norden bomb-sight on, as he called it, "the best goddamn target in the whole of the war" – the very central junction of the Aioi bridge, not 100 metres from the Promotion Hall

I had actually noticed the plane, in fact two planes, a few seconds earlier. It was hard to miss the two bright spots of quick-silver beetling across the clear blue sky. A long way behind them trailed a third plane.

Then something happened that I had never seen before. The B29s were far too high to be hit by any of our anti-aircraft guns, yet from out of the second plane appeared three white parachutes. Were pilot and crew abandoning the bomber?

A number of our citizens certainly thought so, and all about Hiroshima people had started to applaud. One last moment of gilded innocence. It was not airmen that were dangling from the three parachutes, but three aluminium canisters, the better for the Yankees to gauge the full effects of their explosion.

As for that five-ton bomb Little Boy, with its mass of electronics and Uranium 235; well, that had already been dropped. At that very moment, it was already whistling down towards Hiroshima at over 1,000kph, where after 45 seconds it was set to explode precisely 580 metres above the city.

I think that Akiba must also have registered the sight of the planes. They had seemed to split off, each sheering away from the others. "Get out of here," Akiba said, his face tilted up to the mountain-tops. "Get out now. I am sickened by your presence. Go! If it is permitted, I will shoot you with my own hand. Now go!"

I closed the door behind me, and my last glimpse of that office was of Akiba still staring up at the sky. As of Hiroshima herself, she was like some sacrificial cow that had been gently led to the slaughter, unaware that her final moment had come.

Outside Akiba's office, I stare out of the window for a moment before pausing to press my forehead against the metal door. How refreshingly cold the door feels against my forehead and nose after the sweating heat of Akiba's glasshouse. My cheeks, skull and shoulders are tender from Akiba's blows. Watched by the serene portrait of our Emperor, I take the five steps across the common-room to the warehouse door; not a moment to lose now, not one single second. No time to tarry, not a moment left to admire the view. Hiroshima's wheel of fate was finally gliding to a halt, and our entire lives hung on what we happened to be doing during a single split second of time.

Two steps, one step, I stand at the common-room door. Through the door is life. To stay in the common-room for even two more seconds is death. I smoothly turn the handle. A last look over my shoulder at the green mountains. I pause for a moment, surfing that teetering cusp between life and death. And, not that it makes any difference, not that a single second could ever make any difference to the trajectory of our lives, fate makes its decision. I slip through to the cool of the warehouse. The door clicks firmly behind me.

I can see very little in the gloom of the warehouse, but I can hear. I can hear Masanobu Furuta, that calm, soothing voice of Hiroshima Radio: "Chugoku District Army announcement: three large enemy planes proceeding ..."

For many people, those were the last words that they ever heard.

CHAPTER SIX

The Enola Gay. She was about to be immortalised and her name would for all time be inextricably linked with Little Boy and Hiroshima itself.

I have always felt it odd that Colonel Paul Tibbets named his plane after his mother. I am told that on the day before our execution, Tibbets changed the name of his hand-picked B29 bomber. So now and forever more, Enola Gay will be remembered as a bringer of death and a shatterer of worlds. Thanks, Son.

No-one remembers the name of the plane or the pilot that dropped the second bomb, Fat Man. Not one single person, that is, apart from a few old crones like myself who survived Nagasaki. But all the details of the world's first atomic bomb, from its pilot to its plane, have gone into the history books.

For many years, I had felt indifferent to Colonel Tibbets. He was, he claimed, just a man who was obeying orders. Given the chance, he would do it all over again. "I have absolutely no feeling of guilt," he said, 20 years later. "I have learned in all these years of military service to follow orders, so I followed them without question."

Like millions of servicemen around the world, from the Nazi storm-troopers to the guards in the Japanese prison camps, Tibbets was merely obeying orders. But any respect I might have had for the Colonel evaporated when I heard what he did in Texas in 1976. Tibbets, by then aged 61 and a retired

Brigadier General, took part in an air-show. He was flying a B29 identical to his Enola Gay, and there for the benefit of the 40,000 Texan spectators dropped a mock-up of Little Boy, complete with its own mushroom cloud. He landed to wild applause from the hotdog-munching Texans. Grotesque.

But it said so much about Tibbets, who, far from just being his master's tool, was a glory-hunter who revelled in his place in the history. Had he perhaps forgotten that nearly 200,000 people were killed by Little Boy? Had it never occurred to him that some of Hiroshima's survivors might, even 30 years on, be offended by his glorification of the bomb? What next for the thrill-seeking Texans? Why not recreate the use of the world's first torpedo? Or perhaps they might lay on a replica of the world's first concentration camp, built by the British to incarcerate the Boers? Or even a recreation of the first unveiling of the Gatling gun, used to such good effect during the American Civil War?

The true beauty of Little Boy – at least as far as Tibbets was concerned – was that he never had to witness the carnage. Dropping a bomb from 9km up is quite different from having to kill a man as you look him in the eyes. No, Tibbets' one tenuous piece of 'fellow-feeling' with the people of Hiroshima came when his plane was hit by the shockwave. Even though the Enola Gay was some 18 kilometres from the Aioi Bridge, the crew felt as if their plane was being pummelled by flak.

Down on the ground, that same shockwave had already reduced most of Hiroshima to rubble. And what little of the city that survived had by the end of the day been reduced to ashes in the subsequent firestorm.

My introduction to the atomic era was that first enormous flash, as if a spotlight in the heavens had suddenly been turned on to this new global star. Though I have witnessed two atomic bombs, I have never seen the flash directly – but I am told that for two or three seconds it burned brighter than 10,000 suns, burning everything it touched within a radius of one kilometre. Men like my beggar on the bank-steps were not just killed but atomised in the blink of an eye.

At least for them it was quick, which is more than could be said for the majority of Hiroshima's victims. For those who survived the first flash, many had to eke out their last days, weeks, even years, in a miasma of pain, not just skinned alive, but with their eyes boiled out of their sockets and their internal organs macerated beyond repair. And all this was merely the after-effects of the flash and the shockwave; or as it is known in Japan, 'pikadon' which means literally 'flash-boom'.

Only months later would we begin to appreciate the much more insidious harm that was being done by the radiation, which rots away at your insides until your whole body, from head to toe, is nothing but one ragged-raw nerve-ending of pain. There's a reason the radiation sickness is known in Japan as 'Itai-itai'. I can still remember the constant cry of that two-word refrain which, even years afterwards, I was still hearing in the hospitals. It means simply, 'It hurts. It hurts'. For many, death came as a merciful release.

The flash filled the whole of that dingy warehouse with light, as if every wall of the room had been lined with the most brilliant arc-lights. It seemed to come not just through the rooftop windows, but through the very walls. I am told that it was so bright that it was seen from over 100 miles away, by a woman who was blind. Those that saw it close up in Hiroshima were blinded for life, their retinas shaved clean by just a single kilogram of fissioning Uranium 235. Humans, animals, houses and all were instantaneously cremated, and the only thing left of them was their shadows, etched into the concrete walls and the pavements, an echo of their last sad moment on earth.

It was as dramatic an entrance onto the global stage as had ever been seen in history, and thus started a new world order. Over the millennia, the world has had its fill of genocides and mass executions, but never before have so many been wiped out in one single instant.

We were being judged not on our actions, but on what we were doing at the precise moment when the wheel of fate stopped turning at 8.15am on Monday 6th August 1945. One man, a clerk, survived at the very focal point, the hypocenter, of the blast, having just been sent into the office basement to retrieve a file. I heard of a woman who stooped beneath the sink to retrieve her baby's rattle and, by a whisker, missed being flensed by glass shards. A small boy, fleeing from bullies, had hidden himself in the sewer. Yes, every one of us who survived that first blast has their own story to tell about how fate had stepped in to save them.

As soon as I saw the flash, I threw myself to the ground, doing exactly what we all had been trained to do. I lay face down on the floor, head cradled into my arms, my thumbs pressed deep into my eye-sockets and with my forefingers tight over my ears. A thump of hot air seemed to wash not just over me but right through me.

And... nothing.

I could not understand it. I thought the bomb had exploded close by to the warehouse. It had seemed like the most colossal blast. And yet where was the explosion? Where was the noise? It was probably only a few seconds, but it was long enough for me to consciously order my thoughts. For a moment, I wondered if I had been deafened. Was I dying?

And then it came. A terrific wall of noise that drilled through to my very bones. Perhaps they even heard it 250 kilometres away in Nagasaki, a little foretaste of what was to come.

And with the noise came that great rolling shockwave, one enormous tsunami of raw power that flattened everything in its path, as if a meteor had hurtled into the heart of the city. There were subsequent shockwaves, the last little pulses of energy from that one tiny piece of uranium, but it was the first one that did the damage as it steamrollered through Hiroshima.

The shockwave, a great smoking ring, gradually slowed as it rolled out from the hypocenter until it was moving at just over the speed of sound. That is around one kilometre every three seconds. On the foothills of the mountains, people could actually see this unstoppable juggernaut coming straight towards them, tumbling down houses, shrines, trees and bridges, crushing everything in its path. A few of them did not think to get down, to duck, and stood mutely rooted to the spot. Like a deer in the headlights, they died staring death in the face.

In the warehouse, it was as if a giant sledgehammer had been crunched into the side of the building. We were perhaps three kilometres from the hypocenter, yet the warehouse was very nearly blown off its foundations. Every window exploded into a million deadly shards. The walls staggered sideways, the entire building slewing crazily 15 degrees to the side. The roof was suddenly pin-cushioned with light as swathes of tiles were stripped from the beams.

It all happened so fast that only afterwards did I realise that I had been bodily thrown across the length of the warehouse before crashing into a pile of box-kites.

They cushioned my fall; without them I would have broken my limbs if not my neck. Truly those kites found more use in that one second than they would ever have done in the service of the Navy. The warehouse shook again as it was hit by a secondary shockwave. I might have blacked out.

When I opened my eyes, it took a moment to get my bearings. I realised I had been flung across the room. The warehouse was thick with dust, like a murky fog. Up above me, the sky was turning from grey to black.

Apparently I was missing the most extraordinary display of pyrotechnics. Although most people think of Little Boy as being that towering grey mushroom cloud, it was preceded by a rainbow of light, with every colour in the spectrum rippling high over Hiroshima. For a few seconds, the hypocenter was a tower of iridescent vermillion, damson, orange and magenta, a thing of the most unimaginable beauty. Some believe that it was the souls of Hiroshima's dead, liberated from their bodies and soaring straight to heaven. Or was it nature's rainbow wreath of mourning?

Only after this brief flowering did that bleak grey toadstool of death appear in the sky, and forever afterwards it has become Hiroshima's calling card. It is our signature and, whenever you see it, you think of us.

The picture itself, the mushroom picture that has been used a million times over, does have a certain iconic quality. It was one of the defining moments of the 20th Century. One might almost argue that, with its long stem and its billowing, symmetrical cap, it has certain aesthetic qualities. But for those of us who were there, we cannot see that picture of the toadstool without also recalling the thousands of people who at that very moment were in their death throes.

For a while I lay there among the box-kites, wondering if anything was broken, exploring the sensations of life. An incredible silence, I particularly remember that, in stunning contrast to the explosion and its aftermath.

I hauled myself out of the pile of smashed kites and dusted off the worst of the bamboo shards and paper. The warehouse still seemed to be filled with thick mist. My feet, my beautifully booted feet, at least were fine. I pointed my toes, bent my knees and eased my torso and neck from side to side. Akiba's beating was still painful, but it did not feel as if there was anything that would not mend.

From the far side of the warehouse I could hear Motoji moaning. I walked over to him. The dust was so thick that I could barely make out the wreckage on the floor. Motoji looked like a crumpled heap of old clothes that had been tossed into the corner of the room.

"Help," he said weakly. "Help me."

"Can you get up?"

"I will try." I took Motoji's gnarled hand and pulled him up. It was wet with blood. He was shaky on his feet.

"Where are you hurt?"

"My shoulders."

I squinted in the half-light, at first unable to make out what I was looking at. A length of bamboo had been driven right through his shoulder-blade, while another spear of bamboo had lanced through his upper-arm

"What is it?" he asked, nervously. He was trembling and looked as if he was about to faint.

"We must go outside."

Holding tight onto his forearm, I led Motoji through the wreckage and to the door. The handle was jammed by the twisted door-frame. I kicked the door from two paces and it burst open. Motoji followed me, tottering a few steps before collapsing by the wall.

I took a moment to marvel at the infernal tower of dust that was spiralling out of the centre of Hiroshima. The cloud was unbelievable. It did not make sense.

Up until then, I had thought that the warehouse had sustained a direct hit. What else could do so much damage? But as I stared out over Hiroshima, it dawned on me that we had been on the very periphery of the explosion.

The bomb must have wiped out the whole city. Across Hiroshima hung a grey pall of smoke, with shards of red flame darting through the dust-cloud. Above it, like some hellish memorial stone, this tower of smoke and dust was growing before my very eyes. It must have been 10 kilometres high before it billowed outwards. And if ever you have wondered whether the devil has a mark, that grey toadstool was it. Swirling with toxic fall-out, that cloud would ultimately be responsible for many more deaths than the actual Pikadon.

All around us were little wisps of fire, burning in the air, like flaming marsh sprites. They were the last radiated traces of Little Boy, flickering and dancing in the breeze, before with a puff and a sigh they were gone.

Motoji stared blearily out over the river. I knelt down to examine him more closely. The two pieces of bamboo were barely thicker than my thumb, but had been driven through his body with the most incredible force.

"You're badly hurt," I said. "The bamboo has come out the other side."

"I have been punished," he said weakly, eyes flickering up to mine.

"Stop talking nonsense. We have been hit by a bomb."

"I have been punished," he said again. "I have been punished for doubting that we would win the war."

"I very much doubt that." Unbelievable as it may seem, many of Hiroshima's victims did initially believe that they personally were being punished. Later on, they simply switched to believing that this extreme punishment had been visited on the whole city of Hiroshima. And why were we being punished? We were apparently being castigated because, for the duration of the war, we had led such a charmed bomb-free life. Never mind that for months the Yankees had been specially saving Hiroshima for something rather different. But you could never argue with those people.

I stared at the blood that was oozing through the dust on Motoji's shirt. "Let me bind you up," I said. "You need to get to a hospital."

"But what about the Major?" he said. "Go and see that Major Akiba is alright."

"I think you need binding first."

"Go and find the Major!" Motoji said through gritted teeth. "He is more important than I. Go!"

I shrugged. I did not much care either way, though I suppose I marginally preferred Motoji to Akiba. I trudged back through the warehouse, past all the heaps of ruined kites and over to the far door. The entire wall was yawing inwards after being hit head-on by the shockwave. The door was twisted in its frame and I had to jemmy it with a wood-spar. Once I had forced an opening, I grabbed the edge to give it a tug. I winced. The door was hot to the touch and its jagged surface tore at my skin. I kicked it a little further open before squeezing through the gap.

I had walked outdoors again. Our common-room and

Akiba's office had been obliterated, the two rooms reduced to nothing but a pile of masonry and tiles. Akiba's desk had disappeared while the filing cabinets were twisted beyond recognition. There was a slight smell of wood, though the dust had been cleared by the breeze.

I thought Akiba had gone for help. Where else could he be? I was all but on the verge of returning to Motoji when I heard a slight twitch from the rubble. Could there be something alive under that metre-high pile?

I stalked over to where the noise had come from, kicking at the tiles and the wood. Perhaps I was intrigued. I hauled at a piece of board and there under it was a face – a red round face, but so injured that it was unrecognisable.

Over the next two days, I would see much worse. But that first body that I saw was so shockingly grotesque that the sight of it still haunts me. It was Akiba, and his breath was coming in a hoarse rasp, the blood bubbling out from the wounds at his throat. His face, his entire face, seemed to be a sort of shimmering green, as if he had sprouted thick animal fur.

I grabbed him underneath the shoulders and pulled him out from the rubble. The whole of his front, almost to his knees, was covered with this bristling green fur. I tentatively touched his face and he let out a low animal moan.

When I touched his skin, it was the same sensation as when I had levered the door open; jagged, razor-like shards. Akiba had taken the full burst from the windows, the shards of glass driving hard into his body. I saw many other victims with similar injuries, where the glass was buried deep to the bone. The splinters had punched clean through his tunic, while his throat seemed to have sprouted a bloody green stubble. He could not even see me as his eyelids had been peppered with glass.

Akiba's lips opened, trying to form the words that he wanted to say, but the glass splinters had even constricted the movement of his mouth.

From head to toe, his every nerve ending was in torment.

Like many others, for the rest of his short life the only sensation he would know would be pain – nothing else. I doubt that you could have devised a more hideous torture.

For perhaps a minute, I stood over him, intently studying his face. The glass shards seemed to be sprouting out of his puffy red skin. I only knew it was Akiba from his khaki uniform and brown boots.

I knelt down by his face. "Can you hear me?" I asked.

Akiba's face twitched and his lips opened a fraction as he sighed the one word, "Yes."

"What would you like me to do?" I whispered.

The words were indistinct, unclear. But I thought that I could make out, "Please kill me."

"You want me to kill you?"

His head moved forward a few centimetres, nodding his agreement. His voice was barely a sigh easing from his throat. "Please."

My mouth was so close to his ear that I could see the individual puncture marks from the glass, thrusting out like the quills of a porcupine. "I thought that is what you said," I whispered. "Goodbye."

Without a backward glance, I returned through the warehouse to Motoji. How petty, how spiteful, that makes me sound. Yes, if I had been kind, I would have smothered him. Even though I could not abide the man's presence, I could have put him out of his misery.

But I did not. I left him there to fry in the sun, knowing that every moment alive would be another moment of agony.

Just the first of my many misdeeds over the next two days. I am not proud of it. But I must tell my story as it occurred.

At least I hated Akiba. That is not an excuse for my quiet little gloat before I left him to his long death. Anyone with even a gram of compassion would have killed him, regardless of any personal animosity.

But what I will say is that soon enough I would be ill-treating many more of Hiroshima's victims; and the ones that I treated worst of all were the ones that I actually cared about.

With an electric jolt, I remembered Sumie. Was she hurt? Surely not. How could a single bomb have caused such an unholy trail of havoc, stretching for kilometres on end?

But as I looked back to the city, smouldering there in that strange grey twilight, I had a twinge of foreboding. I started to make off for Sumie's boarding house, but had only gone a few metres before I was brought up short by Motoji. Still slumped by the side of the wall, he called out and beckoned me back.

My spirits slumped at the sight of him, but at that early stage after the bomb, my callousness was not quite so deeply engrained. I turned and walked back.

"How was the Major?" he asked.

"Dead."

"And—" Motoji fingered at a scalp wound which was dribbling blood down his cheek. "Where are you going?"

"To get help."

Motoji's eyes flickered over me, almost enviously taking in my lack of injuries. Why was I uninjured while he was hurt? It was a look that I would come to know well over the next week, as if I should have felt guilty for not being maimed.

"Could you find a bandage for my wound?" he asked.

"I will see," I said. "I will see if I can find one."

"Please. I must see my wife." How horribly stricken Motoji looked, hunched up against that wall, with those two spears of bamboo jutting out from his body.

"I will see what I can do." I did no such thing. I started to walk off, as if searching for supplies, but the moment I had turned the corner, I was off towards the city. It is true that it would have taken just a few minutes to have bandaged Motoji up with some canvas from the warehouse. But what concern was it of mine if Motoji was wounded? Would he have done anything for me? I did not give a damn about the man. Besides, I was worried about Sumie. The city, flickering with flame and with that immense roiling cloud overhead, looked like it was coming to the boil.

I did not feel bad about leaving Motoji or Akiba. Takuo, though, was different. I found her lying on the concrete some 400 metres from the warehouse. I assume that after I had chatted to her at the bomb-shelter, she had gone for a walk on the waterfront. She had been caught out in the open in the full glare of Little Boy's explosion.

She was topless. Her top and bra had been blown off her body, her full breasts red and tender. Even then, even while she was in that most pitiful state, a flicker of lust charged through me. I was struck by how the whorls and circles of her patterned shirt had been branded into her skin. Over her shoulders and across her back were etched the black lines of her bra straps. It was a sight which I was to see many times over. Black absorbs the heat, while white reflects it, so fate was even playing its part in the matter of what clothes you wore that morning. Those who had worn black were much worse off than those who had worn white. And those who had even been partially shielded from the bomb fared far better than those who had faced the full flash-burn.

Poor Takuo had never had a chance. I found her slumped on her side, her head pillowed on an elbow. She had been trying to crawl to the water's edge, but had given up.

She was still conscious. Her eyes flicked up at me, but there was no expression on her face. "Water," she breathed. "Water. Water, please."

I looked about me. The river water was tidal and brackish. But a few metres away was a muddy puddle. I scooped up a gritty handful in my cupped hands and brought it to her lips.

Takuo drank greedily, burying her nose into my hands to lick up every drop. "More," she said. "Please."

I scooped up handful after handful. I spent perhaps a minute with her. A minute – that was what this once beautiful woman was worth to me; I was only prepared to give her a minute's worth of water before I went on my way.

After the fifth handful, Takuo let her head fall back onto her arm and gave me a little smile. "Apart from my husband, you are the only person to see me like this."

I caressed the side of her cheek with my knuckles. "Lucky me."

"Will you—" Her gaze never faltered from my own. "Will you take me to him?"

"I—" I paused, deliberating over whether to tell the outright lie. "I will need a handcart."

"Will you find one?" How pathetically vulnerable she looked, just lying on that open piece of concrete, with her dusty black hair cascading over her red raw shoulders. Even the very colours of her shirt, the green and the blue, had been burned into her skin.

"I will."

"Please," she said, her hand fluttering out to catch at the bottom of my trousers. "You will not forget me?"

"No – I will not forget you."

Oh, what a wretch I was. I never had the slightest intention of looking for a handcart, let alone returning to Takuo so that I could wheel her back to her husband.

I did perhaps feel like a brute as I left her there lying on the ground. As a sop to my conscience, I dragged her a few metres to the side of the puddle. But by then I was just saying anything that would allow me to take my leave. If she would have believed it, I would have told Takuo she was suffering from nothing more than mild sunburn. That is my way. Or at least it used to be my way. I would tell lies, any sort of lies, to get out of an awkward situation.

I think that Takuo believed I would return for her. At least she was not crying; I can take almost anything from a woman except her tears.

So that was where I left her. I did console myself that soon enough others would find her. She might even find a trained medic. And what possible point was there in taking Takuo to her husband when more than likely he was dead?

I could come up with any number of cogent, logical arguments about why my behaviour was not anything other than wholly reprehensible. Was I especially beholden to Takuo? Why should I be going out of my way to help her when thousands more were equally injured? And was not my main allegiance to Sumie, who herself might be horribly injured and in genuine need of my help? Who was going to be out there fighting to save my Sumie?

I can dress it up any way I like. But in my heart, I knew that I had lied to Takuo, and that I was probably leaving her to die.

What could I do? What could anyone do in the face of such city-wide devastation?

Still – I said I would not forget Takuo, and nor have I. Even 60 years on, I still squirm at the memory of what I did.

CHAPTER SEVEN

As I walked through the outskirts of Hiroshima, it was like walking into the very centre of hell. Many of its victims have made this comparison. In every way, it was as if hell had been brought to life in the smoking ruins of the city. From the blistered smoking landscape to the thousands of ravaged victims, it exactly captured every child's first imaginings of hell. Buildings had been smeared to the ground, as if wiped away by a giant palette knife. The trees, those wonderful willows and cherries, had been reduced to nothing but gnarled black witches' fingers; telegraph poles bowled over like so much kindling and solid concrete bridges blown from their very foundations.

I was walking down the same desolate road that, just an hour earlier, I had been cycling along. With a jolt, I realised that if I had stuck to my usual Monday morning routine I would have been caught in the absolute heart of the explosion. I might even have been in the very hypocenter cycling over the Aioi bridge – and all that would have been left of me would have been a carbonized stump and a grey shadow burned into the pavement. I shivered. If Akiba had not come back exactly when he did; if I had not left his office door unlocked; if he had not sent me back to the warehouse... If– if – if. We all dwell on what might have been. But perhaps you can understand why I, a man caught up in both Hiroshima and Nagasaki, have pause to dwell on it more than most.

These days, I tend not to think so much about that great infinity of hypotheticals, a single one of which could alter our entire lives. It is utterly meaningless. There is one thing, though, that I never forget: that I, more than anyone else, have been blessed with good luck. I was lucky to survive the bombs and, far more than that, I was lucky to have been in them in the first place and to have been given an opportunity to change my ways. I promise you: there is no greater gift on this earth than the chance of redemption.

All about me as I walked, clambered, climbed, back through Hiroshima were the victims for whom fate had not been so kind. Lying in the rubble-strewn roads were crisped black bodies with no vestige of clothing. You could not tell if they were men, women or even children. Yet somehow they could still move, little jerking twitches with their arms, a last flutter of agonised life before they were spent.

A bus full of charred victims, all crammed statue-like in the same position they had been in when the bomb had burst, one man with his arm still wrapped round the strap-handle; a cyclist astride the wreckage of his bicycle cart, the pair of them tossed against a wall, fused together in a ghastly mass of flesh and metal. And the rivers, Hiroshima's great arteries that had saved her from being fire-bombed, these were already sprinkled with bloated corpses bobbing in the tide. A few were trying to swim, grey skinless arms flapping in the water. By the end of the day, the waterways would be quite carpeted with bodies.

Those that could walk were trudging aimlessly through the streets, rendered into shambling grey ghosts. I saw every imaginable deformity. The first a poor monstrous thing, shuffling towards me with arms outstretched; I never knew if it was man or woman. The victim's clothes were hanging loosely off its red torso in shreds. With a shock of disgust, revulsion, I saw that these tattered strips were not clothes at all. The skin from its arms had been sheered off at the elbow and hung loosely down over its hands like a pair of grey gauntlets. Unseeing eyes stared right through me as the being silently staggered on its way.

I will never forget the crushing weight of the silence in the initial aftermath of the bomb. Later, as the firestorm took hold and people realised the urgency of their plight, there would be many frantic calls for help. But, in that first 30 minutes, it was as if the whole population was suffering from combined shellshock, too stunned to say a word. Those that could walk soundlessly trudged back to their homes to die with their families. As they walked, they seemed to cluster into groups, as if fearful to strike out alone. Those that could not walk would lie on the still hot asphalt, whimpering in formal Japanese, "Help. Please be so good as to help me." Everywhere, it was the same.

Unwittingly, I had walked close to the very hypocenter, the wooden buildings not just destroyed, but atomised, as if crushed by a mighty grinder. All around me, bits of the debris were starting to catch fire. They said later that this was due to all the charcoal burners which had been fired up for breakfast that morning. The bomb's heat had dried out all of Hiroshima's wooden houses turning them into nothing more than piles of crackling tinder. Even the beams were too hot to touch. All it needed was the slightest spark and within minutes these houses had become flaming infernos.

There were a few Western-style concrete buildings that had been able to withstand the shockwave. But their walls were slewed away from the blast, like a sapling in a gale. Even these were starting to catch fire.

It was shocking. Awful. But nothing could touch me. Later, I would regret bitterly my indifference to this wash of wrecked humanity. But on that day, I was cloaked in an icy shroud of heartlessness, and I hugged it close about me.

Pathetic little scenes spring to mind, so vivid that they still make me weep. A little girl sitting on the porch of what had once been her home, nestling the burned body of her baby brother. Her tears drip onto the boy's upturned face as she pleads with him, "Please do not go. Please do not leave me."

A man padding down the street towards me, his bare feet little more than black nubs of charred flesh. His arms are so burned that I can see white bone through the flesh. He is carrying some sort of blanket, clutching it close to his chest.

He spots me as I pick my way through the debris and his juddering gait becomes more pronounced as he breaks into a shambling trot. His face is horribly burned, dusty blood oozing from a wound on his forehead, his wild hair singed and standing upright. As he gets closer, I catch a whiff of a smell that takes me back to my childhood. It is the distinct tang of burned feathers, exactly how it was when my grandmother used a candle to burn off the last feathers of a duck.

The man thrusts out the bundle towards me, pushing it into my arms. "Take her," he says. "Please take my daughter. Her name is Setsuko. She is all that I have."

I look at the slight bundle in his hands. The child could barely have been more than four months old. She is quite dead, her skin already grey and her black eyes tinged with that opaque glaze of death.

"I... " For a moment I shy away from taking the dead girl.

"Please!" His voice is suddenly shrill to the point of cracking, his wild eyes wet with tears. "You must take her! Her name is Setsuko!"

Grudgingly, I accept the girl's body. The very moment that she is in my hands, the man buckles at the knees. I believe he is dead before he has even hit the ground.

I stand dumbfounded, staring at the dead child in my hands. The father's body is huddled into a foetal ball, his head almost touching his knees.

In a rare moment of delicacy, I return the child to his arms, the pair of them locked together for all time. You have never seen such a pitiful scene in all your life. And the horror of Hiroshima was that this was commonplace; all about me children were dying in their parents' arms. Perhaps they were the lucky ones. Thousands of children were orphaned that day, left alone in the world to be tended by strangers.

Of all those incidents on my way back to Sumie's boarding house, there is one that especially haunts me. I was walking past the same building that, just an hour earlier, was being pulled down by a lively band of schoolgirls. The poor girls on the roof must have been killed instantly, blown into the street. But many others who had been labouring inside the house were now trapped in the smoking rubble.

Two of the girls, their smocks, hair and faces grey with dust, trotted over to me. "Please help us, Sir," the smaller one said, pulling at my hand. Her face was red and burned, but still she smiled at me, her teeth beaming white against her grey skin. "Our friends are trapped."

I allowed myself to be led by the hand to the building. It was carnage, a huge heap of smouldering wood and tiles that looked as if it were about to burst into flames at any minute.

I surveyed the scene. A number of half-clad girls were labouring at the debris. I noticed one in particular. She was younger than the others, perhaps ten-years-old, and sat on a piece of rubble staring vacantly ahead of her. A few scraps from her trousers lingered round her legs, red weals all across her front and face.

It was impossible to know where to start. It would have taken a full day to clear it and I needed to get back. And anyway what did I owe those girls?

Truly, my selfishness that day ran so deep that it was like drawing water from the sea.

The two girls that had taken me to the rubble were now hanging onto my arms, one on each hand. Some of the other girls had stopped their work to stare at me.

I cleared the dust from my throat. "Are you sure anyone could have survived this?" I asked.

"Yes, Sir," pleaded the smaller girl. "We have heard two of them. They are trapped in the corner. I will show you."

Still holding my hand she led me up onto a clump of fallen

tiles and woodwork. In parts it was over two metres high. I picked my way over to the corner. From far down I could just make out a little squeak, "Help us. Please help us."

I tried, but my heart was never in it. I did not want to be there and at that stage I did not care whether those trapped girls lived or died. The job seemed insurmountable.

Other girls in the group had rallied round me. All of them were now digging at the same spot, clawing at the struts and tiles with their bare hands. "We are coming for you!" called out the smaller girl, as she wrenched at another shattered plank. "We are nearly there!"

She smiled at me again as I threw another tile over my shoulder. "This is so very kind of you, Sir. Thank you, Sir." Then she started talking inconsequentially, chatting away as young girls will do when they are trying to distract themselves. "My name is Kiyoko. And this is my friend Etsuko. And over there is my friend Fumiko. We have been pulling down the houses on this street all week – and now... now all our work is done. Oh, but now with you here, I am sure we will be able to get them out."

"Yes," I said. "I am sure you will. You are doing very well. Very well indeed." I plucked at a tile and threw it onto the road. "But I'm sorry – I have to be going. I have friends whom I need to check up on and—"

"Oh, but please stay," said Kiyoko, the girl with the scorched face. "We will not be able to do it without you."

"I'm sorry." By now I had retreated back to the tarmac. All the girls had stopped work to stare at me. "I'm sorry. I don't have the time. I can't stay." I cupped my hands in prayer and bowed.

Two of the girls started to cry, suddenly aware that they were all alone in this brave new atomic world, and that now not even the adults would not step in to save them.

"Please—" called out the girl – and her plea was still ringing in my ears as I backed away from that motley cluster of schoolgirls. Unable to bear a moment more of their accusing glances, I started to walk off.

But the worst of it was when the girl who had been sitting all alone, the one with only a few scraps of clothing left on her legs, suddenly awoke from her trance. She got up and began to stumble after me. The smouldering ruins must have been cruel on her feet. "Please help me," she said. "Please help me."

She came tottering towards me, convinced that I was her only salvation. How sad she looked, staggering blindly after me in the smoke. And, to this day, I can still hear her awful words ringing in my ears: "Help me. Please help me."

It made no difference – I would no more have helped her than a rat would help another of its own. Unable to bear any more of her cries, I turned my back on the girl and started to lope away. Anything was better than to be forced to listen to her pleading. As I rounded a corner, I looked back for the last time. She had stopped moving and stood with her arms stretched out to me in supplication. Then very slowly, like a tree toppling full length, she fell forwards. She never broke her fall, arms jolting sideways as she connected face first with the rubble. I did not wait to see if she ever moved again.

Did I feel any guilt? Not then. Not one iota. Though later, in the reflective calm of post-war Japan, I did evaluate my actions. And what I realised was that, when it came to it, when my mettle was tested, I had behaved like a perfect fiend. Most of us, in the fast-flowing 21st century world, are never tested. Our courage is never put to the task. Our loyalties are never heated in the crucible of life. And our hearts, which rule our empathy and our capacity for fellow-feeling, are rarely given the chance to grow.

Many of us claim that we would relish the chance to shine. The world's leaders, I gather, thirst for a crisis so that they can make their mark on history. And in our own lives, we all perhaps wonder how we will fare when that great adventure comes along. Will we, to borrow an expression from the Yankee game of baseball, step up to the plate?

On that day in Hiroshima, my courage, my loyalties, and my shrivelled heart were all finally put to the test. And I failed on every count.

In those early stages after the bomb, I was still able to delude myself that, even as I ignored those girls' pleas for help, I had a higher goal. There were so many thousands of injured and how was I going to help them all? Should I just have helped out the first people that I had come across? No – I was going back to the boarding house to see how the two people that I cared for most in Hiroshima, Sumie and Shinzo, had fared in the bomb.

With most of the major landmarks destroyed, it was difficult to find my bearings. Even the roads had been blown to bits. I would arrive at a bridge, would look at it, stare at it – and, though I might have crossed it a hundred times, I could still not be certain that I had ever seen it before. Through the grey dust, I would sometimes glimpse the mountains on the horizon and I roughly knew that I was heading north. But the maze of waterways and pulverised houses had turned Hiroshima into a labyrinth. One wrecked building looks much like another.

All of a sudden, I came across a place that I did recognise and realised I was nearly home. It was the East Drill Field, which only three hours earlier had been alive with activity as my fellow countrymen prepared for the final defence of the Motherland. Girls and boys had been stabbing at straw sacks with their bamboo spears, urged on to ever greater ferocity by the barking drill sergeants. Old soldiers, the wrecked and the infirm who were the last dregs of Japan's population to be mobilised, had shambled about the parade ground in ill-fitting clothes.

Now, as I gazed at the Drill Field, it was like staring at an old friend whose face had been savagely mutilated. You recognise small parts, the face looks slightly familiar, yet the whole has been so horribly altered that you cannot believe it is the same person.

All about that flat, dusty quad were groups of people, all of them with the most shocking burns after being caught outside in the full glare of the bomb. Like so many of our soldiers, those raw troops had been slain before they had even had a chance to raise a weapon in anger.

Hard by the Drill Field was Hiroshima's main railway station and that also was a shadow of what it had been at break of day. The dead littered the tracks like so many rag-dolls, carriages upended and on their sides, the very rails turned into the twisting shoots of a vine. How quickly I became inured to it. I had only been on this dreadful death planet for a few hours and could already view a dismembered corpse with all the dispassion of a mortician. Scorched children mewling for their mothers, charred men begging for water, and women calling out with melted faces and their breasts shorn clean from their torsos. They all of them left me cold. I could walk past every one of them without a second glance, without turning a hair.

And finally, amidst all this death, I arrived back at Sumie's house. Finally I could stop ignoring the mutilated and the sick. Finally I could help.

Sumie's house, like all the others on the street, had been razed to the ground. From being a handsome two-storey building it was now a disjointed heap of rubble. I would not have known one house from the next, but from some way off I had seen Shinzo and the girl crawling over the ruins.

Shinzo was tugging at a beam, worrying at it, his great flanks wobbling as he wrenched it from side to side. He was wearing patched trousers and a frayed shirt which had had the arms ripped off. On his battered feet, were what was left of two straw sandals. The girl was by his side, face grimaced as she added her gnat's worth of weight onto the beam.

For a moment I stood there watching the pair of them, so very focused on the task at hand – so very different from my own behaviour that morning. Shinzo had let go of the beam, rubbing his hands to clear off the sweat, and as he did so he caught sight of me for the first time.

"He is alive!" Shinzo called delightedly, his blubbery face

wreathed in a great smile. There was such affection in that one look. It is odd to think that there could have been joy in Hiroshima that morning, but all over the city were erupting these little outpourings of ecstasy as parents were reunited with their children, husbands with wives.

Shinzo clambered down through the debris and engulfed me in a monstrous bear-hug. How reassuring it was to be held like that; if only I had thought to do the same with the victims that I had met along the way.

"You are alive!" Shinzo said, now holding me at arms' length as his eyes raked over my face. "We didn't know. The city looks as if it's died. It's good to see you."

"And you too," I said, clutching at him. "And you too!" I was pleased to see him, of course I was, but I could not mask my worry any longer. "Where is Sumie?"

The girl looked up from the rubble she was trying to shift. "She is here," she called out. "Come and help. We still have time."

"The girl is right." Shinzo led the way through the rubble, before winking at me. "How refreshing it is to meet a girl who is always right."

"Thank you, Shinzo-San," said the girl. "And you would do well to remember that."

The girl was standing at the very apex of the rubble, her blue skirt and top grey with dust. But what a jaunty little pose she struck, hand on one hip, and feet in one of those finicky ballet positions.

I ruffled her hair. "You survived," I said. "Well done."

Shinzo knelt next to where the girl was standing and gestured for me to follow. "We think Sumie is here," he said, pointing to a little hole that they had just started to scrape out. "She must have been in the kitchen. The whole house is on top of her. But if you listen carefully, you can hear her knocking."

We knelt in silence, watching the dust drift in from the wind on the sea. You could taste the smoke in the air. Over towards the centre of Hiroshima, sharp jags of flame were flickering up from the murk. Individual ruined houses, spontaneously bursting into flame. It would be perhaps an hour yet before the fires linked up into one single devastating firestorm, so vast that not even our rivers could prevent it from eating everything in its path.

And then I heard it, a little tap-tap-tap from directly beneath us. Three knocks and a pause, followed by another three knocks. Was that her voice I could hear? It was dreadfully muffled, from deep, deep within the rubble, but I was certain that I could hear that one word, "Help".

Immediately I set to work, set to work with a will, as if trying to make amends for my utter self-centredness of the previous hours. Previous hours? Why not make that a lifetime. All that the bomb had done was to magnify the gaping character defects that had been with me since childhood.

I started hurling tiles and handfuls of house rubble onto the street.

"Be calm," said Shinzo. "We are only trying to dig a small hole, not move the entire house. Just throwing a tile four metres should suffice. Watch how the girl does it."

I rested on my haunches to scrutinise the girl.

"Watch and learn," she said, daintily tossing a tile a few metres down the slope.

As we laboured, we discussed the one single fascinating topic that was to dominate the city's conversations for weeks: how we had survived the bomb.

I told them about the events in the warehouse.

"And Major Akiba is dead?" said Shinzo, sweat dripping off him as he eased up a large piece of timber.

"The bastard was dying, I know that," I replied.

"You did not think to help him?"

"He had been sprayed with glass shards. He was caught by the windows when they exploded. There was nothing I could do."

"Perhaps," said Shinzo, "I would have put him out of his misery."

"That, dear Shinzo, is because you always see the best in every one – even bastards like Akiba and Motoji—"

"And let us not forget your good self."

The girl laughed merrily at that. Such a tinkling laugh, she had – a laugh that could, for a minute, even make you forget the bomb.

"And you two?" I asked. "How did you escape?"

"Staying in bed this morning saved my life!" Shinzo said, as he came over to help me shift a beam. With our combined weight, we were able to nudge it back and forth before finally dragging it free. "The flash woke me up. I could see it clear through the blackout blinds. I just wrapped myself in the bedding and rolled onto the floor. The next thing, the windows were blown out, the house had fallen down and I was somewhere near the top of the heap—"

"And I saved him!" said the girl.

"That is so," said Shinzo, not letting details spoil the story. "And I am sure you will save many more. She was here within minutes, digging away like a hound."

"And you?" I nodded to the girl. "Lucky you were not still on your roof-top."

"I was in a ditch behind a wall. When I felt the flash, I threw myself flat. I buried my thumbs into my eyes and my fingers into my ears, just like I had been taught at school." She smiled, twisting a lock of hair between her fingers. "It was fate. For two hours, I had been out in the open. But when the bomb came, there I was in the ditch."

She carried on talking. Even at the age of seven, her natural mode was to chatter. Such incessant chatter. "I wonder what has happened to grandmother. I do hope she is alright. But I think she might be dead. How was it in the city?"

"Terrible," I said. "I cannot believe a single bomb could do so much."

"And the Shima Hospital? The place where my grandmother works?"

"I—" I paused in a rare moment of delicacy. In truth, I

had all but walked past what was left of the Shima Hospital, and it had seemed to have taken the full force of the explosion. It would be months later before analysts were conclusively able to determine that, give or take a few metres, the Shima Hospital was at the very hypocenter of Hiroshima. Little Boy had exploded directly above its rooftop. Not a single person left alive.

"I did not see the hospital," I went on. "But most of the buildings have collapsed."

"Oh," said the girl. "Oh." I can still remember how she stood there in the midst of that rubble, staring vacantly at her feet, twisting a lock of her hair around one finger.

"I am sorry," said Shinzo, breaking off from his work to cradle her shoulder.

"It's alright. I must be strong, otherwise we will not win the war. That is what my grandmother would have said, anyway." She turned her face to stare up at the grey mushroom cloud, which still smeared the sky. "My grandmother is gone. My house is gone. I have nothing but the clothes I am wearing."

"Don't worry," said Shinzo, hand still clapped round her shoulder. "We'll look after you."

Fine words – but I never thought he meant them. I believed he was just trying to comfort the girl. And yet how costly these little promises, given without a second thought, can prove to be.

The girl had walked off to be by herself for a few minutes and Shinzo was continuing to dig with rhythmic stolidity. "How did it look by the Tsurami Bridge?" he asked.

"The one by Hijiyama Hill?"

"My sister Tamiko, you have met her, has been working around there for two weeks."

"I did not see it," I said. "She may have had more luck than the people in the Shima Hospital."

"If there is a chance later, I'll try to find her."

"Very well." It was not exactly a ringing endorsement. At the time, I felt that if Shinzo wanted to search for his sister among the numberless victims, then that was his decision; I certainly did not feel obliged to accompany him. Searching for one single person among that chaos? That carnage? It would have been like searching for a single grain of sand on a beach; and a grain of sand, mind, which you might not even recognise. Many of the dead were only distinguishable by the stopped watches on their wrists, or the blackened rings on their fingers.

By now, our hole down to Sumie was so deep that I had to squat inside it and pass the bits of debris up full height to Shinzo and the girl. It was awkward because although the hole was wide at the top, it tapered inwards. At the bottom, there was barely room enough to stand.

I could hear Sumie's voice quite clearly now. "Help," she said. "Please help."

"I'm coming," I replied.

With my feet on makeshift steps, I tugged and clawed at three pieces of tile which were so tight-wedged they appeared to be interlocked. But I was unable to prise them up.

"Taking your time?" Shinzo called.

The girl also looked down. "The hole must be bigger," she said, her grandmother now seemingly already out of mind. "We must make it wider at the top."

As I worried at those three stubborn tiles, I could hear the dull clonking sound of Shinzo and the girl removing debris from directly above me. I wormed my fingers around the edge of one tile and put my full force on this one point. I felt it move fractionally. I tried the tile next to it, and that too had an imperceptible amount of give. I pulled at each tile in turn, working one after the other, and then with a rending crash one of the tiles cracked in my hand. The other two tiles burst upwards and suddenly I found that I was looking straight down at the top of Sumie's hair.

She was able to lean her head back a little and, when she saw me, she smiled. "I hoped it would be you," she said.

"I came as quickly as I could," I said, reaching down to brush the caked grey dust from her face and hair. I stooped to kiss the top of her head.

"And now you can get me out of here," she said.

"So I shall."

I can still picture her exactly in that dark little hole, only her head above the surface, as if she were drowning in a well of rubble. Still smiling, just for the pleasure of having me with her. Perhaps she knew all along that she would never escape.

It became increasingly difficult to clear the rubble. Although we had found Sumie, there was very little space to work with, and all the fragments had been heavily compacted. Eventually, after what felt like an hour, I had loosened enough to free Sumie's arms. She held her hands loose above her head.

"Much better," she said. "Now I can kiss you properly." Her arms snaked round my neck and she kissed me on the lips. I could taste the dust.

"Come on you two," Shinzo called down. "This is no time for kissing. Let me help."

We swapped places and I caught another glimpse of our-ever-changing city. Every ten minutes, it seemed that something extraordinary, fantastical was occurring to Hiroshima. Long after the bomb was dropped, the city was still in a constant state of metamorphosis.

I was shocked at how quickly the individual fires seemed to have linked together. They were sweeping across the city in a single red rampant wave – and our waterways, our very own natural firewalls, made no difference whatsoever. The hot air was rising and the cold air was sweeping in underneath, creating a vast tornado which could jump streets and even rivers.

I watched the flames as I continued to shift the debris. It was difficult to judge distances, but it looked as if the firestorm was about a kilometre from us. I tried to guess at its speed, but I had no idea. I would have been horrified if I had known it was ripping through the city at five metres a second.

The bomb had also had the most extraordinary effect on our weather system. For some time there had been crackling thunder overhead. I felt the pleasant smack of rain falling onto the back of my head. I had not had anything to drink all morning; I was parched.

I closed my eyes and turned my face to the heavens. I might even have had my mouth open, if only to savour a few drops of rain on my lips.

"Yuk!" said the girl. "Yuk! What is this?"

I opened my eyes. She was looking at the backs of her hands and then rubbing them against her top. She looked as if she had been flicked with black oil.

"The rain is black!" she said. "Are they now dropping oil on us?"

I looked at some of the rain drops on my skin. They felt much colder than normal and had the density and tackiness of black ink. Even when I had wiped the raindrops away, they still left a residual stain. I sniffed at my hands. They didn't smell of oil.

"It is all the muck in the dust-cloud," I said. "The rain is bringing it down. I wouldn't drink it."

That, as it turned out, was an understatement. The black rain did not just contain dirt from the cloud, but radioactive fall-out – an entirely new concept to the world. The Yankees spent years denying that there had been any lingering radiation from the bomb. For those squeaky-clean moralists, their bomb was a good, wholesome US kind of bomb, and the only casualties were those who had been killed in the first explosion and the subsequent firestorm.

It would take the Yankees some years to accept that the radiation from Little Boy – which lingered over Hiroshima for perhaps a month – may ultimately have been responsible for more deaths than the actual blast. Not that this fact was ever going to spoil the Yankees' riotous celebrations after the bomb had been dropped – "It's the best goddamn news in the whole world!" trilled that oaf President Truman. But I may later have given them pause for thought as they realised that they had condemned perhaps 100,000 people to painfully lingering deaths from cancer, leukaemia and all the other foul by-products of radioactivity.

How much it must have vexed the Yankees. They spent years denying that their baby had anything to do with all these thousands of anomalous deaths that were occurring every year in Hiroshima and Nagasaki – in the same way, I imagine, as a tearful mother defends her serial killer son.

The black rain did not – fortunately – stay over us for long. We were on the very eastern outskirts of that hellish black raincloud which was drifting into the countryside to the northwest of Hiroshima. In some places which had hardly been touched by the bomb, some ten centimetres of black rain fell in three hours, and for those that were caught out in the storm, the long-term health consequences were catastrophic.

The firestorm was worryingly close, sweeping up from the south and now also on our flanks. I swapped positions again with Shinzo, pulling him out of the hole before jumping down to Sumie. We had minutes, at best, to free her.

She gazed up at me, proffering her lips, and I kissed her.

"I love you," she said.

"You're not finished yet."

"Still you cannot say it?"

"Plenty of time for that when you are free."

Shinzo had cleared much of the debris around her chest, but Sumie was still pinned from beneath the waist. I squatted above her, hooking my elbows underneath her armpits. "Brace yourself," I said. "This might hurt."

I shifted my feet, like a weight-lifter before the clean and jerk, took a deep breath and rolled backwards. My eyes were shut tight, teeth clenched. I was pulling with all my might. I gave it perhaps ten seconds, every sinew straining upwards, but Sumie did not move so much as a centimetre. She must have been in the most excruciating pain.

I gave it one more try, but, again, nothing. She gave an involuntary yelp, but that was the only indication of her discomfort.

"There is something pinning me," she said. "I cannot feel anything below my waist. Is there a beam over my legs?"

As I climbed out of the hole, I could see the beam that was pinning Sumie down, but there was too much rubble on it, tons and tons of tiles.

We tried, how we tried, to shift it, Shinzo and I straining away and the girl also adding her puny weight, but it would not budge. For a few minutes, I worked above the beam, manically trying to clear debris, then back to Sumie, tugging, tugging, as wisps of glowing ember started to fill the air. I called out to Shinzo for some rope, hoping that together we might pull her out. A last snatched kiss, as I struggled back out of the hole, and that sickening moment as I realised that the flames were all but upon us. The speed of the firestorm was shocking. It appeared almost to have flanked us and even now was licking at the ruined houses at the end of the street.

"Come on!" I screamed at Shinzo, suffused by this rippling flood of panic. I was too late. There was not enough time to save her. All I could do was scream out my rage at Shinzo. "Forget that. Come here! Help me! Help me move this beam!" My breath coming in short, quick pants as a trembling red mist descended over me. Oh, but I felt such brute power then I was not capable of thinking straight. All I could do was throw myself at the beam, again and again, as senseless as a bull that repeatedly charges the red cape. I was clawing at it, mewling with frustrated rage, the tears streaming down my face. Hammering the wood, punching it with my bare fists. It was hopeless.

Shinzo threw himself at the beam. For the first time, I could feel it shuddering beneath our weight, perhaps a centimetre or two. We just needed more time.

"Sumie! Can you move?" I screamed. "Can you move at all?"

I could only just make out her voice. The roar of the firestorm was deafening. "No," I could hear her say. "I cannot move."

Shinzo and I gave one last despairing heave at the beam, but it was never going to be enough.

Shinzo and the girl jumped down from the rubble and were standing in the road. The flames were all but upon us. I could feel the heat washing over me, along with this thunder of a thousand homes being reduced to charred ash.

"There is no time!" Shinzo screamed at me. "Move!"

I looked down at Sumie for the last time. The panic was already starting to ebb, to be replaced by this dull resignation that I had failed my lover.

Her hands were now clasped in front of her face, as if in prayer. She looked up at me.

"You must go," she said. "Save yourself."

"I am sorry."

The flames from the firestorm were within seconds of torching the wreckage of Sumie's house.

That last harrowing plea from Sumie, as she realised that her life was all but over. "Will you live for me?" That is what she asked. The last wish of a person who realises that their life is over and who knows that the very best that they can hope for is that their life be lived vicariously through someone else.

I paused, stumbling over my words, not knowing what to say.

"You will? You will live for me?" she asked again.

"I will try."

The smoke was so thick, so dense, that I could hardly see Sumie at the bottom of the pit. A glimpse of her gazing up at me. And as the flames crackled at my feet, I gave a last despairing wave and bounded down onto the road where Shinzo and the girl were already racing away from the firestorm.

After about 50 metres, I stopped and looked back. Sumie's house had already been engulfed in the inferno, a moving wall of flame which indiscriminately devoured everything in its path. The sound and the fury was intense, like the thundering roar of a storm at sea. I never heard her scream.

CHAPTER EIGHT

After the war, as I came to take quiet stock of my life, I often wondered if I could have done more for Sumie.

Some say that I did everything in my powers to save her: that I reached her house as quickly as I could after the explosion; and that when I was there, I did not stint myself in trying to free her.

That is possibly so. But what I do also know is that, over the years, I have heard of many tales of heroism that put me to shame. One story particularly struck a chord as it was so very similar to my own. A mother was trying to rescue her daughter from the wreckage of their home. Like Sumie, the girl was pinned tight beneath a beam, and the ruins were only minutes from being swallowed by the firestorm. Some bystanders had tried to shift the beam, but had given up. "It cannot be done," they had said. "Leave your daughter and flee."

The mother was horribly injured. Her skin was hanging off her in great bleeding strips, her face had been burned black by the blast. Yet still she summoned the energy to totter over to the beam. She braced her back underneath it, and then with one galvanic thrust lifted the beam clean upwards – by herself lifted a beam that was so heavy that it had already defeated three men. The woman's daughter scrabbled free and the pair of them fled the firestorm.

What a miraculous event, and the pity of it was that by the next day that wonderful woman was dead. But she had done what every parent aspires to do: she had saved her child's life, and I like to think that when she died, she would have had a smile on her lips, and would have known in her heart that she had done everything that a mother can do.

But had I? I suppose I had made an effort to release Sumie. It was not nearly enough, however, and, over 60 years on, I still wonder if I could have done more for her.

I could certainly have eased her last moments. I could have given her the words that she longed to hear – "I love you". But, out of blinkered pride, and that ill-judged conceit of being "true to myself", I had bitten back any thought of kindness.

We ran any which way we could away from the flames. The smoke was all about us, and all we could think was to flee the firestorm, running in any direction that would take us away from that crackling roar.

Shinzo was quickly spent. He stood there, bent over with hands on knees, gasping down great lungfuls of smoky air, and hacking as he tried to talk.

We were on a street corner, I know not where. In the smoke and the chaos, it was impossible to get your bearings. All I could see was the firestorm following us like some unremitting fiend from hell and, no matter how hard we raced, the flames were always licking at our heels.

"You go on," said Shinzo. "I'm done."

Was I, perhaps, in half a mind, to take him at his word? It is all too possible that that odious man that was myself would even have left his best friend to fry in the flames.

But, fortunately, the girl was there. She did the most remarkable thing. She kicked Shinzo – hard – on the ankle, as if cajoling a stubborn bullock. "Come on," she said. "Come on!"

"Ouch!" he said. "Leave me. I cannot do it."

The girl kicked him again. Her foot connected right with the seat of his pants. I watched in slight bemusement as the girl started to dance round Shinzo, poking him in the ribs with her finger. "Come on!" she said. "We're not leaving you."

"Ouch!" he said, as she kicked him again on the shin. "Can a man be left to die in peace?"

"No, not you," said the girl, giving him another kick on the backside. "Even when the flames have taken me and even when my hair is burning and my skin has turned black, with my last breath I will still kick you."

Shinzo caught my eye, the look perhaps of a mule that, stubborn as he is, knows when he is beaten.

"This has nothing to do with me," I said. "If you want her to stop, then just start moving."

Shinzo gave a little smile. "Was she always this bossy?" he asked, crying out as she kicked him again on the ankle.

Like a farmer who knows the exact moment when to switch from the stick to the carrot, the girl took Shinzo by the hand and was leading him down the rubble-strewn street.

He was stumbling down the road, head bowed as he stared at his feet. He coughed down another gasp of air.

"Take his other hand!" the girl ordered.

I complied, taking Shinzo's fat, calloused fingers in my own. I gave his hand a little squeeze for luck, but he did not return it.

"Count to ten!" said the girl. "Count each step as we go."

"What do we do when we get to ten?" I asked.

"We start at the beginning again."

Shinzo was so worn out, I doubt he even had the energy to count. All he could do was plonk one foot in front of the other and then gird his loins to make the next step.

I looked behind. The firestorm was harrying at us, yipping at our heels. Occasionally we would make a little gain, and then it would come sweeping in from the sides in a hail of smouldering embers. They stung as they kissed your skin. Shinzo twisted in pain as a red-hot shard of wood landed on his neck.

One or two people were lying slumped on the road – either dead, or minutes from it. They did not even have the strength to cry out anymore. Not that we would have heard them anyway, as the howling roar of the firestorm drowned out all else.

The girl was trying to break into a trot, gesturing at me with her free hand to pick up the pace. I could feel the heat of the flames on the back of my legs. When I looked back, it was shocking to realise that our path where we had been walking barely a minute earlier was already engulfed in flames.

Shinzo was moaning to himself as we dragged him on, spittle dribbling from his slack ash-grey mouth. He broke into an ungainly trot, but after a minute was back to a stumbling walk.

The girl looked behind us. We would need a miracle to survive if we were going to stick with Shinzo. The smoke was so thick that we had lost all sense of direction. At our hobbling speed, it was only a matter of minutes before we were caught.

"Leave me!" howled Shinzo. "I cannot go another step!"

This time the girl cuffed him round the ear with the flat of her hand. "Save your breath!" she screamed, though I could hardly hear her over that terrible sound of the inferno.

Still clutching onto Shinzo's hand, I darted another peek behind me – and even without this human millstone at my side, it was impossible to believe we could ever escape the firestorm. Our very footsteps in the dust seemed to be sprouting into flames. I had been reduced to nothing but a blind lab animal, scurrying onwards without any thought except to escape the searing heat and those choking clouds of smoke.

"Here!" The girl screamed so loud I could even hear her over the thunder of the flames. "I see something!" She wheeled off to the right, and Shinzo, his slack head bobbing from side to side, dumbly followed.

I didn't know what the girl had seen. Suddenly through the smoke emerged a low stone wall. It had to be one of the river walls. I could not see what lay beneath, but without a thought I jumped over. I dropped perhaps three metres before sprawling into the muddy silt.

"It's fine," I called up. "A bit of a drop."

Shinzo shrieked as he was pushed off the wall. His knees buckled as he pitched forward onto his fat stomach. The breath was punched out of him. A moment later the girl followed, agile as a cat as she landed lightly on the black mud.

We started helping Shinzo out of the claggy silt. He was in it up to his knees.

"Leave me!" he said. "Just go!"

"Will you shut up?" I said. All his bleatings suddenly put me in the most towering rage. "Get out of there now, right now, or I will kick you myself, and I tell you now that my boots are going to hurt a lot more than anything you have had from the girl!"

I channelled my rage into trying to haul Shinzo out of the mud. The girl tugged at one of his ankles which was still planted deep in the silt.

The poor man, the dear man, was snivelling to himself. He might even have been crying. "All I want is to be left alone."

"Shut up! Imbecile!" I was seething. I do not know why I was so mad, but I was a tinder keg ready to explode. Perhaps it was my fury at the loss of Sumie and perhaps I was incandescent at Japan's four wasted years. But the reason matters not for at that moment there was such awesome rage in my heart, and it was Shinzo who happened to be its focus. It was Shinzo who had set me off, Shinzo who was the catalyst for my explosion, and it might well have been that that saved him.

"Get up!" I screamed. "Get up you stinking bastard! Get up! Move!"

I grabbed him by the shoulders and started man-hauling him out of the mud. Through the smoke, still thick about us, the girl was fluttering at his feet, but there was no need as, for one minute, all my anger was concentrated into pulling Shinzo's dead-weight body out of the mud.

I was now dragging him over the silt, my boots sinking ankle deep into the mud. "Get up!" I screamed at him. "If you do not get up I will... I will hound you... I will twist you... I will kick you and I will not stop kicking even when you are dead. Just. Get. Up!"

"Please stop screaming. I will—" he panted for breath "I will try and get up."

I hauled him to his knees and Shinzo used the girl as a leaning post as he got unsteadily to his feet. He eyed me up for a moment and opened his mouth, about to speak.

"Save your breath," I said curtly. "We can talk in the river."

"But—"

"Shut your mouth."

"I cannot—"

"Shut up!"

In silence we stumbled over the silt and made our way to the river's edge. It was muddy but so long as we kept moving, we did not sink down too much. The smell, blown in from the smouldering city, was repellent. Perhaps death does have a smell – certainly I will never forget it.

The smoke cleared a little and I could see that we were on a spit of land that jutted out into the river. Several hundred other people had already sought refuge there. Most of them were clustered about the water's edge, paddling in the river, but for some reason not quite daring to take the final plunge. Many were lying in the water as they tried to ease their horrific burns.

It was hard to tell the living from the dead. Bodies, bloated and burned, drifted by on the current. It was a ghastly river of death.

We reached the riverside and my tide of rage had ebbed into nothing but slack water. It was almost hard to believe that Shinzo's unheeding bulk had galvanised me into such a fury of action.

Still holding his hand, the girl plucked at my fingers and for a minute we stood there with the water lapping at our ankles. The firestorm was still raging in the city, enveloping us in a fog of smoke, but we shared a strange moment of tranquillity. Shinzo, the girl and I, we looked at each other and smiled, and we all had the good sense not to spoil it by uttering a single word.

Some people had crawled to the waterfront and were drinking the brackish water. I was parched and scooped up a cupped hand of water. It was so salty, I could not swallow it.

We had done everything that it was possible to do. So we stood in silence at the side of the river, the mud sucking at our feet, quietly accepting that the die was cast. We had no clue if we were safe from the firestorm, which even then seemed to be trying to burn up the very silt that we stood upon.

As always, it was the patriots who had to spoil it. How I have come to hate the patriots, those swaggering bullies who even yet use the smooth mask of patriotism to hide all manner of brutish behaviour. And it was in World War II that Japanese patriotism reached its absolute zenith. Every single excess, from torturing prisoners-of-war to sending schoolboys into battle, was suddenly deemed not just acceptable but desirable just so long as it was done in the name of 'Patriotism'. The cold-hearted and the callous could behave like mercenaries, just so long as they were acting for the greater good of the Motherland. And every little tin-pot official was suddenly allowed to wield more power than they could ever have dreamed of – so long as they dressed it up under that odious, despicable term of 'doing one's duty'.

It was on that riverbank, as we caught our breaths, that I was to witness yet two more instances of this insane patriotism in action. We were a few metres out into the river, when we heard a shout from behind us. "Make way for the Emperor!"

As I write those words, it seems so utterly fantastic that I can only laugh at the idiocy of it all. If only it had just been that little cluster of crazy men. They exuded that lethal combination of patriotism and righteous fervour: the exact attitude which had been responsible for getting us into the war in the first place. It was endemic throughout Japan – and was to blame for yet one more little tragedy in Hiroshima. Such a waste on that terrible day of waste, but is a man's life worth less just because his fellow citizens have been incinerated by the thousand? I had never thought about that before. I daresay, though, that on the day that Little Boy was dropped, life was indeed cheap.

"Make way for the Emperor!" came the shout again, and through the smoke I could make out a troupe of four uniformed men – carrying, of all things, a picture of the Emperor. It was identical to the picture of Hirohito that I had been peering at that morning in the warehouse. As I may have said already, pictures of the Emperor were almost as sacrosanct as the man himself.

Two of the men had the Emperor's picture hoisted above their shoulders, while the other pair carved a path through the crowds. I still have no idea whether they were trying to save this large black and white photo from the flames. Or whether they were using it as some sort of rallying symbol, as if to say, 'Worry not – we still have the Emperor!'

Many people reverentially bowed their heads as the Emperor's party shouldered its way through the milling crowds to the water's edge. But I could only watch in stunned stupefaction at how in this time of utter crisis, Hirohito's picture was still being paraded like a holy relic.

Shortly afterwards, a boat drifted by with a single man at the oars. It went without saying that the Emperor's party was first on board. And so we watched them escape the firestorm, glad at least that the Emperor had survived. Many of the military men saluted the picture as it sailed away to safety.

The heat from the flames was so intense that we started to move out further into the water. The wind was blowing the blaze directly at us, fingers of fire creeping out over the mud. Still holding hands, Shinzo, the girl and I walked step by step out into the water until it was over our knees.

"Stop!" came a scream. "Do not try and swim the river. It is dangerous! You will not be able to cross the river!"

Although the firestorm appeared to be leaping at us across

the silt, we all momentarily stopped. I could just make out the man who was ordering us not to move, a military policeman in the same mould as Akiba, with short bristling hair. He was standing up to his knees in the water and brandished a pistol over his head. But the heat from the firestorm kept driving us back and as one we edged further out into the water.

Over the roar of the flames, I heard the crack of the pistol as the policeman fired off a warning shot. "Stop that!" he screamed. "No-one goes into the river. It is dangerous! There is a firestorm on the other bank. I will shoot the next person who attempts to swim the river!"

The crowd was skittish, panicky. It felt as if we were about to be roasted alive. The policeman was jostled once or twice, as people bumped past him. He fired another shot overhead.

"Stop! I said stop!" he screamed, voice shrill with excitement. "I will shoot anyone who swims the river! I will!"

For one old man, with grizzled grey hair and wearing only a pair of ragged trousers, the heat was too much. His arms had already been skinned by the bomb, leaving nothing but raw flesh. He lingered at the river's edge, torn between his desire to immerse himself in the cool of the water and his fear of the wild-eyed military policeman.

Eventually, the pain won out. The scorching heat must have been excruciating as it played over the old man's red raw flesh. After a forlorn glance at the policeman, he dived head first into the river, pulling away from the bank in a limp breaststroke.

The military policeman stared at the man who had dared defy his authority. Then carefully raising his pistol with both hands, he drew a bead on the swimmer and shot him through the head. A red splot appeared on the back of the man's scalp. His arms stopped moving and his head lolled red in the water for a few moments. before gradually slipping beneath the waves.

"You will all stop!" said the policeman, his pistol high above his head. "That is what will happen to anyone else who attempts to swim this river. It is dangerous!"

Oh, how I wish that I had been the man to have stopped

the madness. But I wasn't. At the sight of the gun and the dead swimmer, I had once again reverted to being a craven drone who automatically yields to authority. Besides, I was a coward. The policeman terrified me.

But one brave soul did put an end to the nonsense. The military policeman, with arm crooked and pistol pointing to the sky, was still glaring at the cowed crowd – and never noticed the roundhouse blow that caught him on the side of the head. He lurched backwards and was bringing his gun up when another solid blow caught him on the temple. The police officer sank to his knees, arm limp by his side.

His middle-aged attacker was a man slighter than myself, his clothes in ribbons. He stooped down to snatch up the pistol before hurling it far into the river. A ripple of shock pulsed through the crowd. None of us had ever seen such an open act of defiance. It seemed almost treasonable. It was just not within our compass to understand that authority figures could be – indeed should be – challenged.

The hero of the moment politely offered his hand to a woman and, without once looking back, they dived into the river. I do so hope that he survived. I never saw the man again, but if I did, I would shake him by the hand.

Everyone was suddenly pouring into the water, and the three of us followed. The fearsome heat was like a furnace blast. I lost sight of the policeman, who was sitting groggily on his knees and coming to the realisation that no-one cared a jot for his uniform or his threats.

The girl's hand was tight in my own, the water now almost up to my waist. "Will you be alright to swim?" I asked her.

"Yes," she replied. "My grandmother taught me when I was six."

"Good. Do not swim against the current. Go with the flow and we will make for the other bank. Can you do that?"

"Yes." The girl had a little frown on her forehead, aware of the size of the task that faced her.

"Are you ready?" I asked. The heat from the flames was almost unbearable.

"Wait," said Shinzo.

"What is it?"

He cocked his head sideways in apology. "I cannot swim."

I drummed my fingers on my chest, vexed at how he had so speedily wrecked my simple plan. I wondered whether to attempt swimming across holding Shinzo, but did not much like it. He was already nervous. I could almost sense how going into the water would trigger a panic attack. Could we leave him and arrange to meet somewhere later on? Would he even survive?

I stared at the wall of flames that appeared on the verge of eating up the very river itself. "That is... " I said, breaking off to massage my temples. "That is a problem."

"We will be alright," said the girl. "We can go a little further out. We must get as far as we can from the flames. Then we drop down into the water. We only need to come up for air."

"Very good," said Shinzo. "You are so quick."

We waded a couple more metres out into the river – any further and the current would have swept us off our feet – and submerged ourselves in the water. Bodies, brown and bloated, drifted by on the current, a constant reminder of the frailty of the thread that attaches us to life. But you quickly got used to it. Every time you looked out over the river, there would be another dozen bodies bobbing on the surface, their arms sometimes jutting perpendicular out of the water. And if anything went wrong, then in a few minutes I too could be just another body in the river, unrecognisable, merely one more Little Boy victim.

I arched my back so that my face was pointing straight to the sky and only my lips and nose were above the surface – and even then I could feel the raw heat and smell the acrid tang of destruction.

Shinzo clutched tight onto my hand, fearful that he might be swept out into the stream.

Only a few people were lingering with us in the shallows. The rest were taking their chances in the river, preferring a swim to the risk of being burnt to death on that little spit of land.

As I ducked myself fully beneath the water for the first time, it felt as if I had returned to the womb. Even through the warmed water, I could hear the heavy thrum of the firestorm. I opened my eyes to the sting of salt water. The sky had turned pink grey from the fire and the smoke.

I developed a rhythm. I would hold my head under water for about a minute, until I was nearly spent, and then would dip my lips above the surface to take one quick gasp of smoked breath. The heat of the firestorm was arcking out over the water, crisping the wet skin on my face. And as I bobbed for my life in the river, I relived all the shocking events of that day.

For most of us, our days are merely an endless series of routines. All we do, we have experienced before; not just once, but many times over. Then, once in a while, once in a lifetime, something occurs which is wholly outside our experience. Our mettle and our imagination are tested to the full, and we have to rely on that old-fashioned quality known as 'Character'. And when this time of crisis occurs, you can be certain of one thing: your weaknesses will be found out. Like a diamond under pressure, your every flaw will be revealed in all its awful imperfection.

So, for a time beneath the waves as we waited for the firestorm to abate, I was able to take stock. At that early stage, I was not especially proud of what I had done. But I was not ashamed either. I had survived. That alone had merit.

My actions as I had returned to Sumie's house may not have been laudable. I might have stayed longer with the schoolgirls who had been trying to rescue their trapped friends. I could have done more for the little girl who had followed me and begged for help. I might have rescued Sumie. Perhaps.

My behaviour had not been reprehensible. I could not have been faulted for it. Surely anyone else would have acted the same way. Besides, I had never set myself up as a saint. I was just a civilian trying to survive the war in any way I could.

CHAPTER NINE

We spent more than an hour in the river as we waited for a lull in the firestorm. By the time we stumbled back onto the muddy spit, our skin was spongy soft and as wrinkled as an old plum. Those who had been caught in the blast barely had the energy to leave the water. Much more bearable to die slowly in the cool of the river than to face the sting of fresh air on raw wounds.

I am sure that is why the rivers were so thick with bloated bodies. The water at least offered some respite from the pain.

They did not cry out as they left the water, but instead made a numbing low level moan. It is much worse than a shriek, as it is the sound of a soul wracked in torment. Pain such as you would not believe – and pain that would stay with them until the very moment they died. For those that lived longer, they had to endure months of the most unspeakable torture, incapable of thought or emotion, or anything at all except this unconscionable fizz of pain.

We could feel the heat lessening and could now sit easily in the river, our heads above the surface. The firestorm still raged all about us, but at our particular spot on the riverbank, it was all burned out. The thick fug of smoke was easing up and we could make out distant fires in other parts of the city. On the other side of the river, I could make out a cluster of children clinging to the pilings of a bridge. One let go. A desperate scream for help, before a small black head, arms thrashing in the water, was curled away in the current.

The girl was the first out of the water. She took off her top and wrung it out, before shaking herself like a dog, hair flailing from side-to-side.

Shinzo stared out at the firestorm. "There is going to be nothing left," he said.

I also studied the fire. Through the smoke could be seen flickers of fire, like lightning flashes that prickle a stormcloud.

"And it was only a single bomb," I said.

"Perhaps the Yankees have finally invented the matchbox bomb," Shinzo replied.

"Should I know it?"

"They talked of it years ago. There was a theory that if you destroyed a piece of matter, you released the energy that bound the atoms together. No bigger than a matchbox, was what they said."

"The papers spout anything these days."

"That is also true," pronounced Shinzo, with all the stoic wisdom of a Buddha.

He was squatting in the water with just the top of his head above the water. I was suddenly struck by how he looked exactly like a hippo, its eyes and flicking ears above the surface with the remainder of its vast bulk submerged beneath.

"Are you getting cold?" I asked.

"No."

"Of course not – because you have got three inches of hippo blubber to protect you." I smirked at him. "Tell me, Shinzo – how have you stayed so fat? Everyone else is starving. Yet somehow you are as fat as you were four years ago—"

"If not more so."

"How do you do it?"

"I like it."

"Do you have some hidden cache of food?"

"My wife likes it too."

"Likes whale meat does she?"

"Loves it." He smiled, like the good-natured fellow he was. "But tell me – what ever does your wife see in a scrawny devil like you?"

I laughed. "She would still hate me whatever I looked like."

"That is so," he said, pausing a beat before adding, "Your challenging character is not to everyone's taste."

What an extraordinary sight we must have made, chafing each other in the river while all about us the city burned and that never-ending stream of bodies floated past. But it is wrong to think – even on that day of such complete tragedy that the shell-shocked survivors were incapable of levity. No, even during the worst of it, some of us would still quip and make a joke. Not that we were making light of the disaster; but for a few of us, it was our only way of coping. I believe that in English, the term is known as "gallows humour".

"It is freezing," I said. "Shall we get out?"

Stepping out of the water was like emerging into some ghastly charred world, where everything had been uniformly reduced to ash and cinders. We picked our way over to the girl, who was squatting by the bankside wall.

It was already dusk, the flaming city becoming ever starker against the enveloping darkness and the bodies looking like nothing more than black sacks on the river.

The girl proffered up something in her hands. "Look what I've found."

It was an abandoned lunchbox, somebody's little dinner-pail prepared that morning and whose owner was now nothing more than a memory. There was some rice inside, as well as a piece of fish and two pickled plums. All of it had been completely cooked through by the bomb. That was the first time, I think, that I ever wondered what the bomb had done to our own innards. Had we also been cooked through too?

The girl doled out the food. "A mouthful of fish for you – and a mouthful for you," she said, before taking a bite herself. The rice was handed out in the same way.

In all the hue and cry, I had quite forgotten my hunger. I

cannot remember tasting such delicious fish; if I'd had some clean water to wash it down with, it would been a meal fit for an Emperor.

Shinzo wolfed down his meagre portion, barely chewing the fish before swallowing. He rubbed his fingers together, and then – and I had seen this look many times – gazed eagerly down to see what else was left to eat. He stared at the pickled plums for but a moment before, with a wistful shake of his head, averting his eyes to stare out again over the river.

"Two plums between three of us," said the girl. "We'll each have a bite."

"You have them," said Shinzo. "I've always hated pickled plums."

Shinzo not liking pickled plums? Next he would be telling us that he did not like pork ribs. I had once seen him eat a whole dishful, well over 30, in a single sitting.

Still, if Shinzo wanted to play the martyr, I was not going to stop him – and nor was I going to donate my own plum to that chit of a girl. With a shrug, I picked up a plum and devoured it in two lusty bites. And, because I was a loathsome being, because I wanted to show Shinzo that his good-manners were wasted on me, I made sure that I ate noisily, smacking my lips with relish.

"Delicious," I said. "The finest pickled plum I've ever tasted."

"All food will taste good in Hiroshima today," intoned Shinzo. "For the lucky ones who are still able to eat."

A wisp of the moon peeked through the haze of smoke and dust. There were a few other people clustered along the river-bank, huddled together in the lee of the river wall. Shinzo and I sat on either side of the girl, who was so slight that she was quivering with the cold. Shinzo wrapped his arms round her. I could see the warmth return to her body, her shivers gradually replaced with the deep rhythmic breath of sleep.

And that was where we spent our first night in this awful new world. We could have tried venturing into the city, but it would have been pointless. We had no idea where we were, nor where we were going. As far as we knew, Hiroshima had been razed to the ground.

I slept a little, snatches of blissful unconsciousness before I would awake with a jerk, my eyes snapping open uncomprehendingly as I tried to make sense of why I was sleeping rough by the river. Was I grateful even that I was alive? That thought did come to me later, much later, after I had also survived Nagasaki. But that night, all I could think of was my raging thirst and the cold that knifed through my miserable clothing.

By sunrise, Shinzo and myself were fully awake, though we stayed tight in our huddle as the girl was still asleep. I will never forget waking up in Hiroshima that morning. The sound was the first thing I noticed. All I could hear was the ever-same sound of the river as she cascaded into the sea. At first I could not put my finger on it – and then I realised. The moaning and the cries for water had stopped. Many of the victims' torment had come to an end. What a terrible way to die, still tortured by pain even as you breathe your last agonised gasp.

Through the haze, I could see that, as the day before, it had all the makings of another blazing midsummer's day. In other parts of Japan, people would be going about their everyday business, still pushing for the Motherland's ultimate victory in the war. And yet there in Hiroshima, we had been burned so badly by the war that it had become an irrelevance. On that morning, it made no odds to us who won that damnable war. Our only concern was survival.

Perhaps I am wrong. In fact, I know I am wrong. There were many others who, even at that early stage, were striving with every sinew to help their fellow victims. Perhaps what I meant to say was that *my* only concern was survival.

"I would like to try and find my sister," said Shinzo. He whispered so as not to wake the girl. "You do not have to come."

Oh, how invidious those six little words were: "You do not have to come". We have all heard them before, in countless delicate situations – where of course we do not 'have' to do anything, but where courtesy and kindness demand that we have to do it all the same.

It was annoying. In my self-absorbed idiocy, I had rather hoped that amidst all the carnage, Shinzo had forgotten his sister.

It was not that I did not like Tamiko. We had met several times and I had enjoyed her company. Spurred on by her brother, she had moved from Nagasaki to Hiroshima, first working in a communications centre before being ordered to join the demolition teams. She was every bit as engaging as her elder brother; attractive, even.

It really was nothing personal. But in such circumstances, are you allowed to be the realist? Is it permissible to state that some venture is hopeless? We could have spent a week searching every millimetre of the streets around Hijiyama Hill and might still be none the wiser whether she was alive or dead.

What I am trying to express are all the welter of feelings that bubbled up within me at the mention of this fruitless hunt for Shinzo's sister. My every instinct told me that it was a waste of time, that our chances of finding Tamiko and then saving her were – how do the Yankees put it? – a snowball in hell. Actually, I can think of no more appropriate metaphor for Tamiko's chances of surviving Hiroshima.

But I did still have some fellow feeling for Shinzo. I tried delicately to dissuade him from the search.

"She was working somewhere near Hijiyama Hill?" I asked.

"I think so."

"And you do not know anyone who was working with her?"

Shinzo paused and began scratching at his armpit. Despite his two-hour immersion in the river, he was still riddled with lice. "No. Not that I can think of."

"What is the plan then?" I was trying not to be negative.

But I was hoping that, through sheer logic alone, Shinzo would come to the same obvious conclusion as myself.

"I am... I am going to walk around the streets of Hijiyama. I will ask people if they have seen her. There must be aid stations and field hospitals that have been set up. I'll visit them."

"It may take some time."

"Yes, it may take some time."

I paused, giving Shinzo a chance to marvel at the sunrise. Japan is, of course, the Land of the Rising Sun, and every dawn is an affirmation of our nationhood.

"I wonder if our time might not be better spent helping others. If she is alive, then we will find her soon enough. And if she is not, there is nothing more we can do."

"I have also thought that. I would certainly respect your wish if you wanted to serve at one of the aid stations. But I owe it to my sister to search for her. I'm going to look for her."

"For how long?"

"Until I find her. Until I find out whether she is alive or dead."

"But... " I tried to conjure up one last argument to dissuade Shinzo from haring off on this absurd rescue mission. "What about your wife? What about Sakae? She'll be worried. Shouldn't we be getting back to Nagasaki?"

"I have also thought about that," he said. "Nevertheless, I am going to search for Tamiko. Will you come?"

"For a while." I could have left him to it but, even for a swine like myself, that would have too brutish for words.

"And me!" piped the girl, who had been quietly listening to our conversation. "I'm coming!"

"And you're coming too!" said Shinzo, bending over to kiss the top of the girl's head. "Thank you. Now we cannot fail!"

The girl yawned and stretched, fingers linked as she arced her arms above her head. "I'm hungry," she said. "What are we waiting for?"

"We were waiting for you," I said. My dry salt tongue

poked out between thin cracked lips. The girl had reminded me just how thirsty I was.

We walked for a way along the spit until we came to a ladder of rusted iron hoops cemented into the river wall. The bodies still drifted by in their never-ending flotilla of death – and animals too. A horse, flat on its side and with its head submerged, slowly cartwheeling in the eddies.

The remains of a bridge were nearby and a number of bodies had been caught in the wreckage, like stray seaweed that has snatched on a piling. One man still had his infant child strapped to his back, while his older daughter was clasped tight in the crook of his arm; all of them dead.

I was first up the ladder, followed by the girl and then Shinzo, who was breathing heavily even after that modest exertion. And there by the river wall, the three of us stood in disbelieving silence. The firestorm was all but burned out, though right across the horizon could be seen little turrets of smoke. In every direction that we looked, north, west, east and south, the city had been turned into a wasteland. But that simple word does not begin to convey the wholesale destruction that had been wrought on Hiroshima, as its every street and everybuilding had all of them been reduced to ash. It was a desolate, grey moonscape where life had been erased off the earth – so bleak, so dead, that it seemed as if no trace of life could ever exist there again.

Through the smouldering rubble, we could make out about 20 or 30 larger concrete buildings that had somehow survived the bomb. They lingered on like the last remnants of some ancient civilisation. As for the rest of Hiroshima, it had been as comprehensively excised off the face of the earth as Sodom and Gomorrah.

It took some time to get our bearings as almost every single landmark had been annihilated – and those that had not been razed to the ground had been damaged beyond recognition, their concrete walls blown out, and their steel girders buckled away from the blast like storm-blown trees.

"That must be the Exhibition Hall by the Aioi bridge," Shinzo said, pointing seawards. "I can just make out its dome."

"And there's Hijiyama Hill!" said the girl, dancing excitedly. "That is where we start looking."

I squinted through the smoked sunlight as the hill swirled in and out of view. "I want water first."

That morning the city was quite different from the Hiroshima of the previous afternoon. Although there were a few odd patches that had not been caught in the firestorm, most city blocks were now nothing but identical grey squares of ash and rubble. They stretched on as far as the eye could see. It was impossible to believe that anyone could have survived this hell.

Yet, like so many hardy cockroaches, out of the carnage started to emerge the survivors. Many of them were still horribly wounded, their burns turned from red to black, and the loose skin now snipped from their backs to reveal raw flesh. The weakest of the victims had been carried off in the night, cut down by either the firestorm or the cold. We walked past many of them, now black and completely carbonized, their twisted arms captured in the final agonies of their death throes. In one awful knot, two adults and two children were huddled together in a circle, with arms, legs and torsos all now fused together in some grotesque black tableau of a family united in death.

The girl held tight onto Shinzo's hand, watching the horror in mute shock. As we walked down the once teeming streets, there was an unending variety of ways that death had been visited upon these people. And, just when you thought that you were hardened, inured, to it all, up would spring some fresh horror to revolt you anew.

I was still desperate for water, but all the taps and stop-cocks had run dry. The bomb had wrecked every one of the water-pipes, reducing the water pressure to nil. Many people must have died from sheer thirst alone.

The one sight that I will never forget was of fifteen, twenty people clustered around a bone-dry tap, their hands clutching out for water. They had died in a great heap, one on top of the other. The vision that still springs to mind is of flies caught in a honey-trap.

I have not begun to tell you the worst of it. Shinzo, still thinking of his stomach, had spied a small plot of garden that had not been touched by the fire. It seemed to have belonged to some municipal building, now nothing but rubble, and the workers had turned the garden into a vegetable patch. Shinzo had found a sizeable pumpkin. It was quite cooked through and, although it was now cold, we squatted on some concrete blocks and ate every scrap.

"Pumpkin for breakfast," said Shinzo, chiselling the last of the flesh off the skin with his teeth. "Lovely."

The girl was swinging her legs back and forth as she twisted her hair into ringlets. "I don't think my grandmother is alive any more," she said.

"You're probably right," I said, brutal to the last.

"It is difficult to tell," said Shinzo. "Your grandmother was working in the Shima hospital? Then we will go and search for her when we have found Tamiko."

How my ears pricked up that. Not content with getting me to search for his sister, Shinzo was now volunteering me to search for the girl's grandmother too? And why stop there? Why not return to Sumie's scorched house to see if I could pick up a few charred scraps from her body there?

Before I could say anything too unpleasant, I went off to explore the garden. I thought I had spotted a watertank towards the rear.

I picked my way through the scrubby vegetation, all of it glazed with grey dust. I could hear a trace of the girl singing a ditty to herself. Behind some singed trees was the watertank; they used them for fire prevention. The tank was of a good size, I remember, and could have handily swallowed up a large car.

The first thing to assail my senses was the sound. It was the buzzing drone of a beehive.

A black blur of flies was seething above the water. Two crows hopped on the side of the tank, pecking at a piece of gristle. A steady trickle of water dribbled out from the green overflow pipe. And only then – then – did the smell hit me. I almost gagged, whipping my hand up to cover my nose. It was the smell of carrion and flesh that has been left to rot in the sun; it was the smell of a fly infested slaughter house on a hot summer's day. It would come to be Hiroshima's trademark smell of death and over the next two days it was everywhere. But that first time, just 24 hours after Little Boy had been dropped, it caught me unawares.

The moment I smelt the stench I should have turned on my heels and quit the garden. But I found myself drawn to the watertank. What manner of thing had been caught in there to attract so many flies? What could have produced this foul odour?

As I approached the tank, the two crows flew away, but the flies still hovered and swirled – feeding, ever feeding, off the limitless food beneath them.

I peeped over the edge. It took a second to register what it was that I was actually seeing. It was a human stew tank, so thick with bodies that they were squeezed in as tight as sardines in a can. I do not know how many people died in that tank as they sought to save themselves from the flames, but on the surface alone I counted over 15 heads, their empty eye-sockets turned sightlessly to the skies. Their bodies had swollen in death, compacting against each other till the tank was nothing but a solid mass of dead flesh. How could this have happened? How had they all come to seek sanctuary in this same watertank?

My gaze wandered, to be caught by the piece of gristle that the two crows had been eating. It was a single human eye, tinged with the opaque grey glaze of death. It was that, more even than the smell, which made me retch on the spot. Pumpkin cascaded into an orange pool at my feet.

I stumbled back to the others. "Find anything?" asked Shinzo.

"Nothing that you want to know about," I replied, but it made no difference. All around Hiroshima were scores, if not hundreds, of similarly choked watertanks, and Shinzo would soon see them for himself. The very next day, we witnessed some soldiers trying to clear one, but the bodies were packed so tight that they couldn't be shifted. Eventually, the soldiers had attacked the side of the tank with sledgehammers, cracking at the concrete until a large slab broke away. Water and bodies cascaded through the breach. In that watertank alone, crammed from top to bottom, there must have been over 70 bodies.

On we went to Hijiyama Hill, meandering from one pitiful death to the next. It was like some interminable chamber of horrors, for even when you thought you had seen the worst of it, there was always some fresh hell to repel you.

Hijiyama Hill, a spacious clump of greenery to the East of Hiroshima, had escaped the worst of the firestorm, but all about it the buildings and houses had been utterly destroyed.

Searching for Tamiko, as we went from one body to the next, was one of the most dispiriting jobs of my life. We were looking, in particular, for a distinctive square-faced watch with a steel-link strap that had been given to Tamiko by her father. Shinzo said that she might also be wearing a black belt with a steel buckle. As a last resort, we were also searching for a gold tooth that had replaced one of her canines.

These were the ways, then, that we hoped to find Tamiko, and from street to street we worked our way through the ruins, checking for any identifying marks. We were frequently unable to tell the men from the women, and Shinzo would stand there squinting into the mouth of a charred skull, praying that he would not catch sight of that tell-tale gold-tooth. The girl – only seven-years-old, remember – did not show even a hint of distaste as she inspected a blackened arm for any remnants of Tamiko's steel watch.

We found a running tap beside some ruins, from which poured a small but steady stream of water. There were two bodies sprawled beneath, the water still splashing on their outstretched hands. Shinzo and I dragged the corpses away to make room for the girl. How I twitched with impatience, as she sedately knelt before drinking straight from the tap. She seemed to take an age, sipping slowly and letting much of the water fall straight to the ground. She wiped her mouth and, even before she was on her feet, I was flat on my back and letting the water pour into my open mouth. I gulped it down, the sweetest thing that I have ever tasted. When I'd had my fill I lay with my mouth open to the heavens and let the water cascade over my hair, my face, my chest.

How long I kept Shinzo waiting, I have no idea, but he was such a kind man, bless him, that he did not have the heart to tell me to move. Instead, he stood patiently at my feet, and when – finally – I was done, he knelt at the tap without a word and drank up the water from his cupped hands. As we moved off, he found a bucket and filled it with water. It was heavy, but he insisted on taking it with us.

We came across the occasional survivor and Shinzo would seize upon them to ask if they had heard of his sister or knew her whereabouts – to be met with a shrug and a soundless shake of the head. Most did not say a word. There was an awful silence about Hiroshima that morning, as if we were all shrouded in grief.

Shinzo would thank them all the same and would offer them water from the bucket. They would kneel and drink, cupping their hands to draw the water to their parched lips, and would often remain there as we went on our way, squatting disconsolate in the dust.

The girl's energy was boundless. She was like a puppy dog, poking here, ferreting there, and not a trace of squeamishness as she examined bodies and blackened limbs. And she would quiz the victims in the same way, ignoring their horrible suppurating wounds to ask them if they had seen Tamiko. She had found a mug and would cheerfully bring them a cupful of Shinzo's water before taking her leave.

As for myself, what was I doing on that hot day as Shinzo and the girl pointlessly trawled the streets in search of Tamiko? At first I went through the motions. I would follow the pair of them through the ruins and if I chanced on a body, then I would give it a cursory examination. I suppose I kept my ears open for any cries for help. But I had neither the energy nor the inclination to question any of the survivors.

We continued to roam through the ruins until the afternoon. It was as hot a day as I had known all summer and I was in a foul temper. Why was I wasting my time looking for a corpse in this city of corpses? Did I not have a wife and child waiting for me in Nagasaki? I admit that my reunion with Mako was not something that I anticipated with relish; I did not doubt that within five minutes of my arrival back home, the screaming would start – irrespective of the fact that I had just survived the world's biggest bomb. But that boy, our dear little boy, I truly doted on him. I would have crossed oceans to see him – and can only wish that it was mere distance which kept us apart today.

I was mulling over these things as I sat on some concrete steps that led to another house that had been razed by the firestorm.

Shinzo, sweat pouring down his face and still toting his bucket, wandered over. "I thought we might have a look on the hill," he said.

Hot, tired, hungry, I just stared at him, raising a single eyebrow. How much longer did he want to carry on searching for his sister before he got the message? She was dead – and if she was not dead, she was dying, and if somehow she had survived, then eventually they would meet up. What did he not understand?

"Will you come with us?" How forlorn Shinzo looked,

standing there with that stupid bucket in those bedraggled clothes. His hairless paunch bulged through his shirt.

I looked at that great belly, flopping over his trousers – and realised something was missing. "Where is your money-belt?"

"Lost in the bomb. Sorry." He put down his bucket and scratched at his groin. "Will you come?"

I did not reply. With his money-belt had gone half my money too. I stared down at my boots, those heavy work boots that belonged to my father. They were caked in dry mud.

Shinzo moved onto scratching the lice at the back of his scalp. How often had I seen that particular action before? "We'll not be long. You'll still be here?"

I looked past Shinzo to the girl who was nosing through the wreckage of another house. It was all so pointless. Why were we spending another moment in Hiroshima? It had ceased to exist as a city.

"Yes," I said – and when he lingered, feebly mopping at the sweat on his brow, I gave it him straight. "You're wasting your time. You're wasting our time. Your sister is dead. She was a nice woman, a kind woman. But she is dead and there is not a thing we can do about it. So I know that this hunt may be helping you to assuage your grief, but it's hopeless. We can achieve nothing. Nothing! Your sister is dead – so why not start thinking about the living? You have a bride waiting for you back home in Nagasaki – and without a doubt, she currently believes she is your widow."

"Tamiko might still be alive. Lots of people survived."

"It is a waste of time. We could spend weeks here – and for what? So, that at the end of it, you can find a watch or a belt buckle that was once worn by your sister?" I clutched my hands to my head, my fingers kneading at my forehead. The sun and the lack of water had left me with a searing headache.

The girl had stopped roaming the ruins and had sidled over to Shinzo, where she clutched his hand.

"We're going to search the hill," Shinzo replied. "Will you be here in three hours?"

"Yes," I said, spitting the word out in my anger. "You are wasting your time, my friend."

Shinzo smiled, before pronouncing in courtly fashion, "Rejoice that I would do the same for you."

They turned towards the hill – but I am sure that he was still able to hear my tart rejoinder: "Do not expect me to return the compliment."

Then and there I was tempted to leave Hiroshima – and I would hook up again with Shinzo whenever fate decided it. But I was exhausted. I found a little patch of grey grass that was in the shadow of some rubble and cleared it of stones. Then, still cursing Shinzo and his fool's errand, I went to sleep, promptly and with not a thought to my own selfishness.

Did I feel guilty? Not in the slightest. We must each of us take responsibility for our own decisions, and that especially held true for toiling over Hijiyama Hill in the heat of the day. In fact, it was not me that was being selfish, it was Shinzo! How could anyone have been so thoughtless as to take a seven-year-old girl out in that heat to search for a corpse?

I was awoken by the girl's cries and could see from the long shadows that it was already late-afternoon. I had been asleep for over three hours.

I got stiffly to me feet, and could tell from Shinzo's hangdog posture that they still had not found his sister. He looked shattered, his face, hair and clothes all matted with dust. I did not feel a gram of sympathy.

"We know where she is," said Shinzo. "An aid station has been set up in a primary school. A woman thought Tamiko might be there."

"She did, did she?" I asked, brushing off the worst of the ash and dust from my trousers. "Why did she think that?"

"She had been searching for her daughter. She had seen some other girls there from the same work party."

"Very well." I replied curtly. My mind was made up. I wanted to get back home to Nagasaki as quickly as possible.

As far as I was concerned, I never wanted to set foot in that perfect hell of Hiroshima ever again.

"The woman said it is close by," said Shinzo. "It should be minutes away."

It was dusk as we finally walked into the grounds of the Hijiyama Primary School. I was incandescent, steam practically venting from my ears. For although we had known the address, street names were meaningless in the wreckage of Hiroshima. Up and down those hellish streets we had roamed, each of them near identical to the next, as my smouldering temper was stoked into an inferno.

Shinzo had asked more than 20 people for directions before finally, and quite by chance, we stumbled across the school. We had smelt it long before we saw it – a quite horrible stench of cooked meat that wafted on the wind. The building was surrounded by blazing bonfires, at least ten of them and each over two metres high. They burned long into the night. I smelt that awful reek every day for well over a month, and never once got used to it.

The primary school, with those flickering fires all about it, looked the very epitome of a portal to purgatory. I do not know how the main building had withstood both the bomb and the firestorm, but its stark black lines brooded large against the starlit horizon. Satanic looking men laboured in the dark, their shadows stretching long over the rubble and the debris. Over the crackle of the flames could be heard the sound of children screaming; endlessly screaming for their lost mothers. The sound of those high-pitched screams drilled through my ears, reverberating in my skull until all I wanted to do was run for the hills.

Shinzo, holding the girl's hand, led the way through the porch and into the main hall. I followed a few steps behind them. If the outside of the school had been purgatory, then this hall was hell itself, containing such a welter of indescribable misery that it is difficult to know where to begin. Lying in a disordered sprawl upon the floor were hundreds of victims.

From their slight figures, they mostly appeared to be children, but burned and mutilated beyond all recognition. Some of the injuries were so appalling that it was difficult to believe these frail little bodies could still contain a flicker of life.

As I had walked in, my eyes had been caught by the body of a small child lying face down on a blanket, whose legs and back had been scorched quite black. The burns had gone so deep that the scored flesh looked like a piece of over-cooked meat, while through the back of the leg protruded the white tip of a shattered thighbone. I had thought the child was dead – had to be dead from such appalling injuries – and yet suddenly an arm was flung out to the side and she was calling for her mother.

A small boy, barely older than my son, screaming over and over again, "It hurts! It hurts!" His face had been so horrifically burned that it was nothing but a black mask, swollen eyelids sealed tight and white teeth stark against his charred lips.

I walked further into the candle-lit hall. There were a few people who were tending to their relatives, but the main work was being done by a man and a woman. The pair of them were pitifully outnumbered. They could do little more than apply oil to the burns in a vain attempt to ease the pain, before swiftly moving onto the next child. The man had a tub of ointment, while the woman carried a metal jug. She might have been a teacher at the school. Even in her drab clothes, I could see that she was beautiful, elfin – though she looked exhausted. I doubt that she had slept in 36 hours.

She cradled the children's heads as she gave them a sip of water. I watched as she cosseted a boy who was calling for his mother. She was stroking his hair as he died.

I plunged further into the hall. Two young girls holding hands on a blanket – one dead from her injuries and the other about to die. "Don't go," she calls out to her sister. "Don't leave me."

A boy, savagely burned across his chest, thrashes his head from side-to-side as he manically chants, "Water! Water! Water!"

The misery and the pain was unending, and all of it voiced

in a score of screams and shrieks as the children called out for their mothers, fathers, or just an end to the unbearable torment.

"Kill me," pleaded one boy, whose arms and torso had been riven with glass shards. "Please Sir, kill me. Please kill me."

I had to bury my nose into my fingers to mask the smell. It was not just the stench of rotting, cooked flesh. Most of the victims soiled themselves where they lay. The air reeked of death and that sharp, almost heady whiff of urine and all manner of other human waste. The victims would vomit onto their own bedding, just able to turn their heads to the side as they retched up what looked like a thin yellow gruel.

Shinzo had already walked through the hall, hurriedly going from one victim to the next to check if they were his sister. The girl, who had been following, whispered something to him. Shinzo nodded and the next moment stood right in the middle of the hall and bellowed, "Tamiko! Tamiko Wakita!" His voice silenced all the moans and screams instantly.

"Tamiko!" he called out again. "Has anyone seen Tamiko Wakita?" The hall was so quiet that you could even hear the echo.

"Tamiko! Has anyone seen Tamiko?"

Nothing happened, and then from the far end of the hall came a small moan and someone raised their hand. Shinzo and I went over. She was a young woman whose swirling shirt pattern had been scorched into her skin in some ghastly parody of a tattoo.

"I was with Tamiko," she said, timid eyes staring up at us. "She was in charge of our party. She came here with me. She was... " The woman trailed off. "She was burned."

"She is here?" Shinzo said in astonishment. "Tamiko is here? Here in this room?"

"Yes," said the woman. "She was brought here."

Shinzo bustled over to the man in a white coat who appeared to be in charge. The doctor had just finished applying a handful of salve to a boy's legs. He glanced up at us.

Shinzo – still, unbelievably, carrying his bucket – was tongue-tied. "I... I was looking for my sister. I understand she is here, but I cannot find her. Are more survivors in another room?"

"This is all there is," said the doctor, gesturing out over the hall. "I'm sorry. If she's not in this room, then she will have been taken outside. There is a box of personal items that we have been collecting. You may have a look. Again, I apologise. We did what we could."

Like a man in dream, Shinzo weaved over to the corner of the room, where there was a wooden crate on a table. He started to pick his way through the contents, holding broaches, bracelets, earrings and hair-clips up to the light of a lantern before carefully placing them to the side.

He soon came across what he had been dreading to find. Tamiko's square-faced watch with its steel strap, and looped through it her belt. They were positioned near the top of the box; she must have died that afternoon.

How poor Shinzo's shoulders slumped as he clutched those two little mementoes to his chest, the tears falling freely down his cheeks. The girl and I watched from a little distance as that great man stood in the corner, his shoulders quivering in pain, grinding the heels of his fists into his eye-sockets.

"Shall we go outside?" I said to the girl.

"You go. I'll stay." She trotted over to Shinzo and clasped both arms round his midriff, burying her face into his flank. How I wish I had done the same for my friend. But I did not. After a last peremptory look about the hall, and at the doctor and his pretty helpmate, I stalked outside. The hall and all those ravaged children had left me feeling nauseous. And I did not wish to intrude into private grief.

Out in the open air, there was a scene that was different but no less hellish. Three soldiers were hauling bodies over to the pyres. They had dug a shallow pit and were dragging the bodies towards it like so many haunches of meat. Two of them would hold onto the limbs and with a single swing the corpse would be flung onto the mound of bodies with arms, legs and naked torsos all on wanton display in a repellent orgy of death.

I was mesmerised. The three men stolidly went about their work with all the detachment of foresters who had been tasked to clear a wood. For them, the corpses had lost all trace of their humanity and were now nothing more than detritus which had to be cleared away.

The mound was now the height of a man. Who knew – Tamiko might even have been at the bottom of it. A soldier tossed one more body onto the top, a baby's, so light that he slung it up single-handed as if throwing a stick for a dog.

The men conferred for a moment, before one of them picked up a can of kerosene or some other oil and doused it over the bodies. He sprayed all around the mound until the can was empty. Without any further ceremony, he struck a match and held it to a dead woman's hair. With a dull, flat boom, the pyre exploded into flames. Even I, so heartless, spineless, was stunned at the lack of dignity, the lack of honour. Not a prayer, not a single acknowledgement to the victims' humanity, as if they were so much rubbish that had to be disposed of. And now they were not even corpses any more, but had been reduced to one single burning mass of flesh, their only calling card being that awful smell of cooked meat which carried for kilometres in the wind.

All this and more I thought of as I watched the three soldiers at their work. Already they had started work on digging a fresh pit. Perhaps I do them a disservice. Perhaps the only way to have completed a job such as that was to be the automaton, switching your mind off and letting your limbs take over.

Shinzo and the girl had come out of the hall hand in hand and were watching the pyre beside me. Shinzo, his face streaked with tears, had shut his eyes and his mouth was moving in silent prayer. The girl was fascinated by the blazing pyre and how these things that had once been human were melting into ash. The smoke eddied up into the sky, the only memorial that these victims would ever know.

Behind us, we heard a gentle cough. It was the doctor, in his stained white coat. "I am sorry to bother you at a time like this," he said, rubbing his hands down his sides. "I know that you are grieving. But, as you can see, we need help. Could you stay? Could you help us? If only for the night?"

How my stomach turned when I heard those words. Was there no end to the chores that I was being volunteered for? So I had been lucky and I had survived the bomb. But did that mean that I was indebted to every person I met? Did that mean that I had been forfeited into a life of service, where in every instance I had to think first of others? No, no! Never! I was my own man and would do as I pleased. For over a day now, I had – under sufferance – helped out as best I could. But because of my health, was I now morally obliged to tend the sick? And if for one day, then why not another week? A year? Was it suddenly my duty to care for them for the rest of my days?

Shinzo had turned to the doctor. "Of course," he said. "Of course we will stay. We're not trained, but will do what we can."

"What?" I was maddened with rage, like a bull that has been pricked and pricked again until it would gore its own shadow. Who was this man, this idiot, to think that he could answer for me? Never mind that he had just lost his sister. Hiroshima was awash with grief that day. The girl had lost her grandmother; my Sumie was dead. So why did Shinzo suddenly think it was within his boon to offer us up for the night? And without even the courtesy of a 'by your leave'.

The longer I dwelt upon it, the more enraged I became. "Who the hell do you think you are?" I said. "Just who the hell do you think you are? Are you some officer ordering his troops? Is that what you think?"

Shinzo stared at me in puzzlement. "I thought this morning you suggested helping out at an aid station. Did I misunderstand you?"

"I am sick of being taken for granted!" I said.

"I thought you wanted to help."

"Well listen to this – I am off! I am going! I am leaving Hiroshima as soon as I can! I have had it! I have had it with you! I have had it with this city!"

Shinzo nodded in agreement, before bringing up his hands and bowing his head in a deep salaam. "You are right and I am sorry," he said. "I have been thoughtless. I said that we would stay the night – when what I meant was that I would stay the night. It goes without saying that you are free to come and go as you please."

"I am staying," said the girl, agog at my fury.

"Good for you!" I was grinding my teeth I was so livid with anger. "Good for both of you! Do what you want! Spend the night! Spend the week! Save as many of these children as you want! I do not care! I do not care what you do! But please – please – do not bother to include me in any of your plans ever again!"

Shinzo again salaamed, bowing even deeper than before. "I am sorry," he said. "I have taken you for granted."

"Do not worry about that, Shinzo!" I said, my voice almost cracking I was in such a perfect fury. "It is a mistake that I will never allow to happen again!"

"I am sorry."

"Goodbye Shinzo, and I hope to see you again, if and when you ever bother to return to Nagasaki! Goodbye!"

My eyes raked briefly over Shinzo, the girl and that stunned doctor before I turned on my heel. I stalked out of the compound, quite consumed with rage, and all I could hear was the dry crackle of those funeral pyres and the pleading cries of the girl.

The shallowness of that man that was myself almost makes me weep. To think that I could not even have spent a single night tending those burned wretches.

It would be easy to claim that the world was out of kilter

that day and that we all of us in Hiroshima had gone a little mad. But the truth was that I was acting entirely true to form. I had been a beast since childhood. It was in my nature – and it was only in the aftermath of the bomb that my true character, red in tooth and claw, had been unmuzzled.

Though it was quite dark, there was enough light from the sporadic fires to guide me north-west to one of the outlying stations at Hiroshima.

The lethargy that had been hanging over me that day had quite gone, replaced with a vast reserve of energy and determination. I was my own man again; I could do as I pleased. If I wanted to work in a hospital or an emergency aid centre then I could do just that – but it would be my call, my decision. And if I wanted to go directly back to Nagasaki, that was also my decision.

What had happened to Hiroshima was a tragedy. But was it of my making? Was I now bound to stay there until every last victim had been either saved or incinerated? And did I not have some obligation, also, to my wife and my baby boy – or did these thousands of injured strangers have a greater call upon my time?

And so, round and round, went my thoughts in this angry swirl, as I fulminated against Shinzo and all those other parasites who had impinged upon my time. In my rage, I lashed out at a rock. I gave it a full kick with the toe of my boot. It clinked satisfyingly through the ruins.

"Stop!" came a cry. "Stop!"

I didn't stop. I wouldn't have dreamed of stopping. I dug my hands deep into my pockets and continued to walk.

It was the girl and still she came after me, pattering down the street before tugging at my sleeve. "Please stop."

I did not even reply. I shook her with a brisk flick of my arm. But she was having none of it. This time she ran directly in front of me. "Why will you not stop?" she said, holding her ground. "Are you frightened to talk to me?"

I didn't even bother to walk round her. I shouldered her out of the way. She gave a little cry as she fell to the ground – but it didn't stop her coming back for more. Again she darted in front of me.

"Please stop," she said again. "We want you to come back. Please."

This time I cuffed her round the ear with the back of my hand. She let out a squeal of pain.

"How dare you!" she said, and with that she started kicking me with her dainty little shoes and drumming her fists into my chest. "How dare you! You are a beast, a selfish beast, and you have been a beast since the day you were born. You never think of anyone but yourself and you never have. You are a beast! Beast! Beast!"

It was difficult to tell what angered me more. Was it her puny kicks and her feeble punches, or was it that I was hearing the truth?

Either way, my reaction was savage. I gave her a full round-arm slap across the face. Her head jolted to the side. She was flung off her feet, crumpling to the ground.

And what happened next. Did it really happen? Or is it one of those hideous memories which you can only peep at through clenched fingers? Have you ever regretted something so much that the very thought of it still makes you wince? Well, this was that memory tenfold.

Perhaps it did not happen. Now that I am in old age, I sometimes like to fancy that it's just my memory playing tricks.

But in my heart, I know it to be true.

I kicked her.

Not content with knocking the girl across the street, I followed after her and then gave her a scything kick which landed – and I know this precisely – on her buttocks, so hard that she was lifted off the ground. She screamed in pain, mewling on the ground in a foetal ball.

For a moment I stood over her, the boxer triumphant who dares his opponent to get up for more. I glanced back. Shinzo was standing five metres away, his hands clutched either side of his head, as shocked as I had ever seen him.

He rushed over to the girl, cradling her in his arms. He never once looked at me nor said a word.

CHAPTER TEN

The destruction of Hiroshima would, you might have thought, have galvanised Japan's leaders into action. Far from it.

Some, like the war minister General Anami, were all for continuing the fight. "Would it not be wondrous," he said, "for this whole nation to be destroyed like a beautiful flower?"

Others hoped that a peace deal might yet be brokered with Russia; it would need only another 24 hours before the Russians nailed that particular lie.

And that night of 7th August, there was also a third argument going the rounds in Tokyo: that despite President Truman's claims, it was not possible for an atomic bomb to have razed Hiroshima to the ground. It was a physical impossibility. Our scientists knew all about atomic bombs; we had even tried to make one ourselves and knew for a fact that it was quite impossible to have produced enough fissionable material to construct an atomic bomb.

Further to that argument, Admiral Toyoda also stated that even if the Yankees had achieved the impossible and built themselves an atomic bomb, then they were certainly incapable of producing a second. That would have required twice as much uranium or plutonium, which was self-evidently impossible; in fact not just impossible, but exponentially impossible. It was not just doubly impossible, but impossible to the power of two.

So, two days after Little Boy had been dropped, Japan was

not even close to surrendering. They were like the gambling addict who's in so deep that he can never stop – and who yet hopes that everything might turn good on the last throw of the dice.

I shake my head with unconscionable weariness as I think of our war leaders. America had its Roosevelt and Britain had its Winston Churchill – not just great leaders, but perhaps their country's greatest leaders of all time. And who did we have to lead us through the Second World War? The Big Six, those fusty throwbacks to the Samurai era, who still believed it better to die with honour than to surrender.

But did it all turn out for the best? Japan is definitely a kinder, more gentle, more considerate country than it could have ever have been without the war. And perhaps we needed this awful catharsis to break the mould? Perhaps—

I know I certainly did.

As I walked away from the girl, my boiling anger was replaced by the most toxic horror.

We all of us have an image of ourselves. It is our currency, our definition of self-worth.

And, though it had taken me nearly 30 years, I was suddenly going through the most harrowing re-evaluation. How often in our lives do we have a mirror held up to our own awfulness?

I had kicked the girl? I had clubbed a seven-year-old girl to the ground and then kicked her? And all because she had begged me to spend a single night tending the sick children at the Hijiyama Primary School? The girl was right – I was nothing but a beast, a foul-tempered, self-obsessed beast. In the whole of Hiroshima that day, there could not have been a single person who had behaved as awfully, as selfishly, as I had.

Was this what I had become? Had it taken the ending of civilisation in Hiroshima to turn me into an animal? Or, perhaps, I had always been like that.

All this and more I was to dwell upon for many days

afterwards, but at that time, my steps slowed, they faltered, and there in the wilderness of Hiroshima I came to a dead stop and let out a great howling shriek to the moon – not for the dead, but for the monster that I had become.

I drummed my forehead on the heels of my hand and slapped myself hard twice on the cheeks.

If there is anything at all to say in my defence it is that, then and there, I endeavoured to make amends. It would have been easier to have continued on my journey. I could have been the coward and caught the first train to Nagasaki. I might never have seen the girl again – might never have had to stare into her unflinching eyes and apologise.

But, for what little that it is worth, I quickly realised the enormity what I had done.

It was going to be humiliating – mortifyingly humiliating. But if I were to retain even a sliver of self-respect in the future, I would have to apologise.

I retraced my steps, though not quickly, like a boy dawdling on his way to school as he tries to delay the inevitable. I tried to recall my actions of the previous 15 minutes. Had that really been me – me – who had refused to give up one single night to work in a children's aid centre? Who had stormed out in a rage and who had then kicked a girl while she was on the ground? Was that really me?

Yes, it was me, and though I am now able, at least, to accept what I did, even 60 years on I still find the memory of it excruciating.

I found the girl lying on her side in the school hall where the doctor was inspecting her back and her bottom. The bruised skin was already a mottled purple-grey. The doctor delicately probed, feeling his way round the small of her back.

"Can you move your leg?" he asked.

"Yes," she whispered.

The doctor worked his hands up her spine. "There are no broken bones," he said, standing up. "But it will be sore for a while."

His eyes turned to me. "You have returned to join us?"

"I have," I said, before diving into that deep, deep well of remorse and apology. "I am sorry that I left you in the first place. For too long in my life, I have been a very selfish man."

I knelt in front of the girl who was still lying on her side. She looked me gravely in the eye.

"I'm sorry. I truly apologise. I don't know if you will ever be able to forgive me. But, if it is any consolation, I don't think I will ever be able to forgive myself. I'm sorry."

"Beast," she said, and turned her head away. Given the pain, not to mention the humiliation of what she had just been through, I am surprised she did not spit in my face.

"I'm sorry," I said again. "So very sorry."

I stretched my hand to touch her lightly on the shoulder, but she shrugged it off. "Go away."

"I'm sorry."

"Go away."

I had been through this scenario with my wife Mako many times before. If a person was not ready to accept your apology then there was no point in endlessly repeating it. I would wait a while in the hope that she might thaw.

I stood up. "What can I do to help?" I asked the doctor.

"Get some oil," he said. "Any sort of oil – and bandages. We have nothing left."

"I'll find them."

Candle in hand, I poked round the other rooms in the school. There were four or five rooms, though it was difficult to tell what they had been used for. Every room had gaping holes in the walls and ceiling, while the furniture had been reduced to splinters. I stumbled over some rubble, almost dropping the candle. I was in a room that may as well have been pulped by a wrecker's ball. Most of the ceiling was on the floor, while one of the walls had been levelled to the ground. I had all but walked through the room before I saw a couple of metal sinks and the remains of a white tiled wall and realised I was in the school kitchens.

I placed the candle on one of the sinks and methodically cleared the debris, tossing the wood and the tiles straight out of the room and into the garden. Most of the contents of the cupboards had been smashed. Eventually, I came across a large drum of cooking oil.

I hefted it up onto my shoulder and carried it back to the main hall. The stench of the room hit me afresh, though the smell was soon mixed with the sweet aroma of peanut oil. Today, I only need to catch a single whiff of peanut oil and I am instantly back in that school hall with its scores of whimpering children.

I filled up two jugs with oil and steeled myself to do yet one more thing that I could not avoid any longer. Shinzo was in a corner of the room smearing the last of a tub of ointment onto a girl's back. She whimpered at his every touch.

"Here," I said. "I have found some more oil."

He did not look up. "I heard you were back."

"I'm very sorry."

"It is not me you need to be apologising to."

"I've already done that."

He grunted to himself, smoothing the cream onto the young girl until her back looked as if it had been basted with white fat. "You did a wicked thing to that girl—"

"It was unforgivable."

"I don't know about that. But it's good that you came back." For the first time, he looked me in the eye, his black eyes glinting in the candlelight. "These are not easy times. But we learn – and we move on. I think we should start again."

"Thank you. I would like that." And as I walked away, Shinzo clapped me over the shoulder, and, even amidst all those horribly injured children, it gave me such a surge of joy. For even in my darkest hour, it was still possible to find redemption.

And that moment, more or less, was the very beginning of my rebirth. Not that there have not been many slips along the way. But for the first time, I had been granted a glimpse of the correct path, and ever since I have striven to be a kinder, more forgiving person. None of it could have happened though if it were not for three very kind people.

The first of these was Shinzo; the second was the girl; and the third ... well the third we shall come to.

For over an hour, I had been tending to the children as best I could. I poured peanut oil onto their burns and would try to bind their wounds with strips of an old sheet. And always they cried out. How they cried – they cried out for water, for their mothers, or simply called out that perpetual cry of the atomic bomb victim, "It hurts, it hurts".

I was working on the swollen shoulders of a young boy. He had been burned and peppered with glass shards. I was pulling out the splinters with forceps, but most were so deep they could only have been retrieved with a scalpel.

Although I had never done it before, a part of me enjoyed the work. It called for the same sort of precision that comes to bear when making a kite. I am not sure it was of any use. Many of the splinters were so fragile that they crumbled at the first bit of pressure from the forceps.

There was little light, so I was largely working by touch. First I would feel the jagged glass with the tips of my fingers and would then try to grip anything that protruded through the flesh.

"Here. This may help." It was the girl, who had brought over a candle in a saucer. She held it steady over the boy's back.

"Thank you."

I seized on a splinter of glass and pulled it smoothly from the boy's shoulder. It tinkled as I dropped it in the saucer. "Much better. Thank you."

"That's alright, Beast."

"Beast?"

"That is your new name and that is what I shall call you."

"I deserve it," I said.

"You do."

"How long are you going to carry on calling me Beast?"

"I shall decide that." She spoke formally, but did at least have a hint of a smile.

"Thank you," I said again, and then did something that I have never done before. I acknowledged her grace with a deep bow of my head. "Thank you. You are very kind."

And that is what is so very special about children. They can forgive. Adults nurse their grievances and hug them close – and in my time, I had been one of the worst for that. But a child can let it all go in a moment. They do not even want vengeance. All they require is a smile and an apology and it is forgotten. They have moved on.

For me, that one act of forgiveness was one of the greatest gifts I have ever received, for it was the key to my redemption. And ever since, in thought and deed, I have done my best to acknowledge it. I am still fundamentally a sinner. But at least these days I am aware that there is such a thing as a correct path. I strive to take it.

There was one final event from that night which I must describe. Shinzo had shown me compassion. The girl had shown me forgiveness. My third encounter in that reeking, hellish hospital would reveal something else entirely.

I treated many children that night, but the one that I spent most time with was a girl who was but three years old. She had facial burns and some cuts on her back, though did not seem too severely injured. But how she screamed. Her mother had died in the school hall earlier that day. The girl had been found snuggling into her chest, quietly whimpering as if she realised the size of the tragedy that had engulfed her.

It might have been kinder to have left her there for the night, but the mother's body was taken away and, without a second thought, was tossed onto one of the flaming pyres.

How that little girl howled as she saw her mother being carried from the hall. She tried to follow, but was barred from going outside. Instead, she planted herself into a pool of vomit on the doorstep and screamed her lungs out.

I had been nearby, pouring peanut oil onto a woman whose raw flesh had been flensed of its skin. Yet I found myself drawn to this tormented child. I went over and picked her up and, just as I would have done with my own son, I held her tight to my chest and kissed the top of her head.

She still screamed, but I didn't mind. I carried her over to where her mother had died and sat down with her on the blanket. "What's your name?" I asked, but she never replied, only whimpering into my ear as she clutched at my neck.

Back and forth I rocked her. I sang her the same little ditty that my father had used to sing to me. Gradually, the sobbing eased and with a final sniff she was fast asleep in my arms. I wrapped her in the blanket and with a final kiss on the cheek, I placed her on the ground.

I must have been with that three-year-old girl for 30 minutes.

I stood up. A last glance over my shoulder to check that the girl was still asleep.

Gagging at the smell of the entrance porch, which was thick with faeces and vomit. The smell of peanut oil, insanely mixed with the aroma of cooked meat. I went outside to relieve myself, but was back in the hall within minutes – and the three-year-old girl was dead.

I found her lying on the blanket with open eyes staring up to the ceiling. I couldn't believe it. I looked her close in the face and then snatched her up to catch a trace of her breath. And yet – nothing. She had died and I will never know the reason why. Perhaps it was a broken heart.

After nearly two days of unremitting hell, it was that girl's sad little death that sent me over the edge. I sat on the blanket, clutching her tight to my chest, and bawled my eyes out. It could have been my grief for the girl, for Sumie, or for the whole of Hiroshima, but the tears poured silently down my cheeks and would not stop.

I felt a hand touch me on the shoulder, but didn't look up. "Come with me," said a voice. I dumbly placed the dead girl back on her blanket and followed the woman, the doctor's helper, outside. Without a word, she embraced me.

I held her so close, my tears now mixed with a chuckle of laughter. How seamlessly, how quickly, I had moved from momentous grief to the most inexpressible joy at being hugged by a beautiful stranger.

"See death – and embrace life," she whispered into my ear.

"Embrace life?"

"Every time someone dies, it is a reminder to all of us. A reminder to embrace life."

She didn't need to say more.

The woman's arms were still locked round my back, her hands tight against my shoulders, and that hug gave her words an extraordinary resonance. I was not just embracing that beauty, that sage, that angel that had been sent to me from heaven itself, but I was embracing life. Sixty years on, I still say those very words to myself every morning, for they are my abiding philosophy: embrace life.

That is not to downplay death or the grieving process. With every death comes its fair portion of tragedy. But if there is anything positive at all to be gained from death, then it is to serve as a reminder that we must embrace every day, every moment, of this glorious miracle of life.

The woman, that delightful elfin woman who was hugging me so tight, whispered again in my ear. "Thousands of people are dead. We have lived through it. Is that not special?"

In all my years, I have yet to hear the life-affirming nature of Hiroshima explained so succinctly. It was a disaster, a catastrophe. But for those that survived it, Hiroshima could be taken as the most powerful affirmation of life. I know of many bomb victims who are ashamed of their keloid scars and who led their lives feeling permanently embittered. I also have a keloid scar, a shiny stretched ripple of discoloured skin. But thanks to that woman, I wear it with pride, for I only have to glance at it to remind myself that I am blessed, blessed every day that I remain on this hallowed earth.

We gave the three-year-old girl a proper farewell. I wrapped her in her mother's blanket, with only her face showing, as if I were about to put her to bed. Then, with a last kiss to her forehead, I placed her on one of the pyres.

We each said a prayer and I lit the pyre. My grieving was over, to be replaced with the most stunning tranquillity.

We were outside sitting on a piece of rubble. I looked at my angel properly for the first time. Her face was in exquisite profile as she gazed up at the drifting smoke. Lines of tiredness etched round her eyes, but to my mind she was still ravishing. She knew I was looking at her, but her gaze never faltered.

"Even strangers have much to teach us," she said, sitting now on her hands to keep them warm.

"Yes?"

"When you came here this afternoon, looking for your friend, you didn't want to get involved. You were here for your friend. The people in this school were all strangers. We were not your problem."

"I am already quite ashamed at my own selfishness."

"Yet you grieved for that girl as if she were your own child."

"And you gave me a hug when it was the last thing I deserved."

"I did," she said, with a smile. "I gave you a hug because you needed it. And that is why I'm working here – because there are children in there who need help."

"I wish I had met you years ago."

"You would never have listened anyway," she said, clapping me on the knee. "That's all you have to do, stranger. Help those who need to be helped."

"What's your name?"

"Wisdom."

"Seriously."

She laughed and stood up, her short black hair flopping down over her eyes.

"Me? I am nobody." And as she said that, she bent down to give me a brief peck on the lips.

I never did learn the name of my beautiful benefactor. But I have much to thank her for.

CHAPTER ELEVEN

I worked through the night till dawn, when I joined Shinzo in the corner of the room. The girl was there too, curled up on her side.

Shinzo was still awake. "What are we going to do about her?" I asked.

"I don't know." Shinzo yawned.

"We cannot take her with us. We cannot take her to Nagasaki."

"Why not ask her?" Shinzo replied, and promptly fell asleep.

The school hall was quite different when we awoke two hours later. A squad of medics had arrived in the morning and trained doctors and nurses were now treating the victims. They had even started cleaning up the vomit and all the other stinking unmentionables. For a while I just lay there, happy to be in modest comfort and to be allowed to do nothing. I was just as that beautiful woman had exhorted me the previous night – embracing life. I looked about the hall, but could not see her.

The medics had brought a sack of rice and boiled up a tub. When had I last eaten? I was famished. I sat outside with my bowl and savoured every grain of it. Even the pyres, now heaps of smouldering ash with limbs and bodies all burned to nothing, did not seem as awful as they had the previous evening.

They were another little affirmation to embrace life.The girl and Shinzo came out to join me and as we sat there eating, I realised that I was happy. I had not been so happy for a long time. The girl, perched on the edge of a rock, fiddled with her hair. Shinzo scratched at the lice in his armpit. And I revelled in the simple miracle of being born anew.

The doctor in charge came out to talk to us. His white coat was now a tapestry of different stains. "Thank you for staying last night," he said. "You were very kind. And now, as you can see, we have people to help."

"We are free to go?" I asked.

"Yes – and thank you."

"That woman who was working here with you last night. Who was she?"

"I don't know. She came to look for her mother – and then, like you, she stayed." He cocked his head to the side, as if struck by a thought. "I never properly thanked her. I would have liked to."

"She's gone?"

"Yes. A pity. I must go now. Thank you all." He bent down to the girl and cupped her cheek. "And an especial thank you to you. You were very brave."

I was disappointed not to have seen that woman again. But her words – and her elfin beauty – have been cast into amber and that is how they will always remain. Sixty years may have passed since I last saw her, but to me she will always be this angel who bestowed on me both her wisdom and her grace. And perhaps it is as well that I never did see her again, because otherwise her beauty and the simplicity of her message would have become sullied by the whole sordidness of living life.

It was like a short but very intense chapter had come to an end – and, since I will not be returning to the subject of that school hall again, I may as well reveal what happened to all those children there. The school became a place which, after all the horror of Hiroshima, would celebrate the green shoots of the next generation: it became an orphanage.

"That is that," Shinzo said to the girl. "Shall we go and look for your grandmother?"

The girl looked at me almost shyly, was about to speak. But I got in there first. "Let's go and search for your grandmother."

"And then?" said Shinzo.

I mused. "And then we go back to Nagasaki."

The girl looked from Shinzo to me and back again. "I'm coming too."

Shinzo scratched at his fat pot of a stomach. I watched as a man brought out another child's body and placed it on one of the pyres.

"Beast! I said I'm coming too!" said the girl.

"We heard you the first time – and I am a beast and thank you for reminding me," I said. "But it's not that simple. Besides, we might find your grandmother."

"You thought she was dead."

"Well—" I paused. For once, I was thinking, 'Be kind. Be kind!' "I fear that your grandmother might be lost. Do you not have other relations?"

"No – that is why I'm coming with you."

"But... but... " I faltered. "We can't just take you back with us to Nagasaki. Hiroshima is your home—"

"I do not have a home, Beast! Nobody has a home! There is nothing left!"

"That's right. But that doesn't mean we can take you to Nagasaki. Who would you stay with?"

"I'm coming too."

"I think... " I was striving for the right words. I wanted to break it gently to the girl. It just was not feasible to take the girl with us. Let alone that we might well be separating her from her grandmother, the practicalities of taking her to Nagasaki would be enormous. "I think that, after we have searched for your grandmother, we should hand you over to the authorities."

"You're not leaving me."

"Who would you stay with in Nagasaki?" Despite my new

'Embrace Life' mantra being barely more than six hours old, I was annoyed.

"I'm coming with you, Beast."

"You cannot come. It's ridiculous. It's nothing personal. But it would not be right."

Shinzo snorted at that, breaking off from his scratching. "Since when have you ever been concerned about what is right?"

"Well, what do you think?" I said, turning to him.

"If she wants to come, she should come. It's not as if there is anything left for her here."

"Brilliant," I said. "And where is she going to stay?"

"She can stay with me."

"You – you just... " It was absurd. We had been with the girl for, what, two days, and now Shinzo was proposing to adopt her? The man was mad and I was about to tell him as much, when I glanced over at another pyre, and there it was blazing out its message to me: embrace life! Have courage! Be brave and embrace anything and everything that comes your way! "That is the most beautiful thing I have ever heard you say, Shinzo."

I went over and embraced that great gorgeous bull of a man and kissed him on both cheeks. I caught the look of astonishment that passed between Shinzo and the girl. They must have found my sudden about-turn quite incomprehensible – but then they knew nothing of Wisdom's words the previous night.

I said one thing more, and I can still remember my exact words: "May God bless you for it" – and if only he had.

For a short while as we walked through Hiroshima we were a jolly little band, the girl walking in the middle and holding both our hands. That silent city was still the wasteland that it had been the previous day, but those that had survived the bomb were now largely being cared for. I don't remember seeing any survivors pleading for help or water.

There were still many, many corpses, in all their grim variety. They ranged from those black, carbonized statues, to the grey swollen bodies, missing limbs and with cankered wounds. It was the first time I had seen the maggots. They take around two days to hatch, and from that day we saw them everywhere. They were repellent. I have rarely seen anything more disgusting than a body alive with maggots, wriggling and squirming in what looks from a distance to be a rippling mass of live white blubber. Perhaps it was the white, fatty, translucent nature of the maggots that disgusted me so; or perhaps it was the knowledge that they were engorging themselves on human flesh.

But before we arrived at the Shima hospital, we came across one rare moment of the utmost hilarity: we met Motoji.

I am sure you will have long forgotten that sly ferret who worked with Shinzo and me in the kite-factory. He had been with me in the factory at the moment Little Boy was dropped, and the last I had seen of him, Motoji had been lying on the ground and skewered through the shoulders by two pieces of bamboo. I had said I would return to him, but I never had any intention of doing so and had walked off into the maelstrom that was Hiroshima – and that, I'd thought, was the last I would ever see of him. But as it is, that doltish patriot still merits one last mention in my story. I include it chiefly for my own pleasure, as its memory still makes me chuckle.

We had noticed what looked like an old man, bent with age. He was hunched over his stick and tottering through the ruins. We were heading in a westerly direction towards the Shima hospital, while this ravaged man was heading across our path and towards the sea.

We'd given the man a cursory glance when Shinzo suddenly piped up. "I think that's Motoji," he said, before calling out, "Motoji! Is that you?"

It was indeed Motoji, his wounds now bandaged and looking as if he had aged two decades in as many days.

Motoji's eyes went from Shinzo to me, and back again. He

didn't even bother to look at the girl. "Shinzo," he said. "It is good to see you."

"And you Motoji."

There was a pause as Motoji portentously tapped his stick on the ground. "So we have survived and we must all be grateful for that," he said.

"And you got patched up?" I said, ignoring that he had not yet spoken to me.

"Yes, I have," he said. "No thanks to you."

"I'm sure you would have done the same for me," I replied. Shinzo had been carefully examining Motoji, his eyes taking in his ragged trousers and the blood-stained bandages underneath his shirt. "Where are you going?" he asked.

"I'm going back to the warehouse – where else?"

A look of complete puzzlement passed across Shinzo's face. "What is happening at the warehouse?"

"I'm going there to build kites."

The utterly fantastic nature of Motoji's quest was still beyond Shinzo's comprehension. "To build kites?" he repeated.

"Yes, I'm going to the warehouse to build kites. That is what I was tasked to do three months ago and that is what I will continue to do."

"But... But... " Shinzo gaped at the man. "Are you not injured?"

"Hiroshima may have been destroyed, but ultimate victory is still assuredly ours."

"But the kites," said Shinzo. "How will kites help us win the war?"

Motoji leaned forward on his stick, clasping it with both hands. "Three months ago, I was asked to make kites. I will continue to make kites until I am ordered to do otherwise."

I smirked and then, when I caught the girl's eye, I started to titter. Yes, even after America had developed the world's most powerful bomb, Motoji was still intent on building his bamboo kites, the better to preserve our shipping.

In those days, it was far simpler to get through life by doing

153

what you were told, rather than to ever once think for yourself. And as for common sense, that ranked a very poor second in comparison to the direct orders of a commanding officer. Perhaps you can now understand how, even years afterwards, all those lone Japanese soldiers could still be at their posts in the jungle, still fighting a war that was long since over.

Motoji's eyes flickered over me with distaste. "Yes, I will continue to make kites for the good of the Motherland and because it's my duty."

Shinzo plucked at his lips as he tried to stifle his smile, but when he saw the grin on my face there was no holding it back any more. His fingers seemed to be almost smothering his face, but the laughter had to come out.

I was laughing quite openly now, hands at my sides, quivering with mirth. My laugher may seem inappropriate in such a city where we were surrounded by death. But I was not laughing at the dead, and nor, bless him, was I especially laughing at Motoji; like most of the rest of us, he'd had any trace of original thought stamped out of him long ago. But still! In all my life, I have never encountered anything quite so hilarious as Motoji wandering through the ruins of Hiroshima as he thirsted to get back to his kite-making.

When Shinzo let go, there was no stopping him. He stood there, hands on his knees, quite doubled up with laughter, until his face was as red as a ripe pomegranate and the tears were dripping into the dust. I am not sure if the girl knew why we were laughing, but the mood was infectious and so she also started, her arms crossed tight across her chest.

"What are you all laughing at?" said Motoji. "What is so funny? I am going to make kites. That is what I have been ordered to do. That is what you both have been ordered to do! Your behaviour is disloyal to the Emperor!"

It only made things worse. Shinzo was quite hysterical and for all I knew was going to collapse in a heap. The girl with squealing in her high-pitched yip. And as for me, well it was without doubt the best laugh I'd had during the entire war.

Motoji's eyes twitched from one to the other of us. "You devils!" he screamed as he stalked off. "You are treasonous devils! I shall report you to the authorities."

It still brings tears of merriment to my eyes to remember Motoji cursing us amidst the ruins. We were still laughing 20 minutes later, when that bent relic of a man was long out of sight.

A very brief moment of respite in another day of hell.

CHAPTER TWELVE

The Shima hospital, where the girl's grandmother had been working two days earlier, might never have existed. I had been past it many times. But as we walked through the ruins at the bomb's hypocenter, all of them now reduced to crumbled pebbles, it was impossible to tell one building from another.

We spent over two hours there, calling out as we poked amid the rubble. It was only for show. From the moment we'd arrived, Shinzo and I had known that nothing could have survived.

That said, I was certainly not going to snuff out the girl's dreams. I would have carried on searching all day. At length though, she came over, disconsolate, shoulders slumped.

"She is not here," she said.

"I'm sorry," I said, putting my arm round her shoulders.

"She is all I had left."

"I know. I'm sorry."

Shinzo came over. "We could leave a sign here. Just in case."

All about the ruins were scores of hand-written signs, a final plea for those who might have walked away. We wrote two messages with a piece of charcoal, one on a stone step and the other on a plank of wood which we propped in a prominent position against some rubble.

"They will soon have a full list of the survivors," said Shinzo. "In a month's time, we'll get in touch with the authorities. If she has survived, we'll find her."

The girl didn't cry. She was past crying by now. Looking around the site of the Shima hospital was merely confirmation of what she had long suspected.

"And now we're going to Nagasaki?" she asked.

"Yes," said Shinzo.

"Yes?" she said. "Are you happy with that, Beast?"

"Yes," I said. "Very happy." Though how it would turn out having the girl in Nagasaki, I had no idea.

Our plan was to make for one of Hiroshima's outlying railway stations. The main station, as I had already witnessed, had been devastated by the bomb, but there was a chance that trains might still be running from the other stations. Even during the height of the war, the efficiency of Japan's trains was legendary.

We were heading in a north westerly direction for Koi station. If that was closed, we planned to work our way down the tracks until we found an open station.

Almost the first steps of our journey took us over the Aioi Bridge, that famous T-shaped bridge that the Yankee bombardier Tom Ferebee had used as his aiming point for Little Boy. It was still standing, which was more than could be said for most of the bridges in Hiroshima, but had been shorn of its lamp-posts and its concrete balustrades. The river was still teeming with bodies, but by now they were so commonplace that I didn't give them a second glance.

Halfway across the bridge was another body, sprawled on the ground surrounded by clumps of masonry. We all stopped to look. It was the body of a Yankee prisoner-of-war, wearing a US Air Force uniform. He was tall and well-muscled, quite different from our Japanese men. Around his neck was tied a sign proclaiming that it was he who had been responsible for the bomb. The man's head had been battered beyond recognition, the dents in his skin revealing where his skull had been shattered. His face, crawling with flies, was nothing but a black musk of dried blood.

He had been stoned to death.

We stood there in silence, bleakly digesting how this man had died. "We should go," said Shinzo, taking the girl's hand. She darted towards the battered corpse and kicked it again and again, driving her tiny feet into his chest and legs. "I hate him! I hate the Yankees! I hate him for what he's done!"

It was awkward. I had not realised how hard she had been hit by the death of her grandmother. And was there anything so wrong with defiling the body of one of the Imperialist devils? Was it not precisely what all the propagandists had been encouraging her to do for the past four years?

But I found it abhorrent to watch this seven-year-old thrashing away at the Yankee's corpse. It was not right, could not be right, to allow a child to do such a thing.

I went over and clasped her by the shoulder. "Please don't do that."

She kicked the body hard in the head. "I will do what I want. He killed my father!"

"Come away. Please," I said. "You shouldn't be doing this."

"Why not?" Again she kicked him.

"I'll tell you. But only when you've stopped doing that."

She gave the body a final half-hearted poke and as she stepped away, she burst into tears – a forlorn girl not knowing what to believe anymore.

I did what I would have been incapable of doing the previous day. I embraced life. I picked her up in my arms and held her close to my chest. I was still carrying her as we walked off the bridge and could feel her tears on my neck.

"Why was it wrong?" she asked.

"That's not the way to treat a corpse."

"But he's a Yankee dog. He and other men like him dropped the bomb. Soon they'll be invading the mainland. Why shouldn't I kick him?"

On I tramped, with the girl's arms now locked round my neck. So, what was so wrong with kicking a dead prisoner-of-war?

We had been led to believe that the Yankees were the spawn of the devil, a nation of baby-killers. It suited Japan's warmongers very well to depict the Yankees as monsters.

Why were our children and our pensioners learning to fight with wooden spears? Because most of my countrymen believed sincerely – that the filthy Yankees were intent on raping every last woman in the country, not to mention slaughtering every child and torturing every adult. I know – it does sound extraordinary that any of us believed it. But hear it long enough, and loud enough, and eventually you start to believe. After all, if the media and all your friends, your family, are all spouting this garbage, to doubt is to start doubting your very sanity.

I had always doubted the crazy propaganda. I had been to America before the war in my days as a merchant seaman. My father, who had seen considerably more of the world, had described the U.S. as one of the greatest countries on earth. He had found that all their boasts were correct – it truly was the land of opportunity, home of the free. In comparison to Japan during the war, it sounded like paradise.

But now was not the time to say any of this girl. All her life, she had been taught to hate the bestial Yankees. And the bomb had just confirmed everything she had been told.

"That man may have been a Yankee, but he was also some mother's son," I said to the girl.

"And he helped to bomb this country."

"That's true. And I know that you may have lost your grandmother. But it's not the way to behave."

"Why not?"

"Well—"

"Why not?"

"Just trust me. It will take some time. I promise to explain later."

"In Nagasaki?"

"Yes. As soon as we get there."

For a while she didn't speak – and when she did, she changed the subject entirely. "What is Nagasaki like?"

So I told her: like Hiroshima, Nagasaki is another port and has been for many centuries. It has just the one river running through its centre, but its main feature is a long mountainous ridge that splits the city into two parallel valleys, the one short and the other long.

I told her about the kites and the kite-makers; and I told her about the port, far more cosmopolitan than Hiroshima. Once, before the war, it had been Japan's hub for the merchants of the world.

In this way we passed our time until we arrived at another bridge – though I use the term loosely. Most of the structure had been blown into the river and the remnants of its pilings lingered like rotten stumps in the water. The only part of the span that still remained was a single frail girder. It was, as I remember, about a foot's width across and traces of masonry and metal still clung to it, dripping off the girder like singed black ivy.

Shinzo was immediately dubious. He walked from one side of the girder to the other, weighing up his chances, scratching, always scratching. "Can we find another bridge?" he asked.

"Who knows?" I said. "There may be one. There may not."

"It makes me nervous just looking at it."

"Come on!" said the girl. She had already climbed up onto the girder and was prancing back and forth, just as I had once seen her do, a lifetime ago, on the roof of her own home.

Shinzo turned to the river. The current was flowing fast out to the inland sea. Swirling eddies, spumed with white water, bubbled round what was left of the pilings. A snagged body, partially submerged, had caught on one of the metal stanchions, its legs fluttering in the brown water.

Shinzo grimaced as he shook his head "I'll see you at the station."

"Feeble!" said the girl. "It's easy. Watch me!" By now she had pranced out right over the river which coursed five metres beneath her. First she did a pirouette, as comfortable as if she had been on stage, and then she leapt with both feet off the girder. "I'll go first. Shinzo you follow me. We'll look after you."

"You know he can't swim?" I asked.

It was so unlike Shinzo to be goaded. Like a bull that sits in the sunshine, he was generally content to chew the cud. But, for some reason, that jibe irked him.

"Alright," he said. "I'll do it."

And up he went, fat buttocks straining against the seat of his blue trousers as he climbed onto the girder.

The girl was clapping her hands with delight. She was encouraging the oaf on, like a mother raving over the first few steps of her infant son.

I was not quite so overjoyed at the sight of Shinzo clambering onto the girder – because if the idiot fell in, there was only one person who was going to save him.

He started off well enough, shuffling forward on all fours, his fingers gripping the edges of the girder. I warily followed a few metres behind. It was perfectly practicable – so long as you didn't look at the river that seethed beneath. But the moment your eyes drifted off the girder, the sheer pace of the river left you feeling giddy. It was like a back screen lurking in your peripheral vision that was perpetually on the move. Even though you tried to resist, your eyes were forever drawn towards the water. A body might catch the corner of your eye and you could not help but watch as it flicked by.

The girl, who was all but over the river by now, was urging Shinzo on. "This is the only difficult bit," she said. "There's a large piece of concrete in front of you. Stand up and go round it. You can hold onto the metal rod in the middle."

I had come to a halt. There was an uncomfortable piece of concrete digging into my leg, but I ignored the pain to observe how Shinzo edged round the obstruction. It was a clump of concrete, about a metre wide, which was completely blocking the girder. He could have tried going over, but it seemed easier to go round.

With infinite ponderousness, he got up onto his hind haunches, like a bulky walrus begging for a fish. Now he was on his knees, clinging to the masonry in front of him. I heard a sound which I could not readily identify. High-pitched, with little snatched pants of breath.

Shinzo was whimpering with terror.

He was upright and clutching onto the metal stalk that protruded from the concrete when he made the mistake of looking down. Directly beneath him was a body snagged in the water, its legs paddling up and down. From up above, it looked as if the corpse was desperately trying to swim against the current.

Shinzo whinnied with fright and with an effort of will dragged his eyes from the water and back to the concrete block in front of him. It was not easy to climb round. You had to hold tight to the metal rod and then slither round the side before your flailing foot could step back onto the girder.

The girl had come back out and was sitting a short way from Shinzo, legs swinging either side of the beam. She was smiling, encouraging Shinzo on. "You can do it!" she said. Oh, for that sweet ecstasy of youth that is ever the optimist and has yet to be sullied by disappointment. I was so nervous I could barely watch.

Shinzo had both hands on the metal rod and had started to squirm round the block. He still had one foot in contact with the beam and appeared to be in control.

A slight noise from beneath him, an eddy of water gurgling the wrong way. The snagged body slowly turns in the water to reveal a face of exquisite horror: one side is black and swollen, while the other has been sliced away clean.

In my bowels I knew exactly what Shinzo would do. "Keep your eyes in front!" I yelled. "Eyes front!" But he couldn't possibly resist. He peered over his shoulder; shifted his bodyweight to stare at the mangled body; and at that very moment the spike of metal sheared off in his hands.

It was like watching a tower block being brought down in a controlled explosion. First there is the crump of noise, the puff of dust and then, slowly at first but picking up momentum, the whole building crumples to the ground.

Shinzo's stomach seemed to be melded into the concrete, but began to slip. Shinzo, shocked, staring stupidly at the useless lump of metal in his hands. His foot paddling for a purchase. And backwards he falls, arms and legs all clawing at the air to save himself. It is all happening so fast, but the adrenalin has kicked in and I miss nothing. The girl screaming and screaming. Shinzo falling flat on his back into the river, disappearing beneath the surface. His head pokes up above the surface, his hands thrashing uselessly at the water as he struggles for air. I'm already getting to my feet – I will need a huge leap to clear the rubble beneath me. I glance briefly at the girl, over her mouth. She cannot believe Shinzo has fallen in.

I stand up on the girder, swing my arms backwards and then jump as far as I can into the river, landing sort of feet first in a shallow flop. My foot jars with pain as it crunches against something solid beneath the water. Hurts like hell. Might be something broken.

When I draw breath, Shinzo is already five, seven metres downstream from me, screaming like a stricken animal. I strike out after him in a clumsy crawl, the current sweeping me along. Breathe once to the right, once to the left. A few panicky seconds before I catch up with him. He's like a mad thing, arms flailing on the water, fat head gasping for air.

I make the classic mistake that every rescuer is warned about. I try to save him.

The very moment I get within touching distance he has grabbed hold of me, first one fat hand on my shirt, then the other. I have one single moment to grab a lungful of air and then he's onto me, smothering me, locking both arms around my neck. The great fat bastard is drowning me! He has an elbow hard beneath my chin, pressing against my throat. I catch glimmers of sunlight as we roil together in the water. The more I try to get him off me, the tighter he clings. I do the only thing that can possibly save me: I go absolutely mad. I am a berserker.

My mouth is suddenly snapping at his fingers, my legs are kicking. Somehow I manage to wind him with an elbow in his gut, which gives me a little more leeway. Then I punch him as hard as I can, a withering right hook to the head, numbing my knuckles and sending shockwaves up my arm. The blow may have been blunted by the water, but Shinzo's grip slackens and now he's drifting away in the current.

"Get off me!" I scream, still mad with rage. "Imbecile!" His whirling arms are lying limp on the surface. I'm not even sure he can hear me.

I warily approach him again. "No grabbing!" I said.

He lies limp in the water as I cup my hand beneath his chin and I make for the shore with an ungainly backstroke. It's hard to make much headway, but now that Shinzo has calmed – is he even conscious? – we make slow progress. His bulk would keep us afloat for hours. It is soothing to look up at the blue sky while finning through the water. We've travelled a long way, well over a kilometre and the girl and our makeshift bridge are long out of sight.

We come to a bend in the river and, with a couple of hard pulls, we coast into the bank. My feet touch the bottom and I haul Shinzo out of the river and onto the mud. Blood oozes from his nose. I roll him onto his side into the recovery position, and after a time he vomits, over and over again, heaving up every last drop of the brackish water that he has swallowed.

I sit there on the mud, elbows on knees, basking in the morning sun. After the sudden action, my hands are shaking, though not from the cold. My foot is also throbbing, but I decide to leave the boot on until we've reached the train.

Shinzo heaves himself up into a sitting position and fingers his nose, delicately moving it from side to side with the tips of his index fingers. He pats down the rest of his face, searching for other injuries, before spitting out the last of the vomit.

"I think you broke my nose," he said.

"You're lucky that's the only thing I broke."

"Did you have to hit me so hard?"

"You were drowning both of us, you idiot. It was the only way to get you off me."

Shinzo pondered for a while as again he fingered his nose. It looked swollen, but not broken. "Ouch!" he said, after giving it too much of a tweak.

"Leave that nose alone. We still have to cross the river. Do you want another try at that bridge?"

"No, I do not." He was hurting, though I think it was more dented pride than anything else.

"We will find somewhere else then."

We hauled ourselves out of the mud and wandered through the ruins towards the sea – and if only that were the end of this little interlude. If only I had included the bridge incident as another example of Shinzo's cack-handed ineptitude. But I include it because, as you know, in the land of the atomic bomb, it is the trivial little matters of everyday life that decide whether we live or die, and Shinzo's near drowning was one such.

After another kilometre or so, we found a part-destroyed bridge that served to get us over the last river. It was only then that Shinzo could relax enough to thank me.

"I'm grateful for what you did," he said.

"What are friends for?" I said, pleased at least to have evened things out a little. I had not forgotten the grace with which he'd handled my explosive anger the previous night.

"I think I should learn to swim."

"Good."

"My brother threw me into a river once. I've been terrified of water ever since."

"You may find you enjoy it."

"That's what we shall do," he announced, pleased with

himself. "When we get back to Nagasaki, you can teach me to swim."

I laughed at the thought. "Maybe we could get to do it all over again."

"Though without the hitting."

"And without the strangling either." We were both sniggering at the banter, as we each sought to trump the other's put down. What a pleasure it was to be with that man, affectionately teasing each other as we wandered on the final lap through the western outskirts of Hiroshima. The buildings were as much of a wasteland as every other part of the city that we had visited, but we were so inured to the destruction that it no longer registered.

It was Shinzo who brought up exactly the subject on which I had been dwelling.

"Where will the girl be?" he asked.

"I hope she goes to Koi station."

"She knows we were going to that station?"

"I hope so," I said. "I think so. Did we specify a station?"

Shinzo pulled a face. "We didn't. I'm sure she'll find it."

"Will she stay at the bridge?" I asked. "Will she wait for us there?"

"She's a bright girl," said Shinzo, with all his usual complacency. "She'll find us."

After he had said something like that, I absolutely knew the girl would not be at Koi station – and so it proved.

Our Hiroshima journey finally came to an end in the early afternoon, when we wandered in to Koi station. I know that in retrospect this sounds astonishingly naïve, but it really felt like journey's end. But it's only journey's end on the day you die, and for the rest of it, the end of one journey is merely the beginning of the next. And we always hope that after a tragedy in our lives, the next journey will provide a little light relief. We almost feel hard done by if we go straight from one disaster to the next. That, however, is very often how it is in life.

The station had been knocked about by the bomb, but was still very much standing. What a relief that was. Many people were milling around, but it took only took a cursory inspection to know that the girl wasn't there.

I cannot say that I missed her – not then. But it felt odd not having the girl beside us. Without the unceasing prattle of her voice, an unusual silence hung in the air. We had been through so much over the previous two days. Two days! How astonishing that figure still seems; it's no great length of time at all to get to know a person, but for the three of us, it was more than enough to see each other at our very best – and worst.

Shinzo had loose bowels. It came on quite suddenly. One moment we were sitting peaceably outside the station and the next he had got up without a word and was tearing off to find a private spot to relieve himself.

I went to look for food and to see about the trains. Within two minutes, I had found a woman at a nearby stall and had bought almost half of the wares that she had to sell: rice-balls and raw red onions. I bought enough food to get us to Nagasaki, paying with the cash from my money-belt.

It was just as easy finding out about the train. There was indeed a train running to Nagasaki, the last that day, and it was leaving, as I remember, just after 5pm, arriving around 9am on the morning of 9th August. After my labours of the previous two days, everything suddenly started to fall into my lap. I wanted food – and I found it. I wanted a train to Nagasaki – and there it was.

And I wanted the girl to arrive before the train departed – and there she was, with just minutes to spare, a ragamuffin wandering up the road and quite bursting into tears at the sight of Shinzo and me eating our rice-balls in the dust. It was a grand reunion, a quite lovely reunion, with the three of us hugging each other as the girl planted a kiss on Shinzo's cheek – but he was always her favourite.

If I could end my story there I would. The struggle is seemingly over; our happy band could finally quit Hiroshima with heads held high and full of good cheer at the prospect of our new life in Nagasaki.

But looking back, I find it difficult to square my emotions of that moment with how events turned out. That joyous reunion now seems like a little fizzle of light set against the overwhelmingly bleak backdrop of a thundering typhoon.

But did I see it? Did I know what was to come?

I had not the slightest inkling. I only had eyes for that little spurt of light that flickered between the three of us, the smile on Shinzo's face and the shining tears of the girl – and I never thought to look at the storm-clouds gathering overhead.

CHAPTER THIRTEEN

The irony of our last minutes in Hiroshima was exquisite; there is no other word for it.

If only the girl had tarried a little longer at the bridge, where she had waited for a full two hours before following us to the station; if only she had got lost not once but twice along the way; if only she had not been personally led to the station by a kindly old woman...

If any of those eventualities had occurred, we would have missed the last train out of Hiroshima that evening – and there would be no more story left to tell.

But the girl did arrive. Of course she had to arrive; you knew that she had to arrive. We would never have boarded the train without her – and if I was not on the train, then how ever was I going to keep my date with Fat Boy, which was due to explode over Nagasaki approximately two hours after my arrival there?

In hindsight, all my actions seem to have a prickling sense of inevitability about them.

It is like that fabled story from the Middle East, 'An Appointment in Samarra'.

A rich man is with his servant in the marketplace in Damascus. They are browsing through the stalls, looking for food and oddments, when the rich man rounds a corner and with a shock realises that he is staring Death in the face. The Grim Reaper, dressed in ragged black, appears to be stunned, even wrathful; the servant is so awestruck that he swoons to the ground in a dead faint. Without waiting another moment, the rich man races back to his mansion-house and takes two horses. He rides and he rides all through the heat of the day, until eventually it is quite dark and he arrives into the little town of Samarra.

The man is tired but elated at how, through his quick-wittedness, he has managed to cheat Death. He goes to a little tavern to celebrate – and there, waiting patiently for him in the corner, is the Grim Reaper. The rich man is dumbfounded, almost aggrieved. "What were you doing in the market-place this morning?" he demands of Death. "You pulled such a forbidding face that my servant collapsed with fright."

The Grim Reaper stands up and stares placidly at the man – for death is never unkind. "I was shocked to see you," replies Death. "I knew that we had an appointment in Samarra this evening. I never thought that you would arrive in time."

No matter how much a man writhes and turns, he can never cheat fate.

And I was that man.

For over two days in Hiroshima, I had scurried hither and thither, ignoring victims here and brutalising girls there. But always in the background there was this clock ticking away, clicking down the seconds until my appointment in Nagasaki.

Now that I am wizened and have the benefit of hindsight, I do like to think of it as an appointment. It was not just my destiny to be in Nagasaki at 11.02 on the morning of 9th August, but also my blessing. Nagasaki, in small part, was my chance to make amends.

And how did it all turn out? All that I shall come to. But what I do know is this: although one should strive to be kind and to embrace life, one must also be prepared to do battle.

Sometimes, though not often, you have to fight fire with fire.

Sometimes, you may even have to be the brute. And I certainly knew all about that.

We were such a happy little band as we climbed on board the train. It might have been waiting expressly for our arrival. The train was full, packed with people who knew there was nothing left for them in Hiroshima, but we crammed ourselves onto one of the wooden benches. As soon as we had sat down the train pulled out from the station, black smuts of smoke puffing in through the window. The coach was Spartan with little more than wooden benches to sit on, but after Hiroshima, we would have been happy in a cattle-truck.

"Goodbye!" said the girl, waving not at the people on the platform but at Hiroshima herself. "Goodbye!" We stared silently out of the window. It was like leaving the bedside of a terminally ill friend who has finally passed away. We could do no more, and all that was left was to gaze at the ruined city that was as dead as Pompeii.

As I stared out of the window, embedded memories flickered past my mind's eye. And eventually Hiroshima trundled out of sight, and all the passengers aboard the carriage seemed to let out a collective sigh of relief. We had witnessed something terrible in Hiroshima and now we were moving on.

I slept on and off, but my clothes were still damp from the river and eventually I gave myself up to pondering that one rather painful matter that for so long I had chosen to ignore: my wife.

Like most Japanese marriages of the time, it had been an arrangement. She had been suggested to my father, who in his diffident way had mentioned the matter to me. It was not the first time he had come to me like this. I heard the old man out with equanimity and expected that this prospective bride would go the same way as all the others. But then I saw her for the first time. She was one of the most beautiful women I had ever seen. Heart-stoppingly beautiful. She was a science teacher at one of the local schools and, or so I thought, was being offered to me on a plate.

I think that I once loved her. We had married during a

maelstrom of sex at the start of the war; now she hated me. For my part, my love had turned into the most cold indifference.

I do not blame Mako for hating me. Knowing, as you do, how I had behaved in Hiroshima, it will come as no surprise to learn that for the duration of my four-year marriage, I had behaved like the very devil. Let me make a clean breast of how abominably I had conducted my marriage. I was unfaithful, many times over. I had numerous lovers. I was unkind, both in word and deed. I did not give her time to talk and when I listened, I did not even attempt to understand. I hated her when she cried and I hated her even more during those endless deserts of malign silence that broke up the tedium of her screaming. In short, I was a repellent husband who provided Mako with a home and who had given her a son – but beyond that, I was, or at least I had been, a selfish reprobate.

I pause for a moment there to wonder if I have done myself an injustice.

Probably not.

It is true that I brought out the worst in Mako, and that in the middle of her rages, this quite stunning woman could be transformed into a foul-mouthed harpy.

That said, it was I alone who had wrought this transformation. She had never yet caught me out in an act of infidelity. But I believe that, almost from the first, she had intuited it in her heart, and from that she became colder and less obliging in the bedroom, and so I too continued down that same slippery marital slope. By the end, the dear woman seemed to have but three modes of communication: the awesome chill of silence; the whip-crack of a sniper's bullet; and the atomic detonation of the all-out row.

For the first two years of our marriage, there had been the occasional languor, when we could talk about matters of inconsequence without hurting each other. But since the birth of our son, the fighting had been ceaseless. For both of us, it had been such a relief when I had been posted away to Hiroshima to build kites.

And now I was returning home – but a quite different man from the beast who had left Nagasaki three months ago. As the train trickled on through the night, I wondered if it was too late to save the marriage. Were we now so deeply entrenched that there was nothing that I could do or say to win Mako round? I could – would – apologise. I would try to make a fresh start and strive to court her anew. But would it be enough? Or was I destined for another torrent of Mako's abuse, and meanwhile denied the satisfaction of answering her back?

I had been looking out of the window, though oblivious to the spectre of the trees and the smoke sparks that glowed in the night. Shinzo had been watching me for some time.

"I know what you're thinking," he said.

I continued to stare blindly out of the window. "What am I thinking?"

"Will Mako ever forgive you?"

"And what is the answer?" I turned my eyes to look at him.

"I doubt it." He smoothed the girl's hair. She was tucked into his flank, snuggled in the crook of his arm. "Mako is a very beautiful woman. She had high expectations."

"How I hate high expectations."

"Yes, it's always better to be hopeful rather than expectant. But Mako expected much of you and her disappointment has now turned sour." He peeled the skin off an onion that had gone soft with age, stripping the layers back and tossing them out of the window, until with one bite he ate it. "I presume that you'll be going back to apologise. It might be too late."

"It's never too late."

"It's never too late – look what happened to you."

"You noticed?"

"Noticed that this embittered old friend of mine is once again attempting to behave like a human being?"

I laughed and clapped him on the knee. Despite his ample girth, Shinzo was a sly fox. He did not miss a thing. "Should have married a woman like your Sakae? The pair of you define marital bliss."

Shinzo dismissed the thought with a flick of his hand, as if the very acknowledgement of his own happiness would be an invitation to hubris. "We get on well," he said. "She's a fine woman and I love her. You may not consider her a beauty, but to my mind she's beautiful."

"Beauty?" I said. "Beauty? If there is any one thing I have come to understand, it's that beauty is a total irrelevance when it comes to deciding your life partner. Beauty matters for a few months, a year; beauty is useful for engendering envy in others. But beauty is a hopeless basis for a marriage. It's not rational. It doesn't make sense. Yet, still you get idiots like me who decide to marry a woman because they like the tilt of her nose, or the swing of her hips as she walks. Is that good enough reason to cleave yourself to another? It's madness! I must have been out of my mind. I tell you Shinzo, I would rather marry a woman blind! I would rather she had a bag over her head, so that I had talked to her and got to know her, instead of being spurred on by the awesome power of my own libido!"

Shinzo shrugged and scratched at his belly button, digging his fingers in through the folds of his shirt.

"Whereas you... " I paused. "I am not saying that Sakae is not beautiful, but your marriage is based on so much more than looks. You have a comradeship, an affection, that I have never known."

"And the sex is not bad either." He was making light of my seriousness – and I followed his lead.

"I don't doubt it!" I laughed. "I'm sure that the very moment you step through your front door, Sakae will be briskly escorting you to the bedroom and the girl will be left out in the garden to amuse herself."

"I had forgotten about her. But you're probably right. The girl will just have to look after herself for a few minutes." Shinzo smirked at the thought. "Though unlike you, Sakae and I are having sex in order to procreate."

"I remember those days," I said. "It was a long time ago."

Shinzo rooted through the paper bag in his lap and pulled out another rice-ball, which he stared at admiringly. He ate it in a single bite, realised that he was still hungry and had another look in the bag before this time producing a red onion. I have never seen anyone take such delight in a single vegetable; in that moment, as he peeled off the outer skin, he was the very picture of contentment.

The darkest hour had already passed us by and, over eastwards in the direction of Nagasaki, I could make out the sky pinking overhead. We pulled into a station and the hubbub was just as it always is, a little reminder that for the past two days, life outside Hiroshima had continued as normal. A woman came along the platform selling tea. A luckless few clambered on board to travel the final kilometres into Nagasaki before that city was transformed into a smoking ruin. They were literally boarding the last train to hell.

Shinzo grimaced, massaging at his stomach. "That really hurts," he said, both hands smoothing from his flanks to his front. "I've swallowed something bad."

"The river?" I asked.

"The river," he said bleakly. "It must have been the river. The water must have been thick with disease."

He probed at his stomach and the next moment his face had started to go a shade of green. "I have to go," he said, getting up so quickly that the girl was jolted awake. "I have to go right now."

Shinzo lumbered down the aisle and the next thing I saw him getting out onto the platform and looking left and right for any place to relieve himself. For all his girth, he looked quite like a little boy, hands pressed tight into his gut.

The girl rubbed the sleep out of her eyes. "Where has Shinzo gone?" she asked.

"He has a bad stomach," I replied. "From swallowing all that river water."

"He'll be back in time?"

"Certainly."

But he wasn't. The whistle blew, the girl screamed at the guards, and the train began to pull out.

Leaning out of the window to see Shinzo waddling after us, his hands clutching at the waistband of his trousers.

The girl yelling at Shinzo to run faster.

He breaks into a slow trot, desperately trying to catch the last carriage; fingers fumbling at the handle, failing to quite connect; the girl in total despair, calling out the one word, "Shinzo!" And the train chugs into the dawn light and, as the girl and I both crane our heads out of the window, Shinzo stands forlorn on the platform, one hand holding up his trousers and with the other he gives us a little wave. What a sad sight he made, and from that day he would never change for me. When I recall my dearest friend, I remember the laughter, the food, and the interminable scratching. But with all those memories is now entwined that last vivid picture of Shinzo on the platform, stark against the station light as he waved a plaintive farewell.

CHAPTER FOURTEEN

The girl was quiet for some time, arms folded tight about her as she contemplated the loss of her friend. Of course we thought we would soon be meeting up with him in Nagasaki. But as she already knew, nothing is ever as simple as it seems, especially in times of war; anything can go wrong; bombs can be dropped, and loved ones can be snatched away in a matter of moments. So although we might – should – ought – to see Shinzo again, the only certainty in those days was that everything was in a state of flux.

The girl dug into the bag and pulled out a riceball, which she ate in silence, cross little lines on her forehead. I realised I would have to take the girl home. It was bound to cause a row.

"Poor old Shinzo," I said.

She looked up at me, still angry with life. "You'll have to look after me, Beast."

"Yes," I replied.

"Will your wife like me?"

"Her name is Mako." I tugged at my lower lip. "She doesn't like me. She might take to you though."

"And you have a baby boy? Will he like me?"

Just at the mention of that dear boy, a smile unconsciously came to my face. "My boy is called Toshiaki. He likes everyone. He'll certainly like you."

"That's good then. I'll try living with you, Beast, and then I'll try living with Shinzo." A happy thought came to her. "I will have two families, not one. That's sensible in a time of war."

I smiled again and continued to smile as the girl eased out of her shell and began to talk – talk about any inconsequential thing that came into her head. "I think I will enjoy Nagasaki," she said. "I'll make new friends and I'll continue to dance. If you like, Beast, I will dance on your rooftop. And are you still going to make me a kite? You promised to make me a kite on the day the bomb was dropped, I've not forgotten that, you know. And you will have to teach me how to fly it. Is Nagasaki really the kite-flying capital of the world? I'm sure all the other children can fly kites, so I'll have to learn fast to catch up with them... "

How quickly the girl could bounce back – from losing her grandmother, or Shinzo, and yet within a few minutes she could be prattling away with barely a pause for breath. It was, I suppose, an indirect consequence of the war that our children had become surprisingly resilient. They could tolerate any amount of hardship, from poor food and living conditions to family catastrophes. And now that I think of it, I believe that our children were natural-born optimists: whatever came their way, they accepted it without complaint, though always at the back of their minds was this unspoken hope that things might get better.

Which they did – eventually.

But first of all they had to get a whole lot worse: Nagasaki.

I had just two hours in Nagasaki before my appointment with Fat Man, and my abiding memory is that the city was looking tired and unloved. Its pristine parks, which had once been as verdant an oasis as ever I had set eyes on, had become little more than a series of parched vegetable plots, with enormous swathes of land turned over to growing sweet potatoes, pumpkins and any hardy plant that could survive being left untended for weeks on end.

And the people too. When we arrived at Urakami station, they looked as if they were doing little more than existing. The news had just come in from the previous night that our tepid allies the Russians had declared war. The only surprise was that our leaders had expected anything else. At times, I think their naivety was almost a match for that of the populace.

Stalin's hand had been forced by the bombing of Hiroshima. He had realised that if he did not attack immediately, then Russia would be allowed none of the spoils; one outraged writer described them as being like wolves slavering for a morsel of Japan's carcase. So two days after Hiroshima, Russia launched a blistering assault on our western front. Armies of battle-hardened veterans swept through our conquered territories in Manchuria. It was a battle that had been brewing for some months. Ever since the fall of Germany, Stalin had been shipping millions of troops all the way across Russia to the Chinese border. But our leaders never once had the eyes to see it. Even to the last, they were sending our bemused ambassador off to Moscow for yet more peace talks.

It all stems, I fear, from Japan being such an insular nation. We had our own goals and had doggedly set about attaining them. But we never once paused to consider the actions and the motives of our enemies and so-called allies.

We did not dream that America would have the stomach for a full land-battle on Japanese soil. We accepted all Joe Stalin's smiling protestations of peace. And since we had been incapable of building our own atomic bomb, we could not conceive that our most hated enemy might succeed in that same venture.

At every turn, the Japanese were wrong-footed – and yet, as the girl and I walked out of Urakami station, all we could hear was that interminable refrain: "Victory will soon be ours". The country had no food, no raw materials and we were being bombed out of existence – yet still we clung to that single defining mantra: 'Victory will soon be ours'.

You could not question it though. To question the war effort would have been tantamount to questioning your own parentage, your very existence.

How odd it was to leave the station with no luggage. We had eaten the last of the rice-balls and red onions, and had nothing left but the clothes on our backs. After Hiroshima the city was like another world. We could once again savour the sight of trees verdant with green leaves; buildings that stood as tall as the day they were built; and adults, children, all of them eating, walking, talking, without a trace of pain. In place of the maimed and the dead, people were going about their normal everyday affairs. Everyone was busy, doing something anything – for the war effort. It did not matter what they were engaged in, just so long as they were up at dawn and working themselves to the bone.

I had made that journey from the station to my home so many times over the years. As I have already mentioned, Nagasaki is split by a steep ridge into two valleys, and my home was in the longer one, the Urakami valley, on the western side. It was in this valley, naturally, that Fat Boy was due to explode in an hour – where else did you expect that damnable bomb to detonate?

We caught a street-car two kilometres up through Nagasaki, past all the Mitsubishi industries that had made the city such an acceptable target for the Yankees. Many of the more important buildings, like the prefecture and the shipbuilding yard, had been camouflaged with black paint. How strange it was to be there standing shoulder-to-shoulder with those smooth-skinned civilians, none of them burnt, none of them pleading for water. It was like waking up from some gruelling nightmare.

A kilometre from home, we quit the street-car to walk and after Hiroshima, I revelled in every step. Along the way, I told the girl stories, though I was never able to finish them, for always she was on to me asking the next question.

"That is where I went to school for five years," I said, pointing out the place that had taught me boredom and how to deal with it. "Shinzo lives just round the corner. We'll try to see him tomorrow."

"Yes, we must! Dear Shinzo. I miss him," said the girl with

a sigh, before finding something else to distract her. "What's that big building there?"

"Urakami Cathedral," I replied. "It's our Christian capital. There are more Christians here than anywhere else in Japan."

"And if they are Christians, does that mean they're more likely to survive the war?"

One of the things that I love – truly love – about children is that they ask the unthinkable. And – as I now endeavour to do with all children's questions – I carefully weighed up my answer. "This is only my view," I said. "I'm sure many would disagree. But I don't think your survival will depend on whether you're a Christian, Buddhist, Jew, Muslim or atheist. Look at all those Christians walking in there. In a few minutes, they'll be praying for peace and victory and whatever else they want to pray for – and yet on the other side of the world in America, there will be millions of Yankees praying to the exact same Christian God – and yet they will be praying for our total annihilation. So what do you think? Is God going to listen to one side and ignore the other? Or is it all meaningless?"

I was exploring my way through a series of nebulous thoughts, seeing if they could somehow coalesce, before I batted the question back to the girl. "Religion is a personal matter of faith. Believe what you want – but always, I hope, respect other people's beliefs, or even their lack of them. Tell me what you think."

The girl looked over at the white cathedral, where a troupe of young women were walking in past a large statue of the Virgin Mary. "I think that if they believe their prayers work, then that's a good thing. The prayers may help them – even if they're not answered."

I laughed and clapped her on the shoulder. Truly, she had more wisdom between her ears than any number of adults I have known. "Yes, you're right. Praying may well bring them some small solace – even if it doesn't help them survive the war."

And sadly on that day, the Christian God – if you so believe in him – decided to listen to the Yankees' prayers and to ignore those of the Japanese. It was another unsettling little irony of the atomic bombs that Fat Man's epicentre was almost directly above Urakami Cathedral, wiping out more than 10,000 of the Yankees' so-called Christian brethren.

We had arrived – back to the street where I had played as a child and the home where I had been born and where both my parents had died. It was a wooden bungalow with a tiled roof and was of a decent size. It nestled in the lee of one of the steep wooded mountains that surround the Urakami Valley. They are always referred to as mountains, by the way, even though the highest is only 330 metres. But to those of us in Nagasaki, these green hills so totally dominate the skyline that they always seem like mountains, and so that is how they have come to be labelled.

I could just make out the large garden at the back, along with the rock shrine my father had so painstakingly built with his own hands. I had been but four years old when he built it as a memorial to my mother, and helped him mix the cement. My father and a friend had spend two weeks on the job, using a trolley to haul the great rocks through the garden. Some of the stones had been so heavy that the two men had barely been able to lift them. And now, nearly 90 years on, just a single quicklime whiff of cement takes me back to that long summer.

My home had been built at around the turn of the century and my memories had used to be happy ones – though in recent years they had been superseded by ugly moments of rowing with my wife. But still – it was never too late to make amends. I would make amends.

So as I walked with the girl up the front path, I pledged to do my best with Mako. For the sake of our son, not to mention our marriage, I would try to be a new man. And I owed it to Sumie and to all those countless victims of Hiroshima. It is difficult to explain how I felt, but I will try. It was partly to do with my "Embrace Life" revelation outside Hijiyama primary school. But I also had come to have a much greater appreciation of my own good fortune. It almost felt as if I owed it to Hiroshima to be, or to strive to be, a better man. I was not expecting to be the model husband. But I had made a secret pledge to myself to try harder: to be more tolerant, more forgiving, and more faithful.

"Here we are," I said to the girl, trying to smile though my guts were churning up. I knocked on the door. "I hope you like it."

Just as children do, the girl had instantly detected my nerves. They have this sixth sense which always knows when things are awry.

"It looks very nice," she said.

From far inside, I could make out the distinctive sound of Toshiaki screaming – and of my wife shouting at him. The boy's high-pitched ululation stretched on and on; my wife's bark was more staccato. I thought at first they had not heard us, but after one more explosive scream and a smack, I heard footsteps. The girl took a step or two backwards, I think terrified at what was about to emerge.

The clump of footsteps through the vestibule; the rattle of a chain; and the door is flung open to reveal my darling wife, the mother of my child, as beautiful as ever and coruscatingly angry.

"Yes?" she spat, before looking more closely at the vagabond on her doorstep.

"It is you? I thought you were dead."

"Yes," I said. "It is me." I moved forward to give her a hug. It might not have been what she wanted, but it was a token of intent. It would show, I thought, that I wanted to build bridges.

But I might as well have been embracing a block of wood. As I tried to kiss her on the cheek, she ducked her face so that I connected with the hair beneath her ear.

I do not blame her. I do not blame her at all. She had endured much during our four years of marriage; how was she to know that I was no longer the husband from hell? How was she to know I was intent on changing my ways?

"You have been eating onions," Mako said, breaking away to look past me at the girl who was standing diffidently on the path. "Who is that?"

"This is a friend," I replied. "Her family are all dead. Shinzo and I are looking after her for a while. Did you... did you hear about the bomb?"

"I did," Mako snapped. "I heard it on the radio. A new type of bomb. They said it caused some damage."

"Some damage?" I almost laughed at the outrageous understatement. "They said there was some damage? But..." I trailed off, as I caught sight of the great love of my life, who had come tottering out into the hallway to find out what was going on. I had never seen him walking before. He was wearing just a pair of short trousers and at the sight of me, his face lit up into a beam of rapturous delight. Just for that one smile, it was worth getting back to Nagasaki.

"Daddy!" he called, before hurling himself into my arms. I held him as tight as any other human being I had ever held before, and we capered together in the vestibule.

Mako had at last found her manners, gesturing for the girl to follow her through to the kitchen. All I could do was stand there, stand there, with that beautiful brown boy in my arms, who was gurgling with the ecstasy of being reunited with his father. In all my life, and with all of my lovers, I have never had a reunion to match it. Of all the moments that have touched my soul, that is my benchmark, standing there in the vestibule, waltzing with my boy in my arms, him giggling for sheer pleasure as I showered his cheeks with kisses. If there's to be but one single instance of my life that I could live again, that would be it.

It was a moment of perfect happiness, with nothing feigned and just our mutual delight at being reunited.

"You have learned to talk since I have been away!" I said to him.

"Daddy!"

"And you have learned to walk too! Will you lead the way into the kitchen?"

He clutched onto my shoulder as I crouched down to ease off my old sea-boots – boots that had not left my feet for three days. They had been on so long that they seemed to suck at my toes. When I eventually peeled off the damp socks, my feet were soft, white and wrinkled. My right foot was badly bruised, purple and yellow, from diving into the river after Shinzo. It throbbed, but nothing seemed broken.

Toshiaki takes my hand and leads me through to the kitchen, where the girl is sitting upright at the table; for some reason she strikes me as a wild animal, forced into a cage, silently longing for freedom. Everything was exactly as it had been when I had left three months earlier, with cups and plates all cleaned and neatly stacked away. I pulled up a pillow and swept the boy into my lap, where he nestled into my arms.

Mako was making tea. I have to say that she was still a very beautiful woman. She took good care of herself. Her hair, long and clean, was swept back over her shoulders, a match for her black shirt. But her chief endowment was her bone structure, those exquisite high cheekbones, which were set off by immaculate white teeth and the most perfect button nose. Beauty is such a wonderful thing to gaze at. But as I have said, it is such a absurd basis for a marriage.

"How has it been?" I asked politely. "How are you?"

"Fine," she said, banging cups of tea onto the table in front of me and the girl. "Thanks for writing."

I winced. I had written once a month, three curt little cards, but nothing more. I pressed on. "The boy looks well. You've got him walking and talking."

Mako was about to say something when she sniffed – and sniffed again. "You smell. You should have a wash."

"I am sure you're right," I said apologetically. "We haven't been out of these clothes for three days."

I think the expression is that I was walking on egg-shells. I was being careful not to cause offence. But I did know that, whatever I said, more than likely it was going to be interpreted the wrong way.

My eye was caught by a leaflet on the table. It was bright white, quite different from the dirty mottled brown cards that were usually found in Japan in those days. I picked it up – and as I read it, my hands began to shake.

There was a picture of a clock with dates, on which the day of 9th August had been circled. Beside the picture was some poetry, written in the most precise Japanese lettering: 'Back in April, Nagasaki was all flowers. August in Nagasaki there will be flame showers.'

"Where did this come from?" I asked.

"There were hundreds of them lying all round the street," said Mako. "The Yankees must have dropped them."

"But... " My mind was suddenly awhirl with thoughts. "But they dropped these leaflets over Hiroshima just before they dropped the bomb—"

Suddenly, and for the first time, a most sickening thought popped into my head. For the last three days, I had blithely believed that the Yankees would be dropping just the one bomb. But what if they had more? Why stop there? Why not continue bombing our cities until they had reduced every urban area in Japan to ruins?

There ineluctably followed the next unsettling thought in the sequence: if the Yankees were going to target a Japanese city, where else might they choose? Perhaps a city with a good number of munitions factories? Perhaps a city that had specifically not been targeted for any of the standard fire-bomb raids? Perhaps... perhaps... perhaps a city like Nagasaki?

In under ten seconds, I had seen it all. The second bomb, if it was coming, might just as easily be targeted at several other cities: Kokura for example, or Kyoto, or even Tokyo itself.

A prickling sixth sense, for so long stifled, told me that the Yankees would be coming back with another bomb. I simply knew.

I remember this queasy feeling in the pit of my stomach as

it dawned on me that it might have been safer by far to have stayed in Hiroshima.

In my stunned stupor, I had not even realised that my wife was talking "– if it is only one bomb, then how much damage can it do? How can a single bomb do that much damage? I teach science. It does not make sense."

"I do not know," I shrugged helplessly. "They say it's a new type of bomb."

"Did you see it?"

"No – I was working in the warehouse."

She picked up my cup, tossing away the dregs before taking it to the sink. She was almost talking to herself as she scrubbed at the cup. "It is not possible. The sort of single bomb you're talking about doesn't exist."

"There were only three planes, I remember that—"

"If there were only three planes, they could not have been carrying a bomb big enough to destroy a whole city." She dried the cup with a towel and slammed it onto a shelf. "You were probably concussed. It must have created a firestorm. That must have been what destroyed the city."

Three months back I would have argued the point; would have argued the point till we had managed to dredge up all the other grievances from our marriage. I had been in Hiroshima, after all. I had been there when it had happened! Who was she to tell me that, with all due scientific respect, it was just not possible?

But how Hiroshima had changed me.

"Perhaps you are right," I said. "You're the scientist—"

"And you're just the kite-maker." It is amazing the contempt she managed to inject into those last two words. I am aware, by the way, that this conversation is not making my wife sound like a kind woman. But she'd had much to put up with and marriage had embittered her. I blame myself entirely. And as for her perhaps blinkered view of the bomb, I think she found it much more difficult to grasp the concept of an atom bomb because of the very fact that she was a scientist. The idea of a single bomb destroying a city was incomprehensible; it did not make scientific sense. And if it didn't make sense, why then the facts themselves must have been wrong.

I could feel my wife glowering at me as I kissed the top of Toshiaki's head. "And I'm just the kite-maker," I said.

The girl had been sitting in silence, eyes darting from one to the other of us. And she did something so artful, so selfless, that, even at the time, I was disarmed at how easily she changed the subject.

"Can you show me how to fly a kite?" she asked.

I delightedly accepted the life-buoy that had been tossed to me. "Yes!" I said. "Let me show you how to fly a kite. I would love that – and little Toshiaki can learn too." In a single moment, all thought of the bomb was forgotten as I bustled off to my father's old workshop. It was exactly as I had left it, with the old workbench by the window and a score of kites hung up on the walls. I picked up my most colourful kite, a plain diamond of mulberry paper in red, white and blue. They were the colours, as it happens, of the Dutch flag and were a brief nod to Nagasaki's heyday as the most cosmopolitan port in the country.

Much of the garden had been turned into a vegetable patch and by happy chance the dry crusted earth hurt my soft pallid feet. I was forced to go back inside to find fresh socks and after that I once again put on my father's old, slightly damp sea-boots. Fat Man was now only 20 minutes away from making his grand entrance and – as I may have mentioned – good boots are a necessity in the aftermath of an A-bomb.

How fresh all my memories seem of those last few minutes before Fat Man, when our entire lives depended on what we chanced to be doing during one single moment of time.

It had been three months since I had last flown a kite for pleasure; funny to think that I had spent so long making all those box-kites in Hiroshima, yet had never taken one out to fly. Doubtless it would have been considered a frippery, an indulgence, in time of war.

"Shall I get the kite up?" I said to the girl. "Then you try."

Like many things, kite-flying is not as easy as it looks. You launch the kite as you might throw a paper airplane, throwing it forward until it catches the wind. But it is all about timing and that only comes with practice. At the critical moment, you have to flick your wrist and give a tug of the string; if you get it right, she is up and away, jinking into the sky.

In my boyhood, my favourite pastime had been kite-fighting. We would coat the hemp kite-string with powdered glass and try to cut the other boys' lines. You had to yell out a warning before you attacked and then you were duelling, two kites darting this way and that until one or other line was cut.

There was nothing to touch the euphoria of seeing your opponent's kite die in the air. From being a living thing, it was transformed into a piece of dead bamboo and paper, cartwheeling downwards before it flopped to the ground.

Now I have no urge to fight other kites. It must be part of growing up. My kites are my meditation and I am quite content to watch them dancing on the mountain tops, free spirits in the sky. Perhaps I am that kite and when my string is eventually cut, I hope that, for once, I will continue to waft upwards on an unending thermal.

It was very heaven standing there in the garden with the boy slung in my arm and the kite tugging gently at my hand. A zephyr of wind was coming in off the sea and up the valley.

The girl was eager to have a go. I passed her the string and said the kite-flier's mantra: "Speed-o, speed-o". Her face lit up as she took control.

The wind died and she ran backwards, tugging the kite behind her, and for a while it worked and the kite stayed aloft. But, soon enough, she had run out of room, almost colliding with the shrine at the bottom of the garden. The kite gave a little sigh, tossing its nose in the air before falling to the ground in a flat dive.

I laughed as I ambled over to her, the boy twitching and gurgling under my arm. "You don't have to run to keep up a

Nagasaki kite," I said, picking up the kite and spooling in the string. "Most kites you do. But you can keep this kite up just by shortening the string."

I tossed the kite into the wind and with a snap of my wrist flicked it up again into the sky. I passed the string over to the girl. Out of the corner of my eye, I could see Mako watching us.

"If the wind dies, I shorten the string?"

"Shorten the string and jig your arm back and forth. A Nagasaki kite-master would never run backwards."

"And if it gets windier, I let the string out?"

"You let the string out as far as it can go." I smiled at her. I was so happy to see her enjoying the kite. "When I was a boy, I had a kite which I used to send up over 800 metres into the sky."

"That would have been higher than the mountains."

"It certainly was," I said. "My father once climbed the highest hill, Mount Inasa, and my kite was way over his head."

"I want to try that!" said the girl – and on such small things do our lives depend. Because of that, I have lived to tell my tale – and if it had not happened that way, if the girl had decided to keep her mouth shut, then we all of us in that garden would have been burnt to a crisp.

The wind was getting fresher and gradually the girl let out more string. She laughed as the kite danced higher and higher and my spirits soared with it. For me, there is no more uplifting sight in this world than that of a kite flittering in the sky. I could feel the wind and the sun on my face, and, after all the misery of Hiroshima, I could only close my eyes in the most perfect ecstasy.

My son was in my arms and my face was upturned full to the sky. What bliss. I had no thought for anything but the sun and the warmth of Toshiaki in my arms.

I do not know how long I stood like that, but eventually I came to open my eyes and as I did so, I found myself looking not at the kite, but at a thick bank of cloud, shaped like a hand, that was high overhead.

I would never have noticed it otherwise. It was so high up, that it was barely more than a silvery black dot as it ducked through the clouds.

I watched and I watched, now oblivious to the kite. Though it was just a lone plane, it had triggered some switch inside me, for I already half-suspected what it was going to do next.

For ten or twenty seconds, the plane continued drifting on its course. Suddenly it shanked away. This change of direction was not immediately obvious, but as I continued to stare at the plane it became apparent that it had executed a sharp banking turn and was now pulling away hard from Nagasaki.

And unlike almost all the other wretched city folk in Nagasaki, I was one of the few people who realised exactly what had just happened; an aeon ago in Hiroshima, I had seen this peculiar aircraft manoeuvre once before. I had been standing in Akiba's office at the warehouse as three planes had trawled across a clear blue sky. As I had peered out over Akiba's shoulder, each of the planes had seemed to bank sideways. It is, as far as I know, the calling card of the atomic bomber.

It took some moments – precious, precious moments – for me to understand the full import of what I had just witnessed. Had that plane really changed course? Had it? It was difficult to tell as I squinted up into the sky. And then the clangour of alarm bells going off in my head as I realised that it had changed course, definitely, and that I had seen it all before. I had seen it before! But it could not... it could not be another atomic bomb; not after all I had endured in Hiroshima.

The plane, so tiny, so innocuous, drifted away into the haze of clouds. So easy just to have ignored it. But in a single moment of astounding clarity, I realised what was happening: the bomb was already on its way.

The last few sands of fate were fast dribbling out, and every one of us would be judged on what we were doing in exactly 20 seconds' time.

"Not again," I whispered to myself, before screaming at the girl. "Take cover! Run! They've dropped another bomb!"

I was screaming, shouting, at the top of my lungs. The girl was busily trying to wind up the string of the kite. "There is no time for that!" I shrieked, swatting the winder out of her hand. "Take cover! Get into the shrine! Go right to the back! Lie down, face on the floor, head in your arms! Quickly! Now! Now!"

Adrenalin was coursing through me as I barked orders at the girl. I was barely even aware that I still had the boy clutched to my chest. As I charged across the garden to the sanctuary of my father's rocky shrine, I glanced over my shoulder.

Mako was still standing in the doorway. She had her arms crossed, a cup of tea in her hand – and was staring at me as if I had taken leave of my senses.

"Mako!" I screamed at her. "Take cover! It's the bomb! They have dropped another bomb! Please, please listen to me! Take cover!"

I flung myself into the shrine. It was small, with barely room for me and the girl, with coarse rock walls and a little niche in which had been placed a black and white photo of my mother. I crouched over her, with little Toshiaki sandwiched between the two of us.

I looked across the garden. Mako was still in the doorway. "Mako!" I called out. "Please! It's the bomb! Please!"

A moment I will never forget. Mako had one arm cocked onto her hip, effortlessly elegant. Now that I think of it, she cut rather a dashing figure as she leaned against the doorframe. "You are mad!" she called out.

I bury my head into the crook of my arms, with thumbs in my eye-sockets and fingers tight into my ears – and I wait, and I wait.

And what I am thinking is: not again. I cannot believe this is happening again. What sort of ill-luck had drawn me back to Nagasaki for this?

While all these outraged thoughts swirl through my head, nothing is happening. I can hear the wind sighing against the side of the shrine. I can feel the girl squirming beneath me. My son starts to wriggle, kicking his leg out, whimpering as my chest presses down on him. I count to ten.

Have I got it wrong? Had the plane's change of course been pure happenstance?

Is it possible that my mind has been playing tricks with me? Had that little dot of a plane really banked away like the three planes over Hiroshima? Or had Hiroshima made me completely paranoid?

After all – what were the chances of being hit by not one but two of these freakish new bombs? Just what were the chances? I was starting at shadows; what an idiot! And just as I was about to lift my head and slope back into the house for another cup of tea, the last grains of Nagasaki's life trickled out and Armageddon had come again.

CHAPTER FIFTEEN

Even with my thumbs pressed tight in my sockets, I could still sense the flash, along with a warm pulse that singed through my body. I was far closer to the epicentre than I had been at Hiroshima; this time the flash and the booming shockwave were almost instantaneous.

The three of us were bodily hurled against the wall of the shrine; I took the brunt of the blow on my back, cushioning the girl and Toshiaki. With the rolling blast came a fusillade of shrapnel-like debris, clattering against those solid rock walls of the shrine.

I must have been stunned after clouting my head against the wall. I lay there not moving, sending delicate probes out over my body. I could actually feel the ground vibrating beneath me, like the surface of an immense drum. Bits of me ached. I was too shell-shocked to tell if it was anything serious.

The girl and Toshiaki were lying cradled in my arms. I thought they might have been killed outright, but then Toshiaki screamed in pain and the girl started to cough from the heavy dust. The shrine's open entrance had been almost side on to the blast.

We had been saved by those wonderful rough-hewn walls that had been built by my father.

I gently extricated myself from the two children and crawled out to inspect Nagasaki's new world order. And even though I knew what to expect and had seen the like only three days earlier, it was no less shocking.

Nagasaki, my home-town, my favourite city on earth, had been razed to the ground. Already that thunderous mushroom cloud, iridescent with every hue and colour of the rainbow, was soaring into the sky. It seemed to be emanating from almost directly above the ruins of Urakami cathedral.

The air was thick with dust and will-o'-the-wisp flames, burning like bright glow-flies in the haze. Across the horizon, the whole of the valley had been transformed into a swathe of flaming pyres as thousands of wooden houses had spontaneously combusted. There were so many fires that they stretched from end-to-end across the valley, sending a broad blanket of smoke up into the sky.

And my house? My home was no more. It had been blown clean off its foundations and lay smeared across the garden in a welter of tiles and wood that was so splintered it could have been nothing more than ragged flotsam washed up on the shore. I had expected it, but I was still numbed by the violence and astonishing swiftness of the destruction.

I poked my head back into the shrine. The girl was lying on her side, with the boy cocooned in her arms. "Are you injured?" I said.

She shook her head sadly and could only peer out at the slate grey cloud that was blossoming overhead. "I don't think so."

My hands fluttered over Toshiaki's body. From head to waist he seemed fine, but one of his legs felt hot – hot like a piece of cooked meat and when I looked, I saw that it was already red and puffy as if he had been branded. A large splinter of wood, a hand's width in length, had been driven through his thigh. I have often wondered how he came by that injury. I can only imagine that when the bomb exploded, he had somehow kicked his leg out from underneath me and it had been exposed to the blast.

For the first time, I noticed my own wounds. The pain was not excruciating, by any means. I felt remarkably detached.

It was more like the tingle that comes after you have skinned yourself on a rock – though I could tell that as soon as the adrenalin wore off, the pain would be terrific. The sleeve of my shirt had been wrenched off at the shoulder. Somehow my left arm had been exposed and from bicep to wrist had turned an angry red. It was a burn that was to give me much hurt over the years. But despite all the pain and the surgery, in a way I am glad that I sustained some form of injury, however slight. It has given me some inkling of the pain that all those other A-bomb victims went through; it is a sign, also, that I was there. I wear my scar with pride.

I looked at the girl again. Still dazed, she was gaping at the mushroom cloud.

"Can you look after Toshiaki?" I asked. "I must search for Mako."

"I'll help you," she said, trying to get up.

"That's kind. You're very thoughtful." Without even being aware of it, I bent down and kissed her on the forehead. "It would be better if you looked after Toshiaki. His leg is badly hurt. Could you?"

"Yes," she said, and hugged the mewling boy tight to her chest. "I'll wait."

Already my mind was ticking over what I had to do. First I had to try to rescue Mako from underneath the ruins of the house – and quickly too. If I found her alive, I would need to get her and Toshiaki up to the Urakami hospital, which was on the higher hill slopes about a kilometre away up the valley. How would I get them there? Could I carry them both in my arms?

I jogged over to what had once been my home; there was far less wreckage than there had been at Sumie's house, but then my home had only been a bungalow.

Sumie. The name of my lover flashed through my mind. I realised that since she had been burned alive three days ago, I had hardly given her a thought. And as I started to call out Mako's name and work my way through the debris, I did appreciate the awful irony that once again I was trying to dig up the woman that I loved. Did I love Mako? Well, there was still a glowing ember for her in my heart, and I hoped that I might yet coax it into flames

"Mako!" I shouted. "Can you hear me? Mako! Where are you?"

From probing haphazardly about the ruins, I took a few steps backwards to try and gauge where she might have been standing. It was hopeless. I could not even tell the front of the house from the back.

"Mako!" I called again. "Mako!"

I stood quietly on the ruins, listening for a sound – and what struck was that, for the first time in my life, there was no noise. Everything in Nagasaki had stopped and all about me was nothing but void and eerie silence.

Again I shouted her name. Nothing but the sound of the wind. I cock my ear slightly, trying to discern a hint of a noise that might be coming from underneath the rubble. It is so faint that it is like the light knocking of a death-watch beetle. I move to one of the larger heaps of debris – is that a piece of the chimney lying on the top? – and as I squat down, I can hear the tap-tap-tap sound of something knocking against wood.

I had a metre of debris to get through but having learned my lessons from Hiroshima, I shifted it methodically, starting wide at the top and tapering down. I would grab a tile or piece of wood and without even looking would sling it away. Occasionally I would come across bits of smashed furniture, which I would look at for a moment and wonder, 'What in the world was that?', before realising it was part of a table leg or one of the kitchen cupboards. There was even a trace of one of my old kites, the bamboo and red mulberry paper sandwiched between two broken tiles.

As the hole grew, I would pause every so often to give a shout. I could get a better sense of direction on the sound of Mako's taps. I shifted my aim.

Such a glut of thoughts as I dug, all completely random,

one after the next in no sequential order. I had just survived two of these freakish bombs; how many more were coming my way? Surely we had to surrender now – or would Japan keep on fighting until these new bombs had been targeted at every city in the Motherland?

And of course I came to dwell on that eternal question I have been asked so often over the past 60 years: was I blessed, or cursed? And in fewer than 30 minutes, I had already made my decision. I was blessed, blessed beyond belief, to be given not a second, but a third chance.

My second chance, in Hiroshima, I had completely wasted. Yet now, through fate's ineffable grace, I had been given a third opportunity. And what surprises me most of all is that I had the wisdom to see it.

I would make amends. I would make amends for my wastrel life. And I would start with my wife Mako, the woman whom I had treated so abysmally over the years. First I would find her and then I would do everything in my powers to save her. When that was done, I would find more work to do – and there would be no shortage of that in Nagasaki. My arm might be injured, but for as long as I was capable, I would embrace every last flicker of life that was left in Nagasaki.

My left arm was already beginning to throb. It must have been protected a little from the blast by my grubby white shirt, but it was already lobster red and swollen. Every so often I might cuff it against a piece of rubble, and the jarring shock would wring through my whole body. I did my best to ignore it. I did what I have been doing ever since when my arm causes me pain: I gave thanks for the very fact that I was alive at all; and gave thanks that my injuries were not considerably worse.

It had started to rain, that oily black rain that I had first encountered in Hiroshima, leaving cold ink stains on my skin and clothes. Although I didn't then know anything about radiation sickness, I had already conceived the infernal origins of that black rain. But I ignored it and continued to shift the debris. I did not have any option – for there were many more pressing matters. Now that I was in the smouldering ruins of my second atomic bomb, I already had a fair idea of what was coming next.

The firestorm.

The wind was blowing hard in from the sea and the whole of downtown Nagasaki was already a sea of flame – and the Urakami valley, with its high hills on either side, was the perfect wind-tunnel. The firestorm was coming at us like a runaway train and nothing in that Godforsaken city was going to stop it.

Amidst the clatter of the tiles and debris that I was shifting, I noticed some whimpering behind me. The girl had come out from the shrine and was standing a few metres away, cradling Toshiaki in her arms. The poor boy was all shrieked out and all he could do was whimper this unending sob.

I nodded at the girl as I tossed another piece of wood into the garden.

"Can I help?" she asked.

I was about to tell her that there was no room; that I could do the job twice as quickly without her in the way.

But as I looked over at her one more time, I saw she was desperate to join me. "Very well," I said. "Clear a space for Toshiaki and put him on the ground."

Toshiaki, for all his pain, was not going to be any worse off for being left by himself for a few minutes. The girl smiled as she joined me.

"She must be close," I said. "I can hear her knocking."

The girl took a turn down in the hole, worrying at the tiles that were trapped beneath her before passing up bits of wreckage to me.

And it was she who found Mako and that pleased me."Here is an arm!" she shouted.

I swapped places with her. The arm was bare and covered with dust and flecks of stone. It was deeply charred. I cleared away a couple more tiles and found her hand. Very delicately,

I took her clawed, burnt fingers in my own and gave them a gentle squeeze. She pulsed back. It was the first time in two years that my feelings had ever been reciprocated.

Little by little, we unearthed more of Mako's body. Her other hand still clutched the pebble that she had been blindly tapping against a piece of wooden beam. Then a shoulder, before finally we came to her face. And thank God she could not see me, as I winced at the sight of her and had to turn my head away.

Her hair, that wonderful black shock of hair, was frazzled and coming out in clumps. Skin was peeling off in strips to reveal raw flesh underneath. Her face was flecked white with plaster, but was so puffed up it was unrecognisable. Her eye-sockets were swollen shut while a thin dribble of mucous oozed between the lashes. There is no pleasant way to describe what had happened. Her eyeballs had melted.

As gently as we could, the girl and I cleared the rest of the wreckage from Mako's body. I could have saved a few minutes by grabbing hold of her shoulders and dragging her out, but I was quite certain that her skin would have torn off in my hands.

Eventually, there she lay before us, as weak and vulnerable as a new-born; she did not even have the strength to cry out, but could only lie there immobile on her side, head nuzzled on her shoulder. The bomb had clean stripped away her black top and the whole of her front from head to waist had been flash-fried like a piece of steak on the griddle. Oh, but she was savagely injured, with black blood already oozing through the strips of burnt skin. Some wisps of her mompei trousers still adhered to her hips and thighs, though her legs had also been severely burned.

Was there a moment, perhaps, when I thought that Mako had got her just desserts? When I thought that it was a fitting end for the woman who had not believed me about the bomb that had dropped on Hiroshima?

Not for one second did I think that. I swear it. At that time, there was not a drop of anger in my body – no, that would take a full hour to manifest itself in all its glory, and most timely it was too. All I could feel as I took in the enormity of Mako's injuries was this overwhelming sense of pity.

The girl gaped at Mako's ravaged body. She had coped well with tending those strangers at the Hijiyama school just two nights previously. But it was difficult to equate this shrivelled, burned piece of humanity with the beautiful woman who had made her tea only a few minutes before.

I clasped the girl on both shoulders and her eyes falteringly met mine. "It's down to the two of us now," I said. "Can you stay here? I will find some way to get them to the hospital."

"A handcart?" she suggested.

"A handcart would be perfect. Look after them both – you're in charge now!"

"I always was in charge!" she called after me, and it did my heart good to know that, even after this second bomb, the imp was back.

The devastation was every bit as bad as Hiroshima. How can I find fresh words to describe this second wasteland? A wasteland is a wasteland. There are no neat little gradations to describe the varying degrees of destruction. All about me was exactly the wholesale carnage that I had witnessed three days earlier: the smeared houses; the charred telegraph poles tumbled like kindling; the pall of smoke and dust that hung heavy in the air; and just the overall sense that everything in sight had been smashed by a single swing of some gigantic wrecker's ball.

Through the sea of flame, I could just make out some of the factory chimneys, black and clawing at the sky. The great red brick cathedral, the focal point of so many million Christian prayers over the years, was in its death throes. It was already nothing but a decapitated corpse, with its bell-tower and twin domes swept away by the bomb, and now the firestorm was finishing off the job.

Out on the rubble-strewn street, dead neighbours were

locked in all manner of ghastly contortions, all of them in the exact place where they had been snatched away by the bomb.

An old woman who had used to look after me as a child still had the spade in her hand which she had been wielding in the garden. A teenager whom I had known since he was a baby, now nothing but a carbonized husk, hands fused over his face, thumbs covering his eyes just as he had been taught; I only recognise him because of his distinctive brown shoes. And a couple sprawled in front of an ornamental pond, their heads immersed in the water, as if they had used their last drop of energy to crawl there and then expired at the first sip.

All of this I had seen before in Hiroshima. It was just an unending picture of death in all its grotesque variety – but these people were not strangers, but neighbours whom I had known all my life.

There was no time even for shock. I would look and perhaps recognise the charred body of an old school friend – and I would move on. My grieving would have to wait. The dead I could do nothing about; as for the living – well I would do my best.

I took a few seconds to work out which one of my neighbours might have possessed a handcart, or some sort of barrow. Then it came to me, a picture of a smiling, sun-wizened man, pushing a handcart that was piled high with garden produce. I screwed up my eyes in concentration as I tried to remember where he lived; it was not quite that street, but close by. Was it a parallel street?

I loped as fast as I could over the smouldering rubble, picking my way to the end of the road before taking a left. I was sure it was down this street, followed by a left turn, but the roads were now nothing but lines of demolished houses. The further I went, the more I was beset with fears that I was wasting my time; how could a wooden handcart have survived this butchery? Would it not be better just to pick Mako up and try to carry her over my shoulder?

I paused on the street-corner, mind tick-tocking over

whether to go straight back, when I heard a voice call out to me.

"Hi!" came the cry. "Got the time to talk to an old sailor?"

At first I could hardly make the man out from all the rubble he was propped against. It was Yoshito, one of my father's old friends; he had used to dandle me on his knee when I was a small boy. He was covered in dust and seemed to have dug his way out from the ruins of his house. One of his legs had been broken, his foot kicked out to the side at a crazy angle, and for a moment I was struck with how he looked like a puppet with its strings cut.

I stopped and gawked at him. He was lying on the ground with his head pillowed on a broken piece of timber, from where he had a grandstand view of the approaching firestorm.

He nodded at the solid wall of flame, which stretched right across the valley and up to the first of the terraced fields. "There's not going to be much left of Urakami after that."

I looked from Yoshito to the fire and back again – and made a decision. "I'm getting a handcart," I said. "I'll be back."

"Don't worry about me," he said, and I do believe that he had a trace of a smile on his face. "I'm sure it will be quick. We all have to die some time."

"Not if I can help it," I called out, tearing off down yet another street of ruined houses; already my mood was lifting because, even if I did not find the handcart, I would still save them. If needs be, I would carry them both, Yoshito and my wife, one on each shoulder; I would carry them till I dropped; I would find a way. I would do it.

It was still a relief to recognise not the house but the large garden at the back of it – and there, sheltered behind an old brick wall, was the handcart, black and decades old, and with a couple of spokes missing from one of its wheels. I could have kissed the cart I was so pleased to see it.

The wood was hot as I grabbed the two handles, sending a volt of pain up my burned arm. I gritted my teeth and only held tighter onto the cart. It was nothing, I kept telling myself, nothing at all; my very pain was an affirmation that I was still alive.

The return journey was much slower going. I bumped the handcart down the pathway and onto the street. There was rubble everywhere. A couple of times, I had to clear a path before dragging the cart through – and all the time aware of this wild firestorm, like a ravening beast that was breathing flames down the back of my neck.

Yoshito was still lying awkwardly on the ground, with his hands now calmly clasped on his stomach. "You got the handcart?"

"Of course – and you're getting on it."

"I said not to bother. Save yourself and your pretty wife."

I dragged the handcart up alongside him, before squatting down and picking him up in my arms. "Save your breath. You're coming whether you like it or not." I gasped. His legs were now draped over my burnt arm and the pain was agonizing. From what had been just a mild throb, it was like my skin was being played over with a blowtorch. I flopped Yoshito onto the handcart. I did not even like to see what my arm looked like.

"Devil!" I screeched, more in annoyance at my own frailty. If I'd had a piece of leather, I would have stuffed it into my mouth to bite on. As it was, I took out all my pain and rage on the handles of that handcart, digging my fingers deep into the wood.

What a strange sight I must have made, as I alternately cursed and kicked at all the debris that blocked my way. I think the girl must have heard my mad raging screams even before she saw me. She was twitching with nerves, terrified that, true to past form, I had abandoned her, Mako and little Toshiaki; and once upon a time, I well might have.

"Bring Toshiaki over!" I called out, my voice only just carrying over the roar of the firestorm. I pulled the handcart up as close as I could to the ruins of my old home and, as I stepped back over the rubble, I tried to shake some life into my screaming left arm. Was there any way that I could pick Mako up with my right arm alone?

I tried, but I could not even begin to lift her. I slapped myself twice, hard, on the cheek, working myself into a perfect fury, before bending down and picking her up in one smooth movement. My arm sizzled with pain as it was abraded on the jagged ground beneath her. I held her close to my chest, carrying her back over the ruins, and the memory that came back to me was so absurd that I almost smiled. I had remembered how, on the day we had married, I had carried Mako over the threshold of the very house that I was walking on now; what more appropriate way to say goodbye to my old family home than to be carrying Mako out of it?

As tenderly as I could, I placed her on the handcart next to Yoshito. I winced at the sight of her chest. She had been skinned from practically her hips to her collar-bone; her flesh looked like raw whale-meat dusted with grime. The front of my shirt was covered with the flaccid grey ribbons of her skin.

"Put Toshiaki on the cart," I ordered the girl.

"I will carry him." The boy looked from me to the girl with shocked eyes.

"Do as you please."

I led the way, face set in a perpetual scowl of pain as I dragged that black handcart the one kilometre up Motohara Hill. I did not look back. There was no time for thought. I was aware of what was generally occurring around me, of Yoshito's yelps of pain as his leg pitched against the side of the handcart, or the ruts in the road that seemed to be shaking the cart to pieces. But my sole focus was on getting the handcart to Urakami First Hospital, more commonly known as St Francis' Hospital. It was usually a gentle stroll of a journey, I knew it well and had made it so many times over the years. Now, with that hellfire at my heels, it was perfect torture.

There was the dead weight of the cart, the endless debris that clogged up the road, and the searing pain of my arm – and, as if that was not enough, the firestorm seemed to be coming at us from all sides. I remember letting out a great howl of rage – "Devil in hell!" – as I saw that our route up the hill was blocked by a wall of flame. I had no option but to trundle the cart back down the hill, and work my way round the blaze. As for the girl, she followed me in docile silence with Toshiaki fast in her arms; I think she was just letting my rage do its work.

How I howled and cursed as I dragged at that handcart. Mako appeared to be unconscious, but my father's sage old friend was flat on his back and gazing dispassionately at the firestorm.

Amongst the bodies on the road was a woman who was crawling up the hill. "Help me!" she called out, pleading to me with stricken eyes. "Help me, please." She was a woman in her twenties, and one side of her body had been burned, her left arm and leg turning a purplish brown.

I pulled up the handcart alongside her, trying to work out if I could take her up the hill as well. Perhaps she could sit on the end. It would be impossibly slow. I felt that I had already reached my limit.

"Please," said the woman again, before breaking off to cough as the smoke snatched at her lungs. "I want to live."

I was in an agony of indecision. I wanted to help her; I wanted to help everyone. But to pull three people up that hill? Could I?

The girl sidled over. "I will help you," she said. "Can you walk if you lean on me?"

"I – I will try," said the woman.

Yoshito had turned his head and was watching from the handcart. "Let me hold the boy," he said, beaming as the girl passed Toshiaki over.

I stooped and helped the woman to her feet. The girl was brilliant. I know that her unending chatter had, at times, got on my nerves. But on this occasion, she realised she had to draw the woman's mind away from her injuries.

"This is the second bomb we've been in like this," she said as the woman clutched onto her shoulder and made her tentative first step. "We came from Hiroshima this morning – and look what happened! Down comes another bomb. We arrived just in time. Perhaps we're a magnet for these new bombs. Is that possible? Do you think that if we went to another city, they would drop another bomb on us there too?"

Within five minutes, she had already discovered the woman's name, her occupation and where she lived – and, more importantly, they had walked more than 100 metres up the hill without the woman appearing even to notice it.

I was following in their wake with the handcart. I thought the burning sensation in my left arm could not have been any more painful if they had chopped my hand off. Just grasping the cart's handle was bad enough, but pulling it up the hill, with my cooked sinews shaking with the strain, was torture. I remember how my mouth was champed tight shut and my eyes screwed into gimlets as I concentrated on doing nothing more than counting to ten. Head bent down, I would count each step and, when I had reached ten, would start all over again.

We were making headway. There seemed to be a clear path to the hospital. But just when my spirits began to lift, I looked up again to see that the road was blocked – completely blocked by the ruins of two houses.

I was a mule that had been given a task and could think of no other way of completing it. So, with a grunt of pain, I started to drag the handcart up over the rubble. It was insanity. One wheel had caught behind a piece of concrete, yet still I was straining at the handles, believing that brute strength would ultimately win.

I pulled and I pulled and when nothing happened, I pulled some more.

"Stop!" screamed the girl, who was a few metres ahead of me. "You will break the handcart!"

"It's the only way." Again and again, I lunged at the handles.

"Why not take them off? You could carry them over?"

"Because... " I was still so set on hauling that handcart

over that hillock that I could hardly understand what she was saying. Take Mako and Yoshito off and carry them over?

"Because I'm an idiot!" I screamed at her.

I took Mako first, who was like a rag-doll in my arms, and then Toshiaki. Yoshito seemed quite calm as he handed the boy over. "Leave me," he said. "You don't have much time." "Be quiet! You're coming," I said, scrambling back over the rubble again.

Yoshito was the heaviest of them all. He noticed my short pants of breath. "Sorry I am so heavy."

"Shut your mouth!"

The fire was almost upon us now, burning embers flicking past on eddies of smoke. I placed Yoshito on the ground and darted back over the rubble to retrieve the handcart. Even without its load, it was still unwieldy.

I worked myself into a fury of indignation. How could we have come so far, only to be thwarted by something like this? I lashed out at a stone. For once I was able to harness my rage and let it work for me. I had to strain at each wheel, tugging them separately over every blockage. I kicked and shouted and acted like a crazed Samurai.

Sometimes though it works. I would not recommend it. But sometimes rage can give that extra fillip of strength to help you over the line.

And that, eventually, was the way that we arrived into the grounds of St Francis' Hospital, along with a band of other injured vagrants, their hair on end and their clothes in tatters. What a relief it was to have dragged that handcart into the compound and to let go of that infernal torture-machine – and, as I looked about me, I wondered why we had come to the hospital in the first place.

It was completely ablaze, flames spouting from the windows, and smoke torrenting from the roof-tiles.

CHAPTER SIXTEEN

I question the need for Fat Man.

There was a reasonable case for dropping Little Boy. Without that first bomb, Japan would have probably continued the war until the entire country had been crushed like a grape. Among the Big Six were a number of warmongers who were all for committing a nationwide version of Hari-kiri. Their battle-cry was – genuinely, "A hundred million will die together!"

But Little Boy had given our ministers all the excuse they needed to surrender. And I am sure they would have surrendered – especially after Russia had entered the war. But still they dithered and they hummed, and meanwhile the Yankees methodically went about their business of dropping a second bomb. They dubbed it, by the way, 'a quick one-two punch against the Empire'.

But there was never any need for the 'quick one-two'; Little Boy had in itself been a complete knockout blow.

If the Yankees had given us a few more days before dropping Fat Man; if our inept leaders had run up the white flag a little sooner; if Russia had declared war a month earlier; if, if, if...

You may have noticed that I am obsessed by that one little word: *if*. I constantly ponder how differently my life might have turned out.

The reason is because not once, but twice now, my life has been saved through matters of such total inconsequence. In

Hiroshima, I happened to walk into the warehouse a second before Little Boy exploded; in Nagasaki, I was saved by the girl's high-flying kite.

But it is impossible to weigh up these personal hypotheticals without also evaluating how Fat Man came to be dropped on Nagasaki in the first place. We had the most appalling bad luck.

Fat Man – named, so they say, after Britain's plump Prime Minister Winston Churchill – had from the first been earmarked for Kokura. Kokura had one of the biggest munitions plants in Japan, far more substantial than those of Nagasaki.

The B29 that was picked for the job was called Bock's Car. It was a state-of-the-art bomber and the mechanics had been swarming over it for days. And yet on the day that Fat Man was due to be dropped, Bock's Car's reserve full pump would not work, severely curtailing Major Chuck Sweeney's flying time.

And so, inevitably, tragically, Bock's Car hums high over Kokura, desperately hunting for a glimpse of the city through the clouds. Sweeney is under the strictest orders that he can only drop the bomb if he has visual contact with the city. Once, twice, three times the B29 passes over, but each time the cloud cover is so dense that nothing can be seen.

If I were the Mayor of Kokura, I would give thanks every time I saw a cloud. I would have an annual citywide holiday in gratitude to cumuli. I would adopt a cloud as the city's symbol to the world, a sign not just of Kokura's good fortune, but also of the sublime arbitrariness of death. Never before in history has the lot of so many tens of thousands of people depended on a cloud.

With fuel running low, Major Sweeney makes the decision to fly on to Nagasaki to see if he has better luck there. Oh, but the Major was just desperate to drop that bomb and to make his mark on history – but as it is, like Nagasaki itself, no-one remembers who came second and none but the A-bomb diehards have ever heard of Bock's Car or the Major.

There was only fuel enough for the single bomb run over

Nagasaki, but we, also, had thick cloud cover. As the B29 trawled over the city, Sweeney was mulling over whether to drop the bomb by radar alone; would that that happy thought had come to him as he had been flying over Kokura.

Suddenly the bombardier, Kermit Beahan, lets out a shout. "I've got it!" he screams. "I see the city!"

Bombardier Beahan, now in control of Bock's Car, ducks through a chink in the clouds, quickly securing his cross-hairs onto the Mitsubishi Arms Manufacturing Plant. And if I can dally for just a moment longer on one final what-might-have-been: not only was Nagasaki not the primary city, but the Mitsubishi Plant was not even the primary target in Nagasaki. No, Beahan had actually been searching for the Prefecture, three kilometres south. But that tiny gap in the clouds just happened to be above Urakami, and that in the end is what did for us.

There was a journalist, Bill Laurence, in an observation plane behind Bock's Car, the better to record every nuance and detail of the second bomb run. This is just a small piece of the puke-inducing screed that he wrote while he was sitting in the midsection of the appropriately named *Great Artiste*: "Somewhere ahead of me lies Japan, the land of our enemy. In a few hours from now, one of its cities, making weapons of war for use against us, will be wiped off the map by the greatest weapon ever made by man. In a fraction of time immeasurable by any clock, a whirlwind from the skies will pulverize thousands of its buildings and tens of thousands of its inhabitants."

What a gloriously lyrical way to describe an atomic bomb. Laurence, I think, must have fancied himself a poet.There was scant poetry to be had down on the ground – even months, years, after the war had ended.

It would be several days yet before Japan was forced to swallow that bitter pill of surrender – and what a surrender it was. As one, the entire country seemed to break down into hysterical tears. It was probably the greatest single outpouring of grief in history.

There were two people, however, who were not crying when the war finally ended: the girl and me. The girl, as I remember, actually started laughing; as for me, all I could feel was this numbing relief that, just as the whole sorry farrago of a war had come to an end, I had not had my head blown off with an army service pistol.

All in the fullness of time. First there is a burned wife and an injured son to be dealt with, along with a man who was only partly on the way to redemption.

The hospital had not been overtaken by the firestorm, which was a small blessing, as it was at least safe to lie outside in the grounds. But the building was ablaze. It was about 1,800 metres from the epicentre and the bomb had so dried out its tinder-dry roof-beams that within a single hour they had burst into flames. First the roof had gone up, then the third floor, until the smoking timbers had fallen down through the lift-shafts and torched the whole hospital.

In the preceding months, St Francis' had largely catered for TB patients, but after the bomb it was transformed into Nagasaki's primary burns unit. Throughout the afternoon, victims clambered up to the hill for sanctuary – and always, the longer they took the worse their injuries. The first of the victims, who arrived when we did, were at least able to walk. Later in the afternoon, they were nothing but black crawling wrecks, and the length of the hair was the only clue as to whether they were men or women.

The medicines were every bit as basic as they had been at the Hijiyama School two days earlier. The hospital had been well-stocked with creams, bandages and all the other things that might aid a burns victim. But the doctor and his team of nurses had only had time to save their patients from the inferno before all but their most basic medicines went up in smoke.

With the rest of my little troupe lying on the grass in a line, and all the other medics treating people who were more dead than alive, I set to work on Toshiaki. The girl had found me a pair of forceps and she soothed the boy as I started to tug the wooden splinter from his leg. How he bucked and squealed, but the girl kept him pinned tight to the ground. I was fortunate that the splinter had penetrated all the way through the fleshy part and come out the other side, so I was able to pull it out point first. First he watched me, eyes wide with shock, but as the pain grew, he thrashed his head from side to side.

Since our arrival, I'd barely had time to think. The action had been non-stop as we'd unloaded the handcart and borrowed one of the last pots of cream. But, sitting there on the grass, straining to pull that splinter from Toshiaki's leg, it was where I wanted to be. For a while, I even forgot the pain of my singed left arm.

Bit by bit, the splinter began to ease out of Toshiaki's leg, until with a sucking plop it dropped onto the grass. I smeared antiseptic onto his wounds before applying gauze and a final bandage tight round his leg. The burns I could only treat with cream and bandages.

Mako's injuries were just ghastly. Her pulse was weak and I could feel only a trace of breath as I put my ear to her mouth. I did what I could. I snipped away at the worst of the burned skin and tried to clean her up. I hoped the cream might ease her pain.

After I had bound her with bandages, Toshiaki snuggled into Mako's side and we draped the pair with a blanket. If I could have done more, I would.

Treating the young woman who we'd found on our way up Motohara Hill was relatively simple. I applied cream and bandages where possible and when I was done, she said, "Thank you, Sir. Thank you for not leaving me."

"Don't thank me, thank the girl," I replied, nodding towards that fey seven year old who was the true hero of the day. She had even found the only doctor in the place and had cajoled him into coming over and treating Yoshito's leg.

As a man, he was nothing exceptional to look at. If you saw him, with his trim hair and scholarly, rather diffident manner, you would have taken him for being just what he was: a hard-working medic who did what he was ordered.

But, unlike some, Fat Man was to bring out the best in him. That is what crises do. You find out a man's true worth. Some panic; some go to the wall; some think only of themselves; but a few, a rare few, turn into heroes overnight. And Dr Kinoshita was one of the heroes.

He was smiling as he allowed the girl to tug at his sleeve and drag him over. It said much for him that he could be under so much pressure, hundreds of people clamouring for his attention, and yet still have the time to be amused by a bossy seven-year-old girl.

"This is the man, Sir," she said, as she pointed at Yoshito. "I believe he's broken his leg."

The doctor squatted down and with a "May I?" ran his fingers down Yoshito's legs. "You're right," he said to the girl, looking up at her through round, gold-rimmed glasses.

"I am right," she said. "That's because we've already done this for a day in Hiroshima."

"You..." The doctor paused and turned his head from the girl to me. "You have come from Hiroshima? You left Hiroshima and ended up here?"

I nodded.

The doctor gave a little snort of laughter. "At least you have survived," he said. "There cannot be many who have survived both bombs. So you've seen all these injuries before?"

"We have," I replied.

With a professional eye he looked from Toshiaki to Mako to the young woman, sizing up my handiwork. "A very competent job you've done," he said.

I shrugged. "Thank you."

"Could you stay for a while? Could you help?"

The girl eyed me nervously, aware of the flightiness of her charge. "Yes," I replied "I would like that."

"We would like that," corrected the girl.

"That's good. That's very good. Though first let me bandage your arm."

It was a wretched night for many reasons. All I can picture is this unending misery, with blackened bodies constantly calling out for water. It was all the horror of Hiroshima, but tenfold – for every victim that could walk or crawl seemed to be trying to reach our hospital, spurred on by the vain hope that we might be able to ease their pain.

Some of them died the very moment that they entered the hospital grounds. They would totter the last few yards, breast the gateway and then slowly buckle at the knees, like a marathon runner brought to the very brink of exhaustion. All about the grassy grounds were strewn these scores of victims though they represented only a tiny fraction of the misery wrought by Fat Man. If only President Harry Truman had had a glimpse, a single glimpse, of these wrecked lives when he had described the bomb as "the greatest thing in the whole damn world".

The victims were littered all about the yard, and with the smoke, the screams and the funeral pyres flickering in the night, you might easily have believed you were in the very centre of hell. Nothing now could surprise me; there was no injury, how ever horrific, that I had not seen countless times before.

Faces that had been burned into bubbling black masks, yet were still somehow able to plead for water. Black corrugated backs, with the very flesh cooked and crisped like a piece of mutton. Little children whose chests had been so raked with glass shards that they looked like bristling hedgehogs. Shell-shocked mothers clutching long dead babies to their chests. And naked nuns,whose feet had been turned into blackened stumps and who had crawled to the hospital on hands and knees.

All of this I saw and more, and always in the background was that fearful refrain that I would come to know so well: "Water, water! Please give me water!" Others could do nothing more than scream to the world about their own misery. And, perhaps most harrowing of all were the ones who pleaded for nothing more than an end to life itself. "Please kill me," they would call out, and if you had given them a gun they would have quickly pulled the trigger.

The bombs brought home two quite separate aspects of human nature. On the one hand, you were constantly reminded of the frailty of human life, and how easy, how simple, it is for that thread to be cut.

On the other, I also experienced such remarkable resilience, victims clinging on for weeks, months, on end, doggedly refusing to let that last flicker of life be snuffed out.

The bomb had erased all our differences – and by doing so, had emphasised our humanity. In Nagasaki, we were all either victims or carers; if you were not sick, you tended the sick. The equation was now astonishingly simple and for me, it made life not just easy, but enjoyable. I had a sense of purpose such as I had never experienced before I tended the sick.

First I would inquire how they were and whether they objected to me treating them. Then I would patiently snip away at the shards of dead skin, before the girl applied cooking oil. How she chattered, but what I chiefly remember that first night was the smell; it was as if we were preparing for the banquet from hell.

A number of the victims died soon after they had been treated and were tossed onto the pyres; the air was heavy with the smell of cooking oil and that unmistakable sweet smell of roasted meat.

By midnight, we had run out of oils and creams. I sent the girl off to sleep, where she curled up on a blanket next to old Yoshito the sailor. But although I was numbingly tired, I could not sleep. The ghastly images from the previous three days never stopped playing through my mind. So I found an earthenware pitcher and filled it with water from a small indoor well. There was actually a much larger well outside, but that had been blocked up by rubble from a fallen chimney.

The smaller well was housed in one of the outbuildings and was perhaps a metre across, with a scuffed whitewash wall around the edge. Straddled over the middle was the usual winding mechanism, while on the end of the chain was a battered wooden bucket, dark with age. It kept us supplied with the clearest, freshest water imaginable. It took an age to wind the bucket up. And when I had that first sip of water, I realised I had drunk nothing all day.

I drank and I drank, like a hog burying its snout into the river; nothing has ever come close to tasting as sweet as that first mouthful of pure well-water.

I filled a pitcher and spent the rest of the night ladling water into the mouths of those that wanted it. They were pathetically grateful. "Thank you doctor," they would call out, to which I could only reply, "You're welcome," And it was in this way that I came across my own little band of victims.

They all appeared to be sleeping, and even my wife was resting easy. For a while, I squatted beside her, staring at the swathes of stained dressings and what came over me was this overwhelming sense of pity. I saw through her injuries to remember the woman I had once loved. Our honeymoon period had not lasted long – but, compared to most, I was lucky to have had even that. And what a wonderful gift she had given me in our boy Toshiaki. And what had I done, meanwhile, to thank her? I had whored my way through any woman who was prepared to have me.

Mako was lying absolutely motionless. I knelt forward, till my lips were practically next to her ear, and I whispered, "I'm sorry."

She was not quite dead and I fancied that, in the shadows

of the pyres, I saw her lips move, with just the single word, "Love".

Tears sprang to my eyes as I uttered the words I had not used in over three years: "I love you".

She may already have been dead by then, but they say that your sense of hearing is the last to go, so I hope, I pray, that as she passed on from this world to the next, her soul was suffused with thoughts of love.

I stayed with her till dawn, and it was that last vigil which I think crystallised my position: for some reason I had been blessed, blessed beyond all measure with this great gift of life, and I would now savour every moment until I had sucked it dry.

At dawn, I placed Mako's frail body onto the handcart and wheeled her over to one of the pyres. The girl, somehow sensing Mako's death, had silently come to join me. I lifted Mako off her cart and laid her onto a small mound of corpses. What a cheerless way for it all to end.

The girl took my hand as the flames danced. I gave brief thanks for Mako's life and what she had given me.

"Is there anything you would like to say?" I asked the girl.

"That is very, very sad," she said. "She was very pretty."

"She was."

"I'm hungry," said the girl.

"You're hungry?" I said, cupping my hand round her shoulder. "That is because you've had no supper." And with that, we embraced life and went off to find something to eat.

CHAPTER SEVENTEEN

We were by the well. I had hauled up another bucket of the water and the girl was sipping from the ladle. My left arm was aching viciously; from my knuckles to my shoulders it was a throbbing mass of pain. It was always worst when I had nothing to do, as if my brain had dropped out of gear and suddenly all I could think of was my own footling problems.

I was swinging my arm backwards and forwards, hoping that the increase in blood-flow might ease the pain, but it did nothing of the kind.

"This arm is a devil," I said, wondering if the bandages and the oil were hindering or helping the healing process.

There was a shadow at the door. It was the doctor, still spry, though his clothes a lot dirtier than when I had first seen him the previous afternoon.

"I hoped I would find you in here," he said. "I'm sorry about your wife."

"Thank you. A merciful release."

"I fear there will be many more like her. A grave loss for you, nevertheless, and I'm sorry," he said. "How is your arm?"

"Fine. Nothing at all."

Hands clasped in front of him, Dr Kinoshita nodded his head from side-to-side, as if weighing me up. "I don't know if this is appropriate. You may want to be by yourself. But there is something I would like you to do."

"Ask of me what you will."

"Our water position is bad enough," he said. "This well is all we have; I fear it will soon run out. More pressingly, we need food; we need medicine, bandages."

"And?"

"And, now that the firestorm is dying down, I hoped that you might be the man to find them."

"I—"

He bowed to me. "Do what you can."

"I will."

I knew that the girl would want to come too. Even after just four days together, I had already come to know her every mood and whim. But this time, I was adamant. It was going to be hard, arduous work which could take the whole day; it might well be dangerous; and, quite apart from anything else, I wanted her to stay at the hospital to look after Toshiaki. A seven-year-old girl accompanying me through the ruins of Nagasaki? What use could she be? It was preposterous.

"I know you want to come," I said, holding up my hand before she had even said a word. "But who is going to look after Toshiaki?"

There was a lull. The girl pouted. Toshiaki twitched in his sleep.

And Yoshito piped up. "I will look after Toshiaki."

"Thank you for that," I said, attempting to force a smile. "But it's going to be dangerous. Much of the city is still on fire. I don't even know where I'm supposed to be going—"

"I know of one depot in the Nishiyama district," said Yoshito, smiling pleasantly. He was like an old dog, happy in himself. "You could avoid Urakami altogether by walking over Mount Konpira."

"Very good," I said, relieved that Yoshito had put paid to the girl's insane thoughts of accompanying me. I turned back to her. "You couldn't possibly walk over the mountain. It's far too high."

"I'm coming, you Beast," said the girl. "Of course I can walk over that hill."

"True enough," said Yoshito. "I was walking up and down that hill when I was just six years old."

"Thank you," I said. "You have been most helpful."

"So I'm coming?"

"Why do we always have to argue every single time we disagree about something?" I said. "Why can you never accept that sometimes I am right?"

"Because usually you are wrong – Beast!" she said, darting a triumphant smile at the old man. He was leaning against a wall and had Toshiaki in the crook of his arm. I even caught him winking at the girl.

"Look – I'm a lot older than you. I know what's out there. It will be dangerous—"

"All the more reason for me to come with you."

"Why do you always have to make things so difficult? I cannot even understand why you want to come with me in the first place." I was exasperated, but I did also have the wit to appreciate the humour of it all – and it was the first time that morning that I had forgotten about my wife, dead no more than a few hours. The argument had even helped to dull the pain in my arm.

"It's not me making things difficult," said the girl, and already she had started doing a little jig. "Life would be much easier, Beast, if you just agreed with me."

"Yes," I said sarcastically. "Life would be so much easier if I always agreed with you."

"That is so," she said, now dancing in front of Yoshito. "Especially if it's dangerous."

"Keep you out of mischief!" crowed Yoshito, as he cracked a gummy grin.

"Thank you," I said, nodding at him.

"Anyway, how are you going to drive with your bad arm?" said the girl. "You will need me to change gear."

"Of course – and you know just how to do that."

"Yes I do – we learned in class."

"You are so annoying!"

And at that, Yoshito that cackling old devil, piped up, "I think it is just you who is easily annoyed."

If I have learned anything over the years, it is that I know when I am beaten; even when I have been licked by a precocious seven-year-old.

I filled up a water-bottle and with a brief wave at Yoshito, the girl and I were on our way. The doctor had given me a scrap of paper on which he had scrawled a note of authority, which – or so he had written – entitled me to commandeer such medicines and food as I saw fit. Neither of us had any idea if it would have any clout; but then neither of us had any idea if the depot even still existed. For all we knew, the entire city had been destroyed.

As we climbed the hill, we could see a broad sheet of smoke hanging over the Urakami valley like morning mist. A few fires still sputtered through the haze, finishing off the last of the cathedral, the factories and the bigger buildings. But, for the rest, Nagasaki was a grey desert of rubble. A few stick-like figures could be seen wandering down what once had been streets. What struck me most, though, and what kept me turning again and again for a fresh view, was how my once beautiful city had been transformed into such an ugly grey blot.

We walked steadily, traversing Mt Konpira from side to side rather than attempting the much steeper ascent straight up. All the way up, half the leaves on every tree, shrub and plant had been turned from green to black – while the other half hidden from the bomb still remained a dusty green; like so many of the victims, the plants were half-dead, half-alive.

I do not know why I had thought the hill would be too much for the girl. She was like a mountain-goat, bounding ahead of me, and then pirouetting on some boulder as I trudged up behind her. My arm ached. It always ached. I do not think I will even bother to mention it again. If in this story you ever

222

catch yourself wondering about my arm, and think that, as I have not mentioned it for a while, it is therefore no longer causing me hurt, well... that is not the case. As with all pain, you make a conscious decision as to how you wish to deal with it. And as for me, I did my best to ignore it. Though if you caught me on the raw, if, say, you grabbed my arm, that was a different matter altogether. No, whenever that happened, I was off like a rocket.

It took 40 minutes to climb the hill, and it was only when I reached the peak that I could properly survey the bomb's aftermath; it was an astonishing sight, absolutely nothing like I had expected. For the hill that I had climbed, that beautiful Mt Konpira, had saved half the city. On the one side, all trace of human habitation was gone; yet in the adjoining valley, the city did not appear to have been touched. I could see well-ordered avenues, street-cars trundling up the roads, and people who had been not three kilometres from the epicenter, yet who appeared completely unharmed.

The hillside was in stunning contrast to the smouldering ash that I had left behind. Half the city was untouched and the other half destroyed.

"What a pity," said the girl. "It must have been very beautiful."

"It was," I said. "I have been up this hill many times. It always looked lovely from up here. But I suppose it could have been a lot worse."

"It could have been like Hiroshima."

"At least we have half a city left."

"And at least we still have a depot to go to."

As we walked down the hill, we entered this fragrant new world, where the crickets still chirruped, the plants smelled of more than just smoke and ashes, and where, for all the effect that Fat Man had had on their lives, the bomb might have been dropped over 100 kilometres away. It was so very different from Hiroshima, where the drift from carnage to civilisation had been much more gradual – but in Nagasaki, there was this brutal dividing line at the top of the hill which marked the difference between life and death.

After just 100 metres, Urakami was already long behind us; the girl had even started singing a little ditty to herself, a sure sign of contentment. We picked our way down a path and every flower and every perfect house made it seem like a flawless paradise. Gardens that continued to grow pumpkins and vegetables; cicadas that still chirruped; streets that were not blocked with rubble; and houses, hundreds of houses, which did not seem to have lost even so much as a roof-tile.

"Just imagine," said the girl, as we walked down a broad tree-lined street. "If you had lived here."

"If we go down that route, why not ask me why I had to be in Nagasaki in the first place? Perhaps I might have been living safely in Kokura."

"Perhaps. But then you would not have met me."

"And then my life would be very different."

"You wouldn't be having half as much fun." She was snickering as she skipped, hands prettily behind her back.

"You would not be having half as much fun either."

"I always have fun – even with Beasts like you."

This bickering was to be a constant theme with the girl – and was all the more remarkable because she was only seven years old. But she was the sharpest seven-year-old you have ever met. "Whatever I say, you always hurl it straight back in my face."

"It's good for you," she said.

"Tell me, are you ever lost for words?"

"With you? Never!" She laughed, skipping off down the street with her hair bouncing on her shoulders. But she was certainly right. I would not have had half as much fun without her.

In this fashion, we squabbled our way to the depot. They even had a guard manning the gate. He was a callow youth, barely out of school, but had been put into an army uniform and given a gun so that he too could play his part in the war effort. I do not know what he thought he was doing there because he did not even attempt to stop us from entering the compound, instead pointing us to a small office-block on the other side of the dusty brown quad.

People in uniforms were ambling to and fro, but it was all done at a most leisurely pace. The quad was bounded by two long warehouses, each of which had a fresh coat of camouflage paint, in the vain hope it would elude the Yankee bombers. The depot looked trim and in good order, with not a weed in sight.

The office block was made of concrete in the Western style and built to last. I went up two steps, knocked on the black steel door, and there was only the briefest of pauses before I heard the single word, "Come."

I gestured for the girl to wait outside, but of course she ignored me and came straight in behind me.

We walked into a secretary's office, but as no-one was there we went straight on through to the next room, which bristled with all the tools of the quartermaster's trade: pencils, pens, rulers, rubbers, and reams of paper. One entire wall was lined with files. The quarter master himself was sat behind his desk, like a spider at the centre of this great logistical web.

"Yes?" he said, briefly looking up from his papers. On first inspection, he looked like all the other close-cropped, bullet-headed officers that I had dealt with over the previous four years. Yet his appearance was softened by gold-rimmed glasses, not so dissimilar from those the Emperor wore; all that I registered before I even noticed that he had lost an arm and that his empty sleeve was pinned across his chest.

I was about to speak, when the quartermaster spoke for me. "You have come from Urakami? How bad is it?"

"It's a disaster," I said, fishing in my pocket for the note that Dr Kinoshita had given me. "After the bomb there was a firestorm and... and there's very little left."

He tapped his pen on the desk. "It must have been the new bomb that they dropped on Hiroshima. So... " He trailed off, and before my eyes I was witnessing an army officer realise that the war must now inevitably be at an end. His gaze wandered over my shoulder to stare out of the room. "A single bomb that can wipe out a city? Well, then it is over. The war is over. I always thought it was an ill-judged act to have started it in the first place."

"Perhaps."

Again, that tapping of the pen and then the quartermaster shrugged, screwed up his nose, and with those few simple actions had digested the fact that our four-year war effort was at an end. If only his fellow officers had been able to accept our surrender with such equanimity.

"It is the beginning of a new era. We have had four years of destruction and now it's a time to rebuild." A little smile seemed to pass over his face, as another thought came to him. "Though I fear that it might take considerably longer than four years. It is so much more time-consuming to create than it is to destroy. Take your Urakami Valley – hundreds of years in the making, and now gone in the twinkling of an eye."

His eyes moved to the piece of paper that I was holding. "What's in your hand?"

"It is a note from Dr Kinoshita at the Urakami First Hospital. We have no food or medicine. We have nothing. The hospital burnt down last night. Hundreds of people are having to sleep outside."

The quartermaster perused the note, before opening a drawer and pulling out two form-books. He started to write rapidly. "If I am judging this correctly, the army will have little need for any more supplies," he said in almost a conversational tone. "And if I am wrong, then they will probably take me out and shoot me."

He looked up and smiled at the girl. "But that is why I have this job – because I don't need to be given orders. I'm in charge because I make the correct decisions." He signed one form with a flourish and then started writing in the second book.

"So what are you doing?" asked the girl.

"My decision is to give Dr Kinoshita everything that he requests, though we're light on medicines. You also need blankets, so you may take those as well. There's no point in keeping it for an army that's not going to fight."

"But... " I almost burst into tears. I had been expecting such a struggle; everything over the past four days had been non-stop struggle, and out of nowhere I had found wisdom and compassion – from a man who might just as easily have been a hidebound martinet.

"There's one small problem," the quartermaster said as he continued to write. "But for a pair of your resources, it should not be difficult. We have no trucks. We have no cars. We have enough rice to feed an army. But we have no means of transporting it."

"We will find a lorry then," said the girl.

"I'm sure you will. I will write you the names of two places that might still have a vehicle. But one more thing before you go." He opened up a drawer and took out a bag that I had not seen in a long time. "Boiled sweets," he said. "My grandchildren like them."

"Thank you," said the girl. "I will take two."

He laughed as he proffered the paper bag to me. "And you?"

I could not even remember the last time that I had tasted a sweet. "Thank you."

"That is good," said the quartermaster. "And now I can join you. It's not just my grandchildren who enjoy boiled sweets."

For a few golden moments, the three of us were united in that simple delight of sucking a boiled sweet. It is sometimes worth foregoing life's little pleasures, just for the untold thrill of becoming reacquainted with them.

We were still sucking our sweets as we walked out of that office into the brilliant summer sunshine and at that moment, with everything so neat and ordered about us, it was almost impossible to believe what was waiting for us on the other side of a hill.

We did not have far to walk – and our welcome could not

have been more different. The quartermaster had sent us to what had been a one-time training centre for truck drivers. It was where, presumably, teenagers learned how to drive before being sent off to the front to provide more cannon-fodder. But, with fuel in such short supply, the training of rookie drivers had been put on indefinite hold.

Some scrubby vegetables were growing on what had once been a lawn. A rusty gate had fallen off its hinges and was propped against a wall. The remains of some cannibalised cars were littered by a garage. But over in a shed, I could see the outlines of two old trucks.

The girl raced over to them and by the time I had wandered over, she had already swung herself up into a cab and was sitting behind the steering wheel. She beeped the horn a few times and rolled down the window. "Can I drive?"

"Certainly not," I said, as I walked round the truck. It was one of those classic army lorries with a canvas top, and well battered from being mauled about by novice drivers. It had a flat tyre, but the engine looked sound enough when I lifted the bonnet.

"Is the key in the ignition?" I called up to the girl.

"It's not here," she said.

"Try underneath the visor or one of the side-boxes."

I went to inspect the other truck, but the back wheels were off and it was propped up on a pile of bricks.

The place had the still quiet of a ghost-town. The silence was shattered by a shrill barking voice.

"What the devil are you doing?"

I loped round to see an officer, no more than my age, scuffling with the girl as he tried to haul her out of the cab.

"Get off me!" she screamed, lashing out with her feet. "You're hurting me." She twisted out of his grip and slunk to the far side of the cab.

"Get out of there this instant!" roared the officer. "You're not allowed in there."

I walked over to him and said, silky soft, "Please calm down."

The officer, quite tall but just a clone for all the other thousands of soldiers churned out by the Army sausage-machine, turned on me. "Are you responsible for this girl?"

"Not really," I shrugged. "We would like to borrow one of your trucks. We have to take supplies to the Urakami Hospital."

"Out of the question," the officer snapped. His eyes twitched at the girl, who was still sitting in his cab.

"Why is that?"

"These trucks are for training purposes only. Besides, we have no fuel."

I was trying to keep a lid on my bristling anger. Just how many times had I been crossed by these half-wits, these blinkered Army officers who had been programmed like robots to do nothing but obey orders?

"As you must know, half of Nagasaki has been destroyed," I said. "This very minute, there are thousands of people who are dying in the Urakami Valley. They need food and medicine – and I need your truck to deliver it to them."

"That cannot be permitted," he said. "You may not have the truck and even if you could have it, there's no fuel."

I remember drumming my fingers against my thigh as I tried to stay calm. I deliberately paused before speaking. "May I take a truck if I find some fuel?"

"You will not find any fuel. There's no fuel to be had. And you cannot have the truck. That is not permitted."

"Do you have any idea what has happened? There is nothing left of the city. And you are telling me that I cannot borrow the truck?"

"These trucks may not be used for anything except driver-training." His eyes snapped at the girl. "Get down from that cab this instant! You are on army property! Get down from the cab and get out of this compound!"

There was so much I could have said, but much good it would have done me. I tried another tack. "Why not come with us? Why not see what has happened? They are dying in the streets. They need help."

"My orders are to stay here."

"What? To look after two rusting trucks?"

"Get out of this compound now!"

It is difficult to describe my overwhelming sense of impotence in dealing with all things army. Perhaps I might even have been sufficiently goaded to hit him. I was certainly close to it. It felt like the entire nation had undergone a communal brainwash, as every flicker of independent thought had been excised to be replaced with knee-jerk patriotism.

I was seething over all these thoughts and more when help came from a most unexpected quarter. "What's the problem?"

I looked over and there standing in the sunlight just outside the shed was the diminutive form of the quartermaster, very dapper in cap and full uniform. "What's happening?" he asked again.

"This man and this girl, they are attempting to commandeer an official army training vehicle. Sir!" spluttered the officer.

"Very good. That is precisely what I suggested. Why are you not helping them?"

"It's against regulations. Sir!"

In an instant, the quartermaster's icy suave manner changed to thundering rage. "Be damned to your regulations! If you don't have that truck moving in 15 minutes, you'll be on a charge."

"But – but there's no fuel. Sir."

"Of course you have fuel hidden away somewhere. Do you take me for an idiot?"

"But—"

The officer looked at his watch. "Fifteen minutes is all I'm giving you. Off you go."

"I—"

"Trot on."

The officer was in an agony of indecision, looking from

the officer to the truck. "Yes Sir," he said as he darted out of the shed.

The quartermaster watched as the man scurried off to a ramshackle outbuilding, before turning to me. "I should have come with you in the first place," he said. "I'm sorry."

I could not believe it. An officer, a senior officer, apologising to me. "Thank you."

"How I hate these damnable officers. They live their lives by the rule-books, forgetting that first and foremost they are human beings."

"Do you think he will have any fuel?"

"I have learned a little from ten years as a quartermaster. You always keep back a few of the essentials. What if a passing General were to visit?"

"Is that true?"

"Everyone does it. That young officer will have his own personal stash squirreled away round the back. They usually sell it on the side."

By now the girl was hanging out of the door and staring awestruck at her new hero. "Would you like to come with us to the hospital?" she asked.

"I have to stay," he chuckled. "Though I'm sure you'll be more than resourceful enough without me."

We heard a low rumble and looked over to see the sweating officer trundling over with a large blue barrel.

"Well done," said the quartermaster briskly. "I knew you might be able to find the fuel somewhere."

"Yes Sir," said the officer. "I siphoned it off from one of the cars."

"Believe that and you'll believe anything," the quartermaster said with a laugh as he tossed a sweet up to the girl. He turned back to the soldier. "Fill it up and one of the tyres needs more air. And hurry. You only have ten minutes."

I stared at the quartermaster, and for the first time noticed the gallantry awards on his chest. They were almost hidden by his empty sleeve. He was gazing quietly out at the green hills on the horizon – and it was he, another unknown just like my sage at the Hijiyama Hospital, who gave me my last, and perhaps my most important lesson, of the war.

He spoke so quietly that I had to move closer to hear him. "In these troubled times," he said. "It's most important to do what you know to be right. For four years, we have believed that pride in our country and strict adherence to orders will win the war. That is palpably not the case. So all that we have left is our own wisdom and those few that possess it must have the courage to use it. Do you hear me?"

"I do."

"The army's day is over and it will be finished for many years. If we are ever again to become a great nation, we will need industry, which we have in abundance, and we will need wisdom, which has become a rare commodity indeed in this war."

He turned to me, and smiled. "I hope that your arm gets better. But—" and here he gestured at his empty sleeve, "you can prosper very well on one arm alone. I'll see you back at the depot."

It was in this way that the truck was filled with fuel, food and anything else that could be hoisted on board. And, after a farewell salute from the man whom I only ever knew as the quartermaster, we bumped our way back to the hospital, bouncing over the rubble and the ruins. There was never any need for the girl to change gear, as we never made it out of first.

Over the next few days, the girl and I paid several more visits to the depot, which felt like a little island of sanity in that ocean of madness that was the war-machine of the Imperial Army.

And what, meanwhile, of the Imperial war effort? As the Yankees prepared themselves to carpet the whole of Japan with A-bombs, what was occurring in the War Cabinet? By now, the Big Six were fully apprised of this new weapon that had been unleashed against us – the B-29s were now not dropping bombs but leaflets.

In perfect Japanese they explained: 'A single atomic bomb

has as great an explosive power as all the bombs that would be carried by 2,000 B29s. You should carefully consider this fearful fact, and we assure you, in the name of God, that it is absolutely true.'

But among the Big Six there were still men who wanted to continue the war. They described the homeland battle as being like a beautiful orchid, which blooms and then is cut down. It was clinical insanity of the first order – but it was this madness that got us into the war in the first place.

In the end, it was the Emperor himself who insisted on ending the war, though it was some days yet before the surrender could be processed through Japan's immense bureaucratic machine. The Emperor, like my quartermaster, was doing what he knew to be right, rather than adhering to the age-old Samurai tradition that we fight to the last man. It is one of many reasons why I have always admired our seemingly effete leader. But I am biased. I am fully aware that were it not for the Emperor's timely intervention, I would have been shot dead in the very last minute of the battle.

When we were not ferrying back more supplies to the hospital, we were tending the sick, and nursing the boy as well as the woman we had brought along. We snatched what sleep we could.

It was not that I had forgotten my old friend Shinzo. I had been concerned about him from the very first. But it was chaos at the hospital and there was barely even a moment to draw breath, let alone wonder what had happened to Shinzo. I was hoping, of course, that he had been so delayed at that railway station on the morning of 9th August that he had not managed to get anywhere near Nagasaki.

That is my only excuse for why it took me a full four days to make the trip to Shinzo's home. It was a pretty little bungalow situated hard by to the Cathedral in the Urakami Valley. That was why I had not bothered to go there.

CHAPTER EIGHTEEN

It was the chickens which saved her.

How could a chicken possibly save the life of a human being? Can it tend a human? Can a chicken provide food or water? What on earth can a chicken do to save a human life? Well all in due course. But I assure you it is neither a joke, nor an exaggeration: Sakae's life was saved by the chickens. Since that time, and in homage to their great service, we neither of us have ever touched even a single mouthful of chicken meat.

In the four days since the bomb had been dropped, the ruins of Nagasaki had taken on this grey uniformity, with houses crushed into so many million tiny pebbles, as if they had been pulped through a fine sieve.

At that time, I did not believe that I was on any sort of mercy mission. It was more of a pilgrimage to what had been the one-time home of my friend. I was unable to conceive how anyone so close to the epicentre could have survived the bomb.

Shinzo's wife, that homely woman whom he had adored so much, was now presumably dead; and Shinzo, with luck, was mourning his wife from the safe-haven of a village some many miles from Nagasaki.

I was awfully, tragically, wrong on both counts.

The only fortunate thing was that, for the first time in four days, the girl had not accompanied me. It was not a sight for a child's eyes.

Shinzo's house, as I had expected, had been wiped flat by

234

the bomb – though it had not been burned. By some miracle it had escaped the firestorm.

And there, lying in that small front garden, were Shinzo and his wife, with faces down in the grass and their arms almost casually slung round each other's waists. Their injuries were shocking.

Shinzo's back and half of his face had been cruelly ripped away and since it is not an image that I wish to dwell on, I will leave it at that. He was quite dead and had been dead for some time.

Sakae, lying by his side, so close that their legs were touching, had had her shirt ripped clean away. The skin had been flayed off her back to reveal raw flesh. I stooped beside them both, laid a hand on their heads in memory of what we had once shared – and it was only as I laid my hand on Sakae's cheek that I realised it was still warm. At first I thought that it was the sun warming her flesh. But when I pressed my ear to her lips, I could just discern the very faintest breath. She was alive – the woman was alive! My heart bounded with astonishment.

How I ran back to the hospital. I flew over to the truck and within minutes was roaring back to Shinzo's home. I am afraid I had to leave my old friend where he lay in the garden. Later, I would have the time to give him a fitting send off. But while there was even a chance of saving his wife, all my energies were focused on her.

I revved the engine and reversed the truck straight over Shinzo's home and into the garden. There were four or five scrawny chickens that had been rooting around in the ruins and they squawked out of the way as the truck trundled towards them.

Sakae moaned as I picked her up. It was the first noise that I had heard from her. I placed her onto a blanket in the back of the truck. My whole body was trembling, I was in such a fever of impatience to get her back to the hospital. Yet for all my haste, I was nursing the truck back over the ruined roads, trying to stop it pitching too violently from side to side.

The girl was waiting by the hospital gate.

"I have Shinzo's wife!" I yelled, as I jumped down from the cab. "She's still alive." I was already pulling Sakae out of the back of the truck.

"And Shinzo?" she asked.

"He's... " I paused in mid-tug, for a moment taken aback. "He's dead. I'm very sorry."

The girl was so shocked she had to bite her lip. I suppose both of us had believed that sooner or later our fine friend Shinzo would roll back into our lives. And in two short words, I had put paid to all those visions of a glorious reunion.

Perhaps the girl was still in shock, or perhaps she realised the urgency of the situation, but either way she did not waste her breath on words. "Get the doctor please," I had asked, and in a moment she had flown off to find Kinoshita.

The doctor came hurrying over and felt Sakae's weak pulse. "She needs water," he said. "I will apply zinc oxide and bandages."

I fetched a pitcher of water from the little indoor well and dabbed it at her mouth. Her lips moved imperceptibly, opening a fraction, as if to allow more water in. I soaked a cloth and squeezed a trickle into her mouth.

"Where did you find her?" said the doctor, as he cleaned her back. "Is she a friend?"

"She married my best friend. I found them both lying in their garden."

"I'm sorry," said Kinoshita, as he snipped away steadily at a flapping piece of skin that had crisped brown in the sun. "It's very odd," he said. "There are no maggots." I had not appreciated the point. But as I studied Sakae's back, I saw that the doctor was right. It was now a full four days since Fat Boy had been dropped – and almost every injury that we had dealt with had been teeming with maggots. Even the victims who had been with us from the first were not immune to those loathsome white maggots.

They only took two days to spawn into wriggling parasites.

236

A wound might have been cleaned and bandaged, and then three days later, out they would come, working their way out at the edges. Then when you stripped the layers back, the entire suppurating wound would be a white mass of pus and maggots. Just the very sight of a maggot still makes me want to retch.

But there was no way we could stop them. There were flies everywhere, and somehow they could lay their eggs on even the most fastidiously cleaned injuries. A full year after Fat Boy, I was still dressing Sakae's wounds and would regularly find that her body was being eaten away by a fresh outbreak of maggots.

The doctor paused with his scissors to scratch at the corner of his chin. "I wonder why there are no maggots," he asked. "It's very unusual. And you say she was out in the open?"

"She was," I said. "She and Shinzo were lying out in the garden, and... there did not seem to be anything unusual about it. " I paused to recollect what I had seen in the garden. "There were some chickens—"

"Chickens!" said Dr Kinoshita triumphantly. "I knew it!"

"Chickens?" I queried. "What about them?"

"The chickens must have eaten the maggots!" he said. "Perhaps we should bring them up to the hospital."

"Amazing," I said, allowing myself a little smile – and it really was one of those extraordinary imponderables of fate that Sakae's life had been saved by a few pecking chickens. Just one more of those tiny little details that decided whether we lived or died. But on the flip side of the coin, Shinzo lost his life because he fell into a river; and contracted diarrhoea; and missed a train.

Much later, I learned how Shinzo had hitched a lift into Nagasaki on the back of a truck. He had only just arrived back at his home when the bomb was dropped. The pair of them were caught outside embracing in the garden. I still find the arbitrariness of it all quite staggering: a man is killed because he was caught short at a railway lavatory; and his wife survives because she happened to keep a few chickens. It is a neat philosophical point. It is not that small things matter. Most of them don't. It is just that some things matter very much indeed. Though it is only long after the event that we have any clue which of these trifling matters were all-important, and which counted for nothing. But to dwell on it is the route to madness. Instead, we should strive to embrace life and to do right – and to accept that, while small things do occasionally matter, that in general, nothing matters very much at all.

It is in this spirit that we come to the end of my war. It was now six days after Fat Man. The Yankees had dropped another batch of leaflets, complete with the Royal crest of the Chrysanthemum, which read in part, 'For your own sake you should ask his Majesty the Emperor to bring this war to an end and surrender as soon as possible.' But the leaflets were rather wasted on us. Our existence was so hand to mouth, that the war had become an irrelevance.

Sakae, like so many bomb victims, was a long way from being on the mend, but her condition did seem at least to have stabilised. Once, she opened her eyes and tried to smile when she saw me.

I spoon-fed rice into her mouth and tended her wounds. There were other people who I treated, but she was my favourite. If only as a small token to my friend Shinzo, it had become my personal quest to save her. I did what I could for all of the victims, but any spare moments I had, I would spend with either Toshiaki or Sakae. Even though she could hardly speak, I would tell her about Shinzo and how much he had loved her – and how much I had loved him.

Along with the doctor and a few nurses and, of course, the girl, the occasional help squads would be foisted on us. Sometimes, as in the case of a team of Navy medics, they would stay for a morning, would treat the sick in a clinical, efficient manner – and then when their medicines had run out, they would depart.

These teams usually meant well, but they did grate with the routines that we were already beginning to establish at the hospital. Without a word of apology, untrained helpers such as myself would be shoved out of the way to make room for the professional medics. It grated that they all thought they knew best. There was no time for a kind word as they methodically went about their business. When they left, it was always with a sigh of relief that we said goodbye to those self-styled mercy teams.

But if the teams of trained medics were bad, far worse were the roaming squads of civilians who came to help out. It was partly to do with their lack of respect for what we had accomplished at the hospital, and partly – as always – to do with Japan's knee-jerk obeisance for anything in a uniform. You only needed to put a man into a uniform and he suddenly expected people to dance to his every word.

We had just breakfasted and the girl and I were quietly checking our patients' dressings and wounds. We were doing the best we could with our very basic medicines, though at that stage we had not an inkling of the size of the vast mountain that we had begun to climb. All of us were still entirely ignorant of this obscure new disease, 'radiation sickness'. It had not occurred to us that some of these festering wounds would take years to heal.

I was extracting some maggots from a back wound with a pair of forceps. When we had pulled back the bandages a few minutes earlier, the maggots had been as tight bound as a bag of boiled rice. One by one, I dropped the maggots into a bucket being held by the girl.

Then I made a little grunt of surprise. For the first time, I had noticed the man's leg. His trouser-leg had been torn off almost at the thigh, to reveal a long, pale white leg. I stared at the man's footwear – and that was also quite different.

"Know who we are treating?" I asked the girl.

She looked at the man's scorched back and shook her head. "Should I?"

"Look at that hairy white leg," I said. "It has to be a Yankee." The girl peered at the prone man. "This is a Yankee? Is that right, Beast?" she asked in wonderment.

"Must be one of the prisoners-of-war." I tweezered out a couple more maggots.

The girl proffered up the bucket. "A Yankee?" she said again.

"Are you going to start kicking him like you did with that dead Yankee on the Aioi Bridge?"

She twisted her hair into a ringlet, fascinated at having a live enemy specimen in front of her. They were always so big, the Yankees, taller and much better fed.

"No, I'm not going to kick him," she said, decisively making up her mind. "It does not occur often. In fact it occurs very rarely. But on this occasion I'm prepared to admit... "

"Admit what?" I grinned.

"Admit that you were right. This man may be a Yankee – but he also is a victim of the bomb. He needs our help."

"Very well put," I said – and only a fool would have said anymore.

So for two minutes we worked on in contented silence, as the girl quietly digested the fact that she no longer loathed the Yankees.

A shadow fell across my arm. I turned round to see an assistant police inspector standing over me, his clothes in tatters. Somewhere along the way, he had acquired an army pistol, which was slung at his leg in a khaki holster. Behind him stood another uniformed officer, while milling round the gates was a cluster of about 30 civilians.

"Who's in charge here?"

I passed the forceps to the girl and stood up. "Dr Kinoshita is in charge. But he's been up all night and is asleep."

"Wake him up."

"Perhaps I can help," I said. "What is it you want?"

"We have been authorised to open a first-aid hospital." The

man seemed to stand a little taller as he spoke, as if aware of the weight of responsibility on his shoulders.

"You have come to the right place then," I laughed.

"I do not think your humour appropriate."

"Perhaps so. What would you like to do?"

The policeman looked all about him at the clusters of victims sprawled around the grounds. "Why aren't they inside? Why have you left them out here?"

I spoke to the man as I might speak to a slow child. "Where there is space, we have put the victims into the gymnasium and the storerooms. The hospital was gutted by fire and is not yet fit for human habitation. But if you and your men might care to clear it out... that would be most helpful."

"My men must first be fed," he said. "Where is your food?"

I bridled at that. "You have a very abrasive manner."

"This is a national emergency," the police officer said, and as he spoke the second officer sidled up beside him. He was much younger, barely out of his teens, and his fingers trailed over a wispy moustache. "How can you expect my men to work without food?"

"Do we now we ignore all the common courtesies?"

"I have the personal authority of the emergency committee of Nagasaki," he said primly.

What was the point? Why was I wasting my energy on this man, who was no better and no worse than all the other excrescences that had crawled out of the war? I no longer even knew if it was the man's request I was objecting to, or his uniform and his curt manner. And anyway, who was I to say that these 30 hungry civilians couldn't be fed?

"Very well," I said, as I retrieved the forceps from the girl. "Our kitchens are in a semi-basement beneath the hospital. There should be a cauldron of rice there. With luck, there should be some left for you."

The man gave a curt nod, before adding, "That is as it should be – and in future, do not waste my time. I'm here with the full authority of the emergency committee."

"So you mentioned," I grunted, stooping down to once again apply myself to the maggots.

I spent the rest of the morning with the sick. To some, this was a most unrewarding task. But I was different. It gave me joy just to salve a patient's wounds or to bathe a festering body, for there was not a moment that I did not appreciate the blessing that had been conferred on me.

The party of civilians had sated themselves on our rice and had begun to clear the lower two storeys of the hospital. The floors were structurally sound, as they were made of solid concrete that was half a metre thick, but, inside, it was as if the hospital had been shaken like a giant rattle. Everything, from furniture to solid steel machines, had been smashed beyond repair, and the blaze had been so hot that much of the glass had melted. The walls and ceilings were charred black and still stank of smoke. Although the windows had been blown out, the hospital did provide some small shelter, so was a marginal improvement on living rough outside.

I did not really notice what the men were doing. From the periphery of my eye, I would catch them carrying bits of burnt furniture which were tossed on a pile outside the hospital gates. For the larger bits of machinery, it would sometimes take three or four people to manhandle them out of the hospital. When the two floors were relatively clear, they swept up the worst of the glass. Hundreds and hundreds of medicine bottles must have been shattered in the fire, and all the floors were carpeted with sharp, sticky shards.

I suppose it was a useful enough job. It had to be done, and they had done it; though the assistant police inspector might have been a little more gracious.

It was a few minutes before noon, and I remember the moment well because it was the first time that I had begun to comprehend the full ramifications of radiation sickness. We all knew we had been punished by a quite different type of bomb. But it took me nearly a week to appreciate the symptoms of this disease.

I was treating a woman who, on the surface, appeared to have suffered only the most superficial wounds. Her leg had been a little burned and when I had first treated her a few days earlier, I had thought she was going to be walking out of the hospital that afternoon. But her condition had deteriorated markedly over the past three days. She was always tired, her gums had started to bleed and her frazzled hair was falling out. She had not yet developed the purplish spots on the skin which would mean that her condition had become terminal. But she seemed to be dying before my eyes. I remember this feeling of helpless impotence. I had no idea what ailed her, nor how to make her better.

From one of the outhouses, I heard the sound of raised voices – and recognised at least one of them. I jogged over, wincing as I caught my injured arm on the hem of my trousers. How filthy those trousers were. I had been given a crumpled shirt to wear, but my trousers were still the same ones I had been wearing when I had been blown up by Little Boy.

The noise, the row, was emanating from the small shed that housed the hospital's only water-well. I could already imagine what had happened.

In the shed, stood about the well, Dr Kinoshita was in a stand-off with the two assistant police inspectors. By the wall were four of the civilians' troupe, who'd just drawn off a bucket of water. The first police officer, the one who had already berated me, was pointing his finger at the doctor.

I tried to capture that calm poise that I had experienced a few days' earlier from the quartermaster. "What's happening?" I asked.

There must have been something about my look as I stood there in the doorway, for although Dr Kinoshita was greatly my senior, he now deferred to me. "These men... " he said, before trailing off. He had been working so hard that he was on the verge of total exhaustion. "These men have finished their work at the hospital and are now helping themselves to the last of our water. And I... " The poor man shook his head mournfully as he stared at the ground. "I have suggested that they have their fill of the spring-water outside the hospital."

"Well, you heard the man," I said to the two officers.

I will try to describe the exact feeling that tingled through my bones at that moment. It was this awesome sense of confidence, such as I have never experienced, as I finally knew I was fighting for a just cause. "Get out of here and take your men with you."

"I will not be spoken to like that," snapped the police officer.

"Let me say it another way then," I replied. "Would you be so kind as to gather your men and leave the hospital?" But the feeling was just intoxicating. Finally I was taking them on – and it had been a long time coming. After four years, no, a lifetime, of being a supine crawler, I was telling these stuffed shirts where to go. They were an abomination, as vile and disgusting as those fat white maggots, that had somehow been allowed to thrive and prosper during the four years of the war.

"We will do no such thing," said the officer, and for the first time I saw his fingers stray to the army service pistol at his hip. "I am here by the authority of the emergency committee and my men must have water before they leave."

I nodded and I was even smiling at the man, I was so confident. "Perhaps Dr Kinoshita has not explained. This is the only well that we have. There is very little water left and when this runs out, then there will be nothing left for our patients."

I sauntered past the officer and stood by the side of the well.

"This is a time of national emergency," the man replied. I could see the beads of sweat trickling down his cheek. "The army and the militia must come before the injured. We all have to make sacrifices."

I laughed, genuinely laughed at that. "Why are you talking about the army? Have you not read any of these leaflets that the Yankees have dropped? The war is over! Our army is finished."

"That talk is treasonous!" The officer snatched at my arm to drag me away from the well.

I had been enjoying myself up until then, but when he caught my injured arm, a flash of pain lanced through my body. He had tapped into a vast vat of rage that had been simmering since the start of the war.

"Get off me!" I backhanded him hard across the cheek with my other hand. "Get away from me and get out of here, you shits, you scum!"

The officer, trembling, tugged at the gun at his hip. "You have struck a police officer!" he said, fingers working at the leather. "You have struck a police officer who was carrying out his authorised duty! You will leave this room. You are under arrest."

"Get out!" I replied. "I'm sick of the sight of you."

The officer, working at the buckle with both hands, had finally drawn his gun and levelled it right between my eyes. The shaking muzzle was only a metre from my face.

"I am not moving," I said. I was making my stand. I was going no further. It might have been over such a trifling matter as the hospital's water, but, just as the quartermaster had urged, I was doing what I knew to be right.

"I am going to count to three," he said, voice squeaking with nerves. "Then I will shoot."

"Go to the devil – and take your committee authorisation with you."

Dr Kinoshita had been watching aghast. "Let them have the water!" he said. "Give him the water! It does not matter!"

"Of course it does not matter!" I replied. "But for how much longer are we going to be pushed round by these uniformed dogs. They know nothing! All they have done is brought this country to its knees!"

The police officer, shaking all over, had brought up his other hand to steady the pistol. I doubt that he had ever pulled a trigger in anger. "I am counting," he said. "One!"

And what was I thinking? Was I terrified at having that maniac point a gun at me? Did I only have a few more seconds to live before he fired a bullet through my brains?

I was certainly not frightened of dying. I had seen so much death, so much carnage, over the previous ten days, that I was past caring. At least it would be quick – which was more than could be said for most of the deaths in Hiroshima and Nagasaki.

Dr Kinoshita was pleading with me now. "I beg you," he said. "Let them have the water."

"Thank you, Doctor Kinoshita, for everything. You have given me so much."

The police officer looked as if he was about to be sick. "Two!" he shrieked.

As I stood there waiting to meet my end, I was in a rather casual pose, one hand in my pocket, my injured arm hanging limp by my side. I was almost side on to the police officer, and gazing out of the doorway. I could just make out a funeral pyre burning briskly by the gates.

And a thought enters my head – perhaps the last thought of my life: in a few minutes, it will be my lifeless corpse being tossed onto the pyre.

"I mean it!" says the officer. "I really mean it!"

Did he mean it? Surely if he had really meant it, he would have already pulled the trigger? But to that question I will never know the answer – because at that very moment the girl flashes through the door.

"The Emperor!" she screams. "It is the Emperor!"

Yes, it was the Emperor, in person – come all the way from Tokyo to save my life.

The girl was carrying a radio, turned up loud. It took a moment to understand what we were listening to. The voice was high and rather weak; none of us had ever heard it before. It was high noon on 15th August and the first time in history that the Emperor had ever been heard by the nation.

The police officer's face sagged, his mouth drooping open, as the full import of the Emperor's words sank in. It was not at all clear what he was talking about. The actual words were so opaque as to be almost meaningless. But gradually we came to understand what he was saying. We were going to have to bear the unbearable. We had surrendered.

I listened to the Emperor's words with a growing sense of elation. "Despite the best that has been done by everyone – the gallant fighting of military and naval forces, the diligence and assiduity of our servants of the State, and the devoted service of our one hundred million people – the war situation has developed not necessarily to Japan's advantage," the Emperor said with sublime understatement, before continuing, "Moreover, the enemy has begun to employ a new and most cruel bomb, the power of which to do damage is, indeed, incalculable, taking the toll of many innocent lives. Should we continue to fight, it would not only result in an ultimate collapse and obliteration of the Japanese nation, but also it would lead to the total extinction of human civilization."

The police inspector's gun-arm dropped to his side, as if his very muscles had been sapped of their strength. The rest of them in that little outhouse were all in shock, not knowing what to do any more. It was like a decapitation. For the past four years, our nation's sole focus had been on the war – and now that we had surrendered, no-one had any idea what to do next. Two of the civilians were so benumbed they had sunk to their knees.

There was a slight hiccup, almost a stutter, before the Emperor went on: "We have resolved to pave the way for a grand peace for all the generations to come by enduring the unendurable and suffering what is insufferable."

The speech was at an end, and all that could be heard over the radio was the empty hiss of the airwaves.

"Is that it?" asked the girl. "Is the war over?"

I was about to take a step towards her, when in one fell movement the police officer brought the gun up to the side of his head and pointed the muzzle at his temple.

Tears were streaming down his face. "I give my life for the Motherland!" he said, eyes clenched tight shut, steeling himself to pull the trigger.

"Have you learned nothing?" I screamed, leaping forward to smack the gun out of his hands. The explosion was deafening as the bullet caromed into the side of the well.

The gun tumbled to the ground. I stooped to pick it up. The officer was lying on the floor, weeping into his hands as he was reduced to the schoolboy that he had always been.

I walked to the door. "The war is finished," I said to the cowering men. "We have had enough. Japan has had enough." And with that, I scooped the girl up into my arms and kissed her on both cheeks. I was so happy that I was crying, crying not because of the ignominy of surrender, but for the sheer delirious pleasure of being alive.

I put her down and we danced out into the sunshine and onto the grass, brimful with the most intoxicating euphoria.

"No more war," the girl said, smiling up at me as she clung onto my good arm. "Perhaps you will have time to make me a kite?"

I enfolded her into my arms. "It would be a great pleasure." The enormity of what had occurred was beginning to sink in as I let out a primal howl of delight. "It's over!"

It was indeed; our war was over – and my education with it.

CHAPTER NINETEEN

There were still two cities, of course, for whom the war had only just begun: Hiroshima and Nagasaki. For many of the bomb victims, they had years of the most indescribable agony ahead of them.

Much of this was kept secret from the Japanese. The country as a whole knew that two atomic bombs had been dropped, but thanks to a news blackout on any talk of radiation sickness, few people had any idea what it entailed.

The Yankees, in particular, were keen to downplay the long-term effects of their new bombs, trying to pretend that Fat Man and Little Boy were really nothing more than a couple of giant-sized incendiary bombs. They spent years smothering news stories and fudging papers in their bid to prove that the A-bomb was just another wholesome, Honest-to-God Yankee killing machine.

There was one man, General Leslie Groves, whose comments about radiation sickness were so outrageous, I did not know whether to laugh or cry. It was Groves who had been the main driving force behind the Manhattan Project and without his constant belly-aching, the Yankees would probably have taken another year to develop the bomb. Groves not only created the bomb, but also helped pick the target cities – and, before the Emperor's surrender, had been all for bombing Japan into oblivion.

Groves made many ludicrous comments after the war, but

there were none quite so far-fetched as when he stated of the typical A-bomb victim: "He can have enough [radiation] so that he will be killed instantly. He can have a smaller amount which will cause him to die rather soon, as I understand it from the doctors, without undue suffering. In fact, they say it is a very pleasant way to die."

The truth, for any of us on the ground, was that the radiation sickness turned out to be one of the most terrible tortures ever inflicted on mankind. It would be months before we learned how to treat those raw, maggot infested wounds; it was a sickness of which none of us had the slightest comprehension, and we only learned by trial and error how to cure it.

I know this well – because after Japan's surrender, that hospital was my second home. In rather a loose fashion, I became a nurse. I did not have to take any exams, or jump any hurdles as such, but the good Dr Kinoshita kept me on as a general fixer at his hospital.

I am not by any means qualified. But then I like to style myself as something different from a nurse. I am a carer – and that is what I still do now, and that is what those two awful bombs have given to me: I care. I have cared, very deeply, about each and every one of the humans that entered our wards, and whether they were with us for a few days or a few years, I always strived to make their lives that little bit more bearable.

I loved them all, the girls, the men and the pitiful old ladies, but the two that I loved the most were my son Toshiaki and Shinzo's widow, Sakae.

Even though it is now 60 years since I last saw my dear little boy, it still pains me to the think of him. After the end of the war, he clung to his life for another year. It would be nice to say that they were happy days, but I fear that he spent most of it in the most unspeakable torment.

I can truly say that I would have given up my life for his – and, when Toshiaki died, I focused my grief on my patients. I would work 18, 20 hour a day on the wards and when my withered arm throbbed and ached, I only ever considered it to be a reminder of my own good fortune.

By this strange alchemy of reasoning, Sakae's fragile link with life came to have the most extraordinary hold over me. I had to save her. If I could save her, then I would be saving a little bit of Shinzo, of Toshiaki, of Sumie and Mako and all the others I had lost.

And, after over two years in that hospital, and with the skin on her back as brittle as parchment, I like to think that I did save her.

What I could never have guessed was that over those two years, as we chatted amicably and learned to make light of our pain, I would fall in love. And our love was based not on ephemeral beauty but on companionship, on mutual respect, and on a deep understanding of our pasts and our dreams.

Of all the many gifts that were bestowed on me by the bomb, I would not have dared to dream that I might also find my soulmate. We married three days after she left the hospital. It would have been very fine, perhaps, if we had been able to have children. But I can only count my blessings; I have no time for regret.

Sakae and I have, in a small way, become ambassadors for Fat Man and Little Boy. We have toured the world, telling people about the bombs in the hope that they may never be repeated. For a while, we even lived in America. How strange it was to be dwelling in the land of our one time enemies. Only a few years earlier, we had been trying to wipe each other off the face of the earth, and yet the matter of race is fast becoming an irrelevance. As I queued up to order a Big Mac and fries, my skin and my nationality were of as little consequence as the shoes on my feet.

As for Japan after the war, the Motherland was not crushed into the dust and nor were our womenfolk raped and tortured. It took some years, but I believe that once again we have become a great nation – though a kinder, less arrogant nation. It is difficult enough to change the mindset of a grown man, let alone that of a country; but the bombs changed me and they most certainly changed Japan. From being a nation of rampant warmongers, we became the most fervent pacifists, with every victim of the bomb becoming a symbol, in their own right, of the unparalleled horror of war.

And I am pleased to say that as part of my country's rehabilitation into the world, our gentle Emperor also received his dues. At the start of the war, nations from around the world stripped him of every one of the medals and orders of gallantry that had been conferred upon him. Yet 30 years later, our Emperor was once again back in St George's Chapel, Windsor, and there amidst all the white-gowned choristers, he became one of the few men in history to be reinvested into that noble and ancient Order of the Garter.

And with that little bow to the Emperor, I believe that I am nearly done.

But is there anything yet left to tell? Is there anything that I have missed?

Well perhaps there is the one last matter I should attend to: The Girl.

I feel that now it is time to make a clean breast of things. You will have noticed how, throughout my little book, I have never once referred to the girl by name. She is always 'The Girl'.

The reason is because, at the start of this story, The Girl was nothing more than just 'a girl'. To me, she was yet one more of Hiroshima's numberless dispossessed. She had a name, but at that time I was not interested in people's names – and nor was I much interested in people.

It would be some time before I came to appreciate The Girl's worth and to realise that there was considerably more to her than this yakking, chattering seven-year-old waif. So The Girl does have a name – and now I give it to you. Her name is Katsuko.

For other, quite different reasons, you do not know my

name either. Apart from my injured arm, you know next to nothing about my looks. But that is because I am a nobody. It is my story, but I am a mere cipher, just another of the selfish dogs that was allowed to prosper during Japan's years at war. And that is the way that I would like to keep it.

At the start of this book, I wrote about the dilemma that I am always asked when people learn that I am Mr Two-Bomb, the man who survived both Little Boy and Fat Man. Am I lucky? Have I been blessed – or cursed?

I can unequivocally state that I am the luckiest man alive. Through the bombs, I have learned how to care; and I have learned how to love. But perhaps the greatest gift to be bestowed on me by the bombs was that they brought The Girl into my life.

And she has never left it.

She is standing over my shoulder now, watching me as I scratch away at these last few paragraphs, still correcting me on the composition of my sentences. She is even more nagging, more talkative and more bossy than she was 60 years ago – and I would not have it any other way. Every day, I give thanks for this woman, this wonderful woman.

Now in this story, I have called her everything from 'That chit of a girl' all the way through to her given name, Katsuko.

But it would be several years before we hit upon a name with which we both felt comfortable.

It was a name that I felt I had earned – and I can only hope that she is as proud of her name as I am to use it. For the name that suits her best, and the name which reflects how much she means to me is this: I call her my daughter.

ACKNOWLEDGEMENTS

My thanks to the foreign correspondents who used to inhabit News Corp's New York bureau in 1998. They included Geoff Stead, Cameron Stewart, Tunku Varadarajan and Oliver August – and not forgetting my stalwart photographer, Shannon Sweeney.

Also in this diverse cluster of reporters was Andrew Butcher – and it was Andrew who first told me of an extraordinary interview that he'd once had with the original Mr Two-Bomb. I thank you!